behind**closed**doors

alina reyes

behind**closeddoors**

translated by David Watson

Grove Press
New York

Originally published in France as *Derrière la Porte* by Editions Robert Laffont, Paris
This translation first published in Great Britain by Weidenfeld & Nicolson in 1995
First Grove Press edition published in May 1996

Printed in the United States of America

Library of Congress Cataloging-in-Publication Data

Reyes, Alina
    [Derrièrre la porte. English]
        p.   cm.
    ISBN 0-8021-1589-6
    I. Watson, David, 1959–   . II. Title.
    PQ2678. E8896D4713   1996
843'.914—dc20   96-2103

Grove Press
841 Broadway
New York, NY 10003

10 9 8 7 6 5 4 3 2 1

behindcloseddoors

an adventure in which you are the heroine

Contents

Welcome, woman, to the lair of Eros. I, its humble servant, want to be with you everywhere your desire impels you as you enter the doors of this kingdom, for my sweetest joy will be to be your companion in all the pleasures you indulge in, to share with you all the men, all the passions we have dreamed about, and, with the same ardour, to satisfy the most secret impulses of our souls and our bodies.

Woman, my beautiful equal, should I address you familiarly or more formally, with admiration? At least know this, my passionate friend, that once we have passed through the doors of Eros, once we have been introduced to the labyrinth of fantasy of the god who lies deep inside the hollow of our bellies, I will be your most devoted accomplice, I will be the hand which guides your hand, with you I will feel the fabulous fire-breathing monster which will split open your body and the kisses which will send flames of lava flowing over our flesh.

So, if you are willing, let us play. For the only guide to losing yourself in this kingdom is the game, with its pleasures and its risks. At the entrance to the cave you will choose a thread, then another with each new adventure, these threads leading you through the maze according to the uncertain laws of your desire and of chance.

It is up to you to enter the labyrinth, to choose the doors you want to open, so as to trace your own route, your own book, your own destiny.

Come, see how dark it is inside. Now everything is possible.

1

The Little Circus

I had been on the road since dawn. I had been woken by a bad dream. I had taken a long bath, perfumed myself, put on my white lace underwear and, next to my skin, my black leathers. I looked at myself in the mirror and thought I looked beautiful. Then I went out, straddled my motorbike, revved the engine and set off.

I had dreamed of this bike since I was a child. Twenty minutes' walk from my parents' house there was a bike shop where I went every day to admire the red 1000cc on display in the window. When the shop-owner saw me he teased me about my passion, which I didn't like. I desperately desired that machine, but I knew I was too young to satisfy that desire. It was my secret, and I didn't like anyone talking about it, even less making fun of it.

And now I lived alone and free, and nothing could stop me, if I so wished, from setting off at dawn, naked and perfumed inside my second skin of leather and riding for as long as I wanted, solitary and wild, my red bike between my legs.

It was summer. Around midday, I slowed down to pass through a deserted village in the middle of nowhere. The heat was oppressive. A small travelling circus was set up in the main square. I stopped in front of the only bar and went in to quench my thirst.

I sat at the counter, near three local men who were drinking aperitifs. They looked at me with a mixture of boldness and shyness, then they carried on drinking and chatting in fits and starts, occasionally glancing across at me.

I was starving, too. The landlord agreed to make me a mushroom omelette, and I ordered a good red wine to accompany it. I went and sat down at one of the four tables, next to the window. I ate and drank, taking my time.

I was on the coffee when a white convertible parked in front of the bar, next to my bike. A man got out of the car, and I felt as if someone had punched me in the stomach.

This man was the one I had seen in my dream, that very night, in my bad dream in which I desired him passionately but could never attain him, never sleep with him. This man was here and he was about to enter the bar.

There was the sound of a tiger growling softly, and the man seemed to change his mind; he headed for the circus and I lost sight of him. I waited. His car was outside the door, he had to come back. After a while, it seemed as if my nightmare was starting again. The man had been there, right next to me, then in an instant he had escaped me. I couldn't sit there any longer. I left the bar.

There was no one in the square. I went towards the dozing tiger. A muscular young man in a vest stepped out from behind the cage and said that if I wanted to become an animal-tamer, he'd hire me to work with him. I asked him whether he had seen the man from the convertible. He pointed to the black caravan.

A small, dark-haired woman appeared before the door, under a sign in gold letters: *The doors of Eros.* 'He's in there,' said the pretty traveller, pointing to the curtain behind her. I paid the entrance fee and went inside.

At the end of a dark corridor I found two doors. I opened one of them at random.

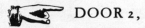 DOOR 2,

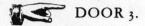 DOOR 3.

The Bull

Behind the door a man, slumped on his bed, quickly withdrew his hand from inside his trousers, where he was gently rummaging as he flicked through a magazine. I excused myself and made to leave, but he protested that, on the contrary, he was delighted to receive a visit, and if I was looking for something he would gladly give me directions.

Naturally I thought about the man from the convertible, but I was unwilling to broach the subject straight away, and I sat down with him at the low table where he offered me a drink and a cigarette.

The man was no young buck. He reminded me more of a bull. But he was very courteous, and managed to make me forget that I had surprised him in a rather inelegant position. His thick eyebrows almost met in the middle, his deep-set eyes shone like tiny precious stones, his wide nostrils flared and retracted in a regular rhythm, his mouth was remarkably fleshy.

As we exchanged a few travellers' tales, a few remarks about the beauty of the world, I tried to make out the shape of his body beneath his slightly shabby clothing. Perhaps I had become a little excited by the sight of disturbed intimacy which he had presented on my arrival; or perhaps it was due to the mixture of robust sensuality and self-mastery which emanated from his person . . . I told him point-blank that I wanted to make love.

Without answering, he got up, took my hand with a reassuring smile and pulled me towards the bed. He was so friendly that a wave of warmth took possession of my whole being. I wanted to thank him, take care of him, do him good. I told him that I would make love only on the condition that he would allow me to direct the entire operation.

He turned to look me in the eyes, and I said again, gently but with determination:

'Do you agree to let me do anything I want, without protest?'

He agreed, and I knew I could trust him.

I told him to undress. Meanwhile, I wandered round the room in search of interesting objects. I found a candle and a mirror, which I placed on the bedside table. I unzipped the pocket of my leathers, took out my lipstick and, in front of the mirror, made up my lips and cheekbones.

When he was standing naked, I walked around him to get a good look at the massive bulk of his body. He was averagely hairy, and had a firm bottom, a quite short but thick cock and large testicles. I pressed my nose to his armpits to savour his smell.

I asked him to stretch out on his back on the bed. I still held my lipstick tightly in my hand. I used it to paint his mouth, which became bright red, and to buff his nipples.

'Look at yourself,' I said, holding up the mirror.

The three touches of red on that powerful body made him uncommonly beautiful, but I didn't know how to tell him. I retracted the lipstick and did up my leathers.

I ordered him to get up on all fours on the bed. Without removing my boots or my clothing, I lay down beneath him, so that his sex was hanging above my face, but without him being able to touch it himself. I began to suck it gently, hoping to make the transition from detrimescence to complete erection last as long as possible, but his cock very quickly became as hard as a bone. So I knelt down behind him and began to lick his bum.

When he became less stiff, I picked up my candle and,

delicately, taking as much care as I could, penetrated him and forced it inside him. Still on all fours, he lowered his head and hung onto the bars of the bed, saying nothing, keeping his promise. While pushing the candle in and out I began to wank him, holding his cock from below, as if I were milking a cow. It became extraordinarily hard again, and so big that I couldn't close my hand around it. He stuffed his head into the pillow and groaned like an animal. At that moment I loved him more than anyone else, and I came on my own, inside my leathers, which had ridden up between my legs. An instant later, his sperm spurted out between my fingers.

We fell back onto the bed. The pillow he had been writhing against was covered with lipstick. I wiped his mouth and his sex with paper tissues. I felt intoxicated with happiness, but I acted calm and gentle, to excuse the strange violence of my desire. I undressed and went to sleep in his arms, naked and completely happy.

When I awoke, he had disappeared. I had a shower, left my underwear on his pillow as a present, slipped back into my leathers and left.

In the corridor, I hoped to find the Man of my dreams behind one of the following doors:

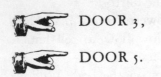 DOOR 3,

DOOR 5.

3

Three Blind People

I found myself in the semi-darkness of a square room. The walls were completely concealed by drapery, which fell in ample, darkly gleaming folds to the floor. A bit of daylight entered from the back of the room through a partially uncovered window. The only piece of furniture, a wide, deep bed, glimmered softly.

Suddenly I felt extraordinarily weary. As if in a trance, I looked at this huge, soft bed and felt an irresistible need to sleep. I went to the window, drew the curtains, and the darkness was complete.

I undressed, letting my clothes fall to the carpet. I couldn't see a thing. I pulled back the covers and slid between the sheets. They were old-fashioned sheets, like your grandmother's, made of thick cotton and with wide embroidered hems. Nestling in the feather pillow, I imagined that a young girl, decades ago, must have embroidered her initials on them in long, slender letters, to make up her trousseau, to prepare for her life as a woman.

Perhaps these sheets were the ones in which she had spent her wedding night; perhaps, on this cloth through which her white fingers had pulled the needle, she had shed her blood and lost her virginity, discovered men and the pleasure of orgasm. Or perhaps they had stayed piled up in some vast wardrobe all her life, her trousseau turning out to be so well stocked that they weren't able to use everything.

Plunged into this ink-black night, I sank slowly into sleep, still thinking in snatches about this young bride, trembling all over with fear and desire in her large nightdress, and also about the man I had come here to pursue. And in a half-dream, I saw myself in the virgin's body, waiting for this man, for the first time, to lay his hands on me and finally penetrate me, for since my birth I had aspired to nothing else. Then, curled up in a foetal position, I allowed myself to be carried away by sleep.

I don't know whether I slept for a long time or not. At first, I thought I was dreaming. I felt a hard, warm bar against my buttocks, but I was so weary that I was unable to open my eyes or make a movement. There was no sound, it could only be an illusion, one of those erotic torments that take hold of you at night, which nothing can banish.

Soon, however, I felt a whole body pressed against my back, and the warmth of a stifled breath on my neck. A man's arm passed delicately beneath my bust, and two hands, like the wings of a dove, were placed on my breasts. Now I was wide awake, but I didn't move, so as not to interrupt anything. I didn't want to notice anything, I wanted to carry on sleeping.

The bar worked its way into the split between my buttocks where it started rubbing softly. All the man's movements were slow and careful, as if he were trying hard not to drag me from my sleep, as if he wanted to turn the rape into a dream. And that pleased me to the utmost, I wanted to do nothing, I had a burning desire to play along with this and do absolutely nothing.

However, I couldn't prevent myself sticking out my bottom, as discreetly as possible, so that he could find more quickly and more easily the route that I wanted him to take. And indeed his member slipped from my buttocks to my pussy. Motionless, my eyes still closed, I convinced myself so completely that what was taking place was unreal that I managed to stop myself crying out. I wanted to be nothing more than a receptacle of desire, an abandoned body, unconscious, totally submissive to this rape fantasy.

His member penetrated me and started moving gently in and out, sliding wonderfully. Immersed in darkness, I felt as if nothing else existed but this succulent pleasure machine. I had a deep mouth between my legs, an ogress who sucked and feasted like a glutton.

I quickly achieved my first orgasm. I wanted to say: 'I'm eating you, I'm eating you.' But I stayed as calm and silent as possible, just enough that my trembling and moans could still seem like those of a dream.

However, I almost let out a cry when something landed on my cheek. Surprised, I opened my eyes. I still couldn't see anything, but a soft, musky smell filled my nostrils. That thing hardening against my cheek was another cock. And the tender bullets of flesh brushing against my nose, with their intoxicating perfume, were a pair of balls.

The first cock was still pumping in my belly, which was now at a pitch of excitement. When the other one thrust itself to the back of my throat, I thought I had never been so happy. It pushed in and out between my lips as it would have attacked any orifice, without allowing me any choice.

Now no one was bothering to play at being a ghost or being asleep. The two men were urging each other on, they invaded me, manhandled me, shook me without any consideration, but now I was in a state of permanent orgasm, my whole body mad with a pleasure which would not subside. I heard them, between moans, mumbling incomprehensible words, and they both ejaculated together, while I, my mouth wide open, screamed with joy under the spurts of sperm.

I implored them in a whisper to stay a while inside me. We arranged ourselves in the bed and, this time, I really sank into the sleep of the just, one cock in my mouth and the other between my legs. I already knew that when I awoke I would have to choose between:

— trying to extract new pleasures from my unknown lovers, at the risk of seeing them lose their appeal in the light of day:

  DOOR 4;

— or do a bunk and continue my quest, in the hope of successfully evading all the traps that the place seemed to have in store:

 DOOR 9.

4

The Two Friends

I woke up with a smile on my lips, wonderfully rested. My night-time companions were no longer there. A ray of light poked my stomach like a finger. I remembered my delicious adventure, the two virile members I had feasted on, and I said to myself that there was nothing on earth worthier of adoration than men. These cocks had done me so much good that I suddenly regretted not having one of my own, for then I would jerk it off constantly, to pay homage to it and to tell it how precious it was to me.

I got up and opened the curtains. Daylight entered the room. I had a look round. There was something which intrigued me. I could hear faint sounds of conversation, yet there was no one there. I stood still for a moment, straining to hear. The sounds grew ever clearer, like someone singing quietly.

Stealthily, I went over to one of the walls, masked like the others by the dark curtains which enveloped the room and made it look like a photographer's darkroom. It seemed as if there were two people talking behind them, but I couldn't catch what they were saying. It was a bit like when people talk in their sleep: you can hear them saying something, but you often don't understand what it is. It occurred to me they might be speaking in a foreign language. Indeed, it sounded a bit like German, or some Nordic language.

My curiosity was aroused, but I didn't dare show myself. I easily found a gap in the curtains, and carefully opened it, just wide enough to peep through. And I was very pleased with what I saw.

The curtain hid a crescent-shaped alcove, furnished as a sitting-room. On the sofa sat two very beautiful young men. My first thought was that they were my companions from the night before, and I congratulated myself on having stayed with them.

They were both tall, slim and blond, with angelic faces – blue eyes and pink lips. They looked like brothers. They were both barefoot and dressed in faded jeans and white T-shirts, which accentuated their bronzed skin. They were talking almost in a whisper, and I still didn't understand a word.

I was about to go through the curtains to join them when a gesture by one of them, whom I will call The One, stopped me in my tracks. The One moved close to The Other to whisper something in his ear. The Other laughed, then they kissed on the mouth, slipping their hands inside each other's T-shirt to caress each other's back, stomach and chest.

I watched their lips meet with a surge of emotion, as if the action were taking place in slow motion. I hadn't expected that at all, and it was so exciting that I ached between my legs.

With bated breath I remained behind the curtains. From my position I could see that the swelling in The Other's jeans was now stretching the cloth taut. The One put his hand on it, then went down on his knees at the feet of The Other, who remained sitting on the sofa, and undid his flies. The Other wasn't wearing underpants. His long dick, curving back a bit near the tip, sprang up between the buttons of his jeans. The One freed his firm, round, blond balls, licked them, moved his tongue up as far as his glans, then pushed his cock inside his mouth and began sucking slowly. The Other, his trousers round his ankles, his mouth open, his arms and legs spread wide, his head thrown back over the sofa, lay back and gave out little moans.

Then The One undressed his companion completely and

undressed himself as well. He was already erect, and his cock was like The Other's, long and elegant. Their bodies were perfect in the way young men's bodies are: lean and muscular, with golden skin and only a little blond hair. They kissed again, mouth against mouth, body against body, cock against cock.

My excitement made me bolder. I took the risk of opening the curtains wider, enough to be able to see through the gap without having to hold it open. My two friends were too wrapped up in each other to notice anything. Still standing, my legs apart, I began to caress myself with both hands, without taking my eyes off them. These two men who had made me come were now exchanging male pleasures. It was a sort of combat in which their two virilities sublimated and annulled each other at the same time, and it was the most arousing sight imaginable.

The One knelt down again before The Other and licked his way between his legs. Like a penitent, he ran his tongue over his friend's cock, his balls, then between his buttocks, and, when he was through on the other side, he stood up and, with a precise thrust of the hips, penetrated him.

The movement was so perfect that all three of us let out a moan of satisfaction together. Then The One began to move in and out with vigorous thrusts of his graceful bottom, holding his companion round the chest and nibbling his neck and shoulders. The Other masturbated to the same rhythm, as did I, behind my curtain. A clandestine spectator, I had already come several times. I was no longer standing up, I had fallen to my knees, but I was enjoying the spectacle so much that I could still find the means, with my legs still wide apart, to give myself all possible pleasure, devouring with my eyes the erotic passion of the two friends.

I reached my final orgasm when I saw their back muscles tense and their faces contort under the effect of a violent, sinewy ecstasy. They ejaculated together, The One into his friend's behind, The Other in his own hand. I cried out at the same time as them, my body convulsed again, as I watched the lovely white liquid of The Other spurt and splash way out in front of its source.

I got up and went back to the bed. With the virgin's sheet I wiped the inside of my thighs, which were soaking wet. Then I got dressed. Now the two friends had given me enough, I wouldn't ask any more of them. I had decided to continue my journey.

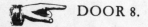 **DOOR 8.**

5

The Lame Woman

This long corridor and all these closed doors really excited my imagination. I was dying to know what might happen behind these walls.

Approaching the first door, I noticed that the keyhole was ornately fashioned and exceptionally wide, and I said to myself that the key that opened that lock must be one hell of a beautiful object and pretty big besides. I knelt down and pressed my eye to it.

Behind the door a small, round room, upholstered in black rubber from floor to ceiling, was bathed in a filtered red light. A woman was lying on her back, naked, her arms and legs spread wide and attached by chains and iron bracelets around her wrists and ankles to four hooks stuck in the floor. She was alone, motionless, and her eyes were closed.

I thought at first she must be asleep, but soon I feared that she might be unconscious, or even dead. I had made up my mind to open the door, when a second woman appeared from the back of the room, making an entrance like an actress in the theatre.

She was dressed in a nurse's white overall. Although she was about fifty, she had her hair tied back like a young girl, in two broad, shining black plaits which fell over her bosom. Her sad face was partially masked by a pair of sunglasses with reflective lenses which concealed her eyes. She was limping, and it seemed such a shame, for she was tall and had a good figure, albeit a bit on the thin side. She was carrying a large white flannel over her left arm, and in her right hand a bucket the weight of which seemed to exaggerate her limp.

She approached the woman spreadeagled on the floor, stood in front of her, at the level of her thighs, and in a single movement threw the bucket of water over her body from her feet to her head. This woke the inert woman with a jolt; she gave a shudder, opened her eyes and looked fearfully at the nurse. The latter took a bunch of tiny keys from her pocket and unlocked her patient's iron bracelets.

Although she was free, the woman didn't move. She seemed exhausted. She was beautiful, slim and shapely at the same time, with very white skin, and she looked so helpless it made you want to take advantage of her. Kneeling down, the nurse began to wipe her with the flannel.

Soon it was obvious that she was not so much wiping her down as caressing her. She had turned the young woman onto her stomach and was lovingly drying her neck, her back, the backs of her arms and legs, and was now lingering over her adorable bottom. She kneaded it, patted it, nibbled it and finally began to cover it with kisses. She was like a mother with her baby.

The nurse took off her overall, beneath which she was naked. Now she was wearing nothing but her white leather shoes, which were large but had low, square heels, her blank glasses, and her tresses which lightly brushed the tips of her pointed breasts, unusually generous pears on so thin a body. She turned the young woman onto her back, lay down next to her and gave her a long kiss on the mouth. Then her hands moved down over her small, round breasts, her flat stomach, her lovely, plump thighs, and back up to the flower now opening between her legs.

Her legs wide open, yielding to the expert caresses of the lame woman, whose mouth was sucking her small, swollen breasts and whose fingers were opening her pretty, pink shell, the beautiful patient was now reduced to imploring in a weak but fervent voice: 'Your mouth, please, your mouth now!' Then the nurse pushed her face between the legs of her tender friend, who let out soul-rending moans of pleasure, and finally shrieked like a mad bird, arching back with great, heaving jerks of her hips.

Expert Tongue lay on her back in turn, opened her long legs and asked her partner to kiss her on the mouth and fondle her breasts while she masturbated. The lame woman came herself, then they embraced and seemed ready to go to sleep in each other's arms. During this whole time, I had wanted to join them, but I didn't dare make a movement. Now would I go to see what was going on behind the next door,

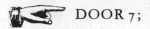 DOOR 7;

or would I succumb to the temptation to join the two women,

 DOOR 6?

6

The Hoods

I opened the door gently and approached the sleeping women. When I was at the centre of the room, they opened their eyes and greeted me with a smile. I felt somewhat reassured. The lame woman invited me to make myself at home, to rest with them. I undressed and lay down next to them.

Now that I was there, naked with these two naked women, I didn't know what to do. Luckily, they took the initiative. They enclosed me, kissed me on my mouth, each in turn, made me touch their breasts, their bodies. I began to get excited, enough to take the initiative and pull the young woman onto me, the better to feel her body against mine, while she gave me her deliciously soft mouth and tongue.

I savoured her kisses and the tender contact of her thighs, her stomach and her breasts against mine, when suddenly there was a sharp click. At the same moment, I felt the iron ring close around my ankle.

I wanted to leap up, but the girl pressed down on me with all her weight, digging her nails into the flesh of my arms. I would have easily got the better of her if the nurse hadn't immediately come to her aid. I struggled the best I could, but they succeeded in fastening one wrist, then the other, and finally the other ankle.

Everything happened very quickly. As soon as I was completely immobilized, lying on my back, naked, my arms and legs apart, just as the young woman had been before the arrival of the lame woman, they disappeared. Now I was completely powerless, forced to go along with whatever was going to happen next, of which I knew nothing. Would they abandon me here? Leave me to die? Assault me? Rape me? Or maybe the lame woman would come back and make love to me, like she did with the young woman? Would they give me pleasure, or torture me? I waited, for a long time, alone, tormented by these questions. In the end, I dozed off.

It was a dog barking which woke me up. I opened my eyes and saw above me, all around me, lined up tightly all along my body, an army of male sexes. Their owners were dressed from head to toe in latex. Standing motionless and deep in thought, the men in black seemed to be praying in silence around my body. They were wearing boots, and their hands were free, but the only openings in their rubber armour was between their legs, leaving their genitals free, and in their hoods, around the mouth and eyes.

Once they had finished their silent prayer, the masked men knelt down all around me and began touching themselves and becoming aroused, while they exchanged coarse comments about me.

'Here's the new whore.'

'What do you think of the slut?'

'I'd love to fuck her up her arse.'

'I'd do it in her mouth.'

'Have you seen these tits?'

'And her cunt?'

'Do you give head, you pretty bitch?'

'Do you swallow, slut?'

'Do you know you excite us?'

'Like to see us wank ourselves?'

'Do you know what we like?'

'Wanking over a slut like you.'

'Have you ever seen so many dicks at the same time?'
'Have you seen how hard they are now?'
'Which one do you like best?'
'Look how moist she is, miss la-di-dah!'
'Don't worry, my love, we'll make you glisten.'
'Here, darling slut, taste mine.'

One of them who was wanking above my face stuffed his cock into my mouth, while another stuck his into my pussy. They both made a few thrusts between my lips, then they took turns between my legs, or often chose instead to bugger me. All this time, the others continued wanking quietly around me. Every now and again, a dog barked nearby.

All these cocks poking between my quartered legs, all these balls wagging in front of my eyes, all these dicks being rubbed by all these hands above me drove me wild with desire, but they always pulled out of me exactly at the moment when they saw me about to come. There were dicks of all sizes and colours, long, short, fat, thin, veined, black, pink, brown ... Between them they gave off a heady smell ... They grew harder and harder, I saw them straining, ready to explode ... Over me, all over me ... Then they stopped to let them deflate a little, then started manipulating them again. Some of them, with their spare hands, put a finger in their anus or fondled their balls, others kneaded my breasts, my stomach, my thighs, my ankles, whatever part of my body was nearest to hand. One or other of them would give a few thrusts between my legs then leave me as soon as I began to cry out. My pleasure remained suspended, incomplete, terribly painful. Now and again they had me suck them, and their balls hit against my face without my being able to touch them.

As they wouldn't let me reach orgasm, but constantly brought me to the pitch of excitement, I thought I was going mad. Abandoning all restraint, I begged them to make me come. They made me repeat it several times.

'You want to come?'
'Yes.'

'Then say it.'

'I want to come.'

'Really?'

'Yes, yes, please, I really want to.'

'You are ready to come in any way?'

'Any way, but please make me come ... I'll do what you want ... I beg you, quickly ...'

Then they brought the dog. A handsome alsation, which one of them led on a lead to between my legs.

I knew the end was near. The masked men were all motionless around me. Their eyes, behind their hoods, had hardened. The dog moaned and wagged its tail, and pulled against its lead to sniff between my legs. 'Lick it,' said the man, and he let go of the lead.

The dog began to lick my pussy with its large, rough tongue. The hooded men began wanking themselves, faster and faster. I saw the dog's head stuffed between my legs, I felt its tongue prise me open tirelessly, I saw the large cocks beginning to ejaculate over me, and I climaxed in convulsions, crying out like an animal, in the dog's snout and showered by come.

The hooded men got up and left the room. The dog, now upright, followed them meekly. I was covered in sperm and exhausted. I slept.

When I was woken by the lame woman's bucket of water, I knew everything would happen again as it had done with the first woman. The damp rubber floor made suction-pad kisses on my body. I let myself be loved by the nurse, who, after all that violence, offered me a pacifying form of pleasure. When it was her turn to come, I kissed her tenderly on her face, her neck, her pointed breasts and, at the moment of orgasm, I took off her glasses to see her eyes turn up.

Then I got dressed and went out into the corridor.

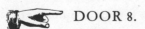 DOOR 8.

The Apple

The door opened onto a luxurious, warm, fragrant garden. Animals, birds and serpents of every species lolled, slid or flitted around among the astonishing variety of trees. A river flowed through the middle, dividing into four branches which spread out through the vegetation. Near the tip of the delta, a handsome, naked man lay stretched out in the foliage, sleeping or dreaming, his face suffused with a smug contentment.

I slipped out of my clothes and, naked as Eve, walked slowly across to meet him. In a few steps I was next to him. I knelt down in the grass to contemplate his sleeping, soft, muscular body and the sweet basket of fruit offered by his lower belly, a delightful banana languishing on two love apples round enough to eat.

Adam was still sleeping, and I was happy to devour him with my eyes, which did not fail to awaken appetites within me that I attempted to contain by squeezing my thighs together with my hand pressed into my apricot. Soon I saw the eyes of my fine friend start to move beneath his closed lids, while his banana took on the volume of a fritter about to be flambéed. It was clear that desire had begun to haunt him in his sleep.

Seeing his lower belly adorned in such a favourable manner, I couldn't resist reaching out with my hand. But before I could touch it, he woke up, grabbed me brutally by the hips to force me onto all fours, and took me, saying: 'Here you are at last, bone of my bone, flesh of my flesh!' Sweet words, albeit strange ones, which had absolutely no effect on me, especially as the act was consummated in three quick thrusts.

No sooner had he finished than my premature ejaculator lay back down in the grass and dozed off to sleep again. Should I, in response to his bad behaviour, give him a slap and leave him to his solitary dreams, or try to give him a little education? In view of the fact that, firstly, he was a bit of a hunk, and it would be shame to waste him, and secondly, duty impelled me to show solidarity with the next woman who would fall into the hands of this animal, I concluded that the best option would be to have another gentle go at opening his eyes to a few facts of life.

In the middle of the garden a magnificent apple tree, courted by flocks of birds, bent under the weight of its abundant crop. I went and picked a lovely red apple, which I wiped in the grass to make it even more shiny.

I came back and sat down next to the slumbering brute, and bit noisily into the apple. He gave a start and, finally, deigned to look at me.

'Do you want some?' I said, offering it to him.

It was firm, juicy and sweet. We ate it down to the core, taking it in turns to sink our teeth into it. And thus the first exchange of complicity and good humour took place between us.

When I saw him smiling and satisfied with this first pleasure, I set about teaching him other physical joys. I placed my fingers on his cheek and started stroking his face and his hair. He clumsily reached out his hand towards me, and I helped him recognize my features by touch.

Then I moved closer to him and nibbled his neck, his ears, his lips, his tongue. He did likewise, the best he could, laughing a little. I stroked his chest and rubbed my bosom against him, to draw his attention to the fact that our differences were a source of interest.

Thank God, he was quick on the uptake. Off his own bat, he took my breasts in his hands, felt them and looked at them for a long time before venturing in with his mouth. I began panting and moaning with pleasure. He looked at me, a tad frightened, but I didn't give him time to get more worried. Taking his hand, I guided it over my hips, my stomach, my legs, to the hot, damp nest between my thighs. The tension had been so great that I came almost at once, my head pressed into his shoulder, and in silence, so as not to scare him.

I caressed him in turn, massaged his back, his buttocks, his feet, sucked his toes, his ankles, his chest, licked his navel, the hollows of his elbows and knees, I gently scratched the inside of his thighs before finally plunging my head down between his legs, where I bit and tasted the fruits which I had so desired and coveted from the start.

Neither he nor I could wait any longer. I sat on top of him, facing towards his feet, and made him penetrate me. In this position I moved up and down the whole length of his member, almost letting it come out of me, then pushing it fully in with each movement. In this way, while enjoying a languorous and extremely efficient rubbing against a particularly sensitive part of my anatomy, I hoped to lead him to discover, by offering him a new point of view on the action, all the pleasure that one can also derive from the spectacle of intercourse. He was quick to come, but not before I had another magnificent orgasm, which I didn't try to hide this time, and which left me panting with happiness.

We continued our exploration until nightfall. He was young, vigorous and curious, and we could experiment at our leisure, especially as he learnt to hold back sufficiently to amplify and extend his pleasure. He even had the idea of giving me a spanking, without my having to ask him for it. Every now and again, we had a short break to go and bathe or drink at the stream or to munch one or other of the fruits which the trees disgorged all around us. We were the happiest, most exultant of beings, sailing tirelessly from new pleasures to new orgasms.

But at nightfall, when we rested in each other's arms, my partner's face became gloomy. He stared at the sky, where some pretty dappled clouds were gathering in the lurid colours of the evening, and gradually his face took on an expression of unease, which soon changed into genuine terror.

'Let's hide!' he said, leaping to his feet and pulling me by the arm.

'Why? What's happening?'

'Because! We are naked! Can't you see we are naked!'

'So what?'

'He mustn't see us like this!'

'Who he?'

'Him! The Lord of Heaven! I can hear him! He's walking in the garden! He's coming!'

Now he was getting delirious! I saw his adam's apple jerking in his throat, things didn't seem to be going too well. And yet it had been so good only a moment ago ... I chose to reply in a jokey manner, hoping to defuse the atmosphere a little.

'Of course,' I said. 'Everyone knows that: it's the time when the Lord of Heaven takes his dog for a walk on earth so it can answer the call of nature ...'

'Be quiet, unbeliever,' he said, distraught. 'It's because of you ... because of you I ate the forbidden fruit ...'

This time he almost made me angry.

'Oh, so that's it!' I shouted at him. 'You were delighted to learn about pleasure, but now it sticks in your throat, doesn't it! And do you know why? A few hours ago you were nothing but a beast. And now you are a man you are afraid, that's why! The truth is, being a man really puts the wind up you. And rather than admit that you're afraid of yourself, you invent a master, up there, and make out he is laying down the law for you ... Perfect! I'll leave you alone with your evening visitor ... You go for it, if you still can!'

'Poor boy,' I thought, as I left the garden. 'He'll be inflicting no end of torments on himself now ...'

I slipped on my leathers and walked a short way in the corridor before deciding to open one of the two doors I stopped in front of.

 DOOR 9,

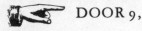 DOOR 8.

8

The Clown

The moment I placed my hand on the latch I felt two breaths on my neck. The shock made me turn round. I heard two sighs, which seemed to fade away into the distance.

The corridor was dark, deserted. For a few moments I peered into the shadows, convinced I had glimpsed two presences at my back. Everything was calm, silent. I could make out the dark rectangles of the doors in the corridor, but if one of them had been opened, I would have heard it. Perhaps the ghosts had disappeared at the end of the corridor, at the point where I could see it turn at a right angle into another corridor. I decided not to worry about it and I opened the door.

I arrived at the end of the bare-back rider and trapeze artist act, when the former, standing on her horse as it trotted round the ring, threw her hands up to be hoisted into the air by her flying partner.

The big top was full of people. I walked down the auditorium and found a place at the front, at the end of the first row. It was a little circus, similar to the one in the village square, suffused with a mixture of happiness and melancholy, which was instantly heartrending.

The following number was an animal act; this turned out to be a group of rats, which, if the cries of the audience were to be believed, were just as frightening as lions or tigers. Armed with whips, which they cracked as they shouted their throaty commands, the tamers made their rodents perform all sorts of acrobatics, such as jumping through hoops of fire. Before leaving the arena, and after a drum roll, each tamer picked up a fat, grey rat by the tail, between two fingers, and arching their mouths wide open, lowered the creatures' heads into their throats, unleashing a crescendo of screams and shudders in the audience.

Then the clowns entered the ring, wildly applauded from the moment they started their grimaces and pirouettes. The strange thing was that there were no children in the audience, but the adults behaved like excited kids. This phenomenon was particularly noticeable with the arrival of the clowns.

'Hello, boys and girls!' said the white clown.

'Hello, Zinzin!' the audience replied with one voice.

I saw them all fidgety with impatience, balancing on one buttock on the edge of their benches, their faces lit up with a feverish joy.

Zinzin and the funny man began their buffoonery, to universal enthusiasm. When a pantomime bull, animated by a couple of extras, appeared behind them, men and women started screaming stridently, like youngsters at a Punch and Judy show when the policeman turns up with his truncheon.

The clown started a bullfight with the cloth bull, with the help of a large red handkerchief which he had pulled out of his sleeve and in which he noisily blew his nose between passes. The crowd rocked with silly, exaggerated peals of laughter. The awful thing was, no one seemed aware of the aberrant nature of this type of jollity, and everyone seemed genuinely to be having fun.

Suddenly, a rider disguised as a barbarian galloped out from the wings on a black horse, did a tour of the ring and, when he reached me, grabbed me so forcefully by the arm that he dragged me off my bench. In a flash I found myself sitting behind him, hanging onto his shirt as I bounced around the circle of light to the jeers of the crowd.

Then, as violently as he had picked me up, he threw me into the middle of the ring between the two clowns, who began tossing me back and forth between them, like a rag doll, in a slapstick routine that delighted the audience. Their accomplices inside the pantomime bull joined in the mayhem, butting me in the back with the bull's head.

Finally, the white clown took me in his arms, miming pity. Pretending to be transported by an excess of romantic sentimentality, he held me firmly in a bone-crunching grip. Meanwhile, the funny man tied me to the horns of the bull.

When I was tied up, the clown stepped back to look at me, gave a whistle of admiration and, opening the huge buttons of his flies, took out his penis, which he showed off to the audience while rubbing his stomach like someone about to tuck into a meal. People started shrieking with joy.

This was really beyond a joke. I began to protest vehemently, jerking about to try to free myself. The bull I was tied to started butting me to knock me off balance. These clowns and this stupid crowd were making me mad. I tugged violently against the ropes, but only succeeded in making them dig into my wrists where they burned my flesh. From a sheath he was wearing on his belt the funny man took out a sword, which he passed to his assistant. With the point of the blade he began to cut open my leathers. Obviously I was paralysed, at the mercy of the slightest slip. The audience held its breath, went 'Ahhh ...', amazed each time the clown completed a cut and another piece of my clothing fell to the ground, uncovering my body bit by bit.

The operation lasted an eternity. This ridiculous fat pig of a clown got more and more of a hard-on the more he stripped me. When he had completely unpeeled me, glowing with pride, he displayed his little erect prick to the gallery and adorned it with his red nose to milk the applause raining down on him. The people were getting carried away and began stamping their feet in unison. In the general din, the clown came slowly towards me.

I aimed a kick at his goolies, which he evaded. The funny man placed the sword at my throat. I gritted my teeth and looked witheringly at the seedy little clown, who returned to his burlesque with his never-ending grimaces. That didn't prevent him from spreading my legs and taking me by force, egged on by the delirious audience.

I had no choice but to give in, attempting to stay completely cool so as to make this misadventure as painless as possible, mentally as well as physically. Seeing I was determined not to move, the funny man withdrew his arm from my neck. The clown was pumping away inside me like a rabbit, but still hadn't achieved his objective. I could hardly feel him, my attention was so concentrated on my right hand, which I was managing bit by bit to slip out of its tourniquet.

Round the ring and up in the stands the people were too wrapped up in their voyeurism to notice me freeing myself. Thus I was finally able to grab the sword and stick it through Zinzin's arm. He recoiled from me screaming, his miserable little purple thing still stiff. A wave of hysterical panic ran around the big top. I slipped out under the stands, found an exit and started to run, stark naked, down the dark corridor.

I was livid, I wanted to die rather than be reminded of the stupidity of these people. I ran at random through the labyrinth of corridors, and the more I ran the more my anger turned to rage and, in the end, to a fierce desire to laugh.

I stopped and began to walk calmly, until I felt I wanted to open another door.

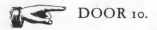 DOOR 10.

9

The Firemen

The moment I pushed the door I thought I saw in the corridor two fleeting, furtive silhouettes, which moved behind me and disappeared before I had a chance to take a look at them. A few moments before I thought I had felt two people breathing on my back, though I didn't want to believe it. Had I been followed by ghosts? This labyrinth of corridors was so dark that it was difficult to make anything out clearly, and I gave up trying to throw light on this mystery for the time being.

I entered a large, well-furnished room. A woman in a dressing gown came to meet me and smiled as she took me by the arm.

'I am happy to welcome you here,' she said. 'You have chosen a good door ... if you like pleasure, that is ... I would be delighted to share mine with you.'

She led me to the back of the room, behind the bar, poured me a glass of bourbon and said:

'Do you like firemen?'

Then she explained that she was preparing to receive a regiment of them, a fine, carefully selected group of lads in their bright red uniforms.

'Although I'm rather partial to them myself, I will happily share them with you,' she added. 'Please accept, my dear, and I guarantee you won't forget this little treat for some time...'

I succumbed to the temptation. My hostess had me undress

and we both slipped on delicate lingerie and elegant shoes, all in red. We had an agreeable session in front of the mirror, arranging ourselves, applying perfume, doing our hair and each other's make-up, growing warm at the thought of what was in store for us.

When we were ready, she pressed a button, a siren sounded, and we ran across to sit down on the sofa. A moment later, a battalion of firemen made their entry into the room. They lined up in front of us, straight and dignified. They were magnificent. Their uniforms marvellously accentuated their strength, their helmets glittered, their bearing, their shoulders and chests aroused an irresistible desire to throw yourself against them.

I glanced across at my companion, to indicate my satisfaction and my impatience to see the festivities begin. I looked at the men avidly, and I felt – like I did when I was standing in front of a Jaguar – that I was going to start coming just by looking at them.

The hostess organized them into two groups, one for her and one for me, and commanded them to drop their trousers, which they did in an orderly and disciplined fashion. When she had passed among them to examine their manly equipment, with which, incidently, they were well endowed (I guessed that she had also selected them by this criterion, and not only by their proud demeanour in uniform), she came back and sat on the sofa, her legs apart, and waited.

The men had lined up in two single files, and each of them rubbed his fireman's hose in order to present it to us in its optimum state. When my companion saw that the first two were able to offer perfectly hard and erect cocks, she clapped her hands and straight away they detached themselves from their squad of comrades and trotted up to us, in spite of their trousers shackling their ankles.

My first fireman had barely reached me when I cried out with excitement. I ripped off my knickers and bra and impaled myself on him with dreadful impatience. He was a handsome boy, and he had an air of innocence about him which only inflamed me further. I set off on an uninterrupted series of orgasms which finally made my head spin, to the point where I feared I would pass out. When my pretty fireman had come in me, I hung on to him, begging him to stay and start again. At that moment I felt madly in love with him. But he withdrew to make way for the next one, who proved to be equally charming.

I consumed the first four or five men with the same excessive eagerness, that's how long I needed to begin to quell the flame that all these males had ignited in me. I cried out my pleasure without restraint, like my companion in delight, who also seemed to be endowed with a lively temperament and an immoderate passion for these gentlemen.

When I felt completely drained of strength, I handed the initiative to my partners, authorizing them to take me according to whichever of their fantasies. After a while, I'd have had difficulty saying exactly where I was or even who I was. I was no more than a being fused into time, and time was a long, dizzy delight.

I came to myself again finally when I suddenly recognized the Man, the one I had come in here to look for, disguised as a fireman, taking his turn with my companion. A sharp stab of excitement, quickly tinged with sadness, spite and jealousy, ran through my heart. Why did he have to be in the other group? He didn't know it, but he was my man, he was for me...

However, it was another fireman who penetrated me, who guided his sting to the heart of my burning belly ... I forgot everything, I was carried away by pleasure.

When the men had all retired, their mission bravely accomplished, I went to sleep on the sofa, with my hostess. Later, she suggested a shower and a light meal, and I borrowed a flimsy little dress from her, which I wore without underwear, for I was tired of my leathers and anything else that would constrict my body.

Then I kissed my companion and went back out into the

corridors, where I wandered for a long time, deep in thought. The ghosts were following me again, I felt their presence behind me and I turned round frequently, terrified, but they didn't show themselves, and I refused to succumb to my fear as I dashed through the first available door.

I thought about that man, whom I had almost caught up with. He had looked at me, but he went to fuck the other woman, like all his friends. 'Bastard,' I whispered. But I regretted it immediately, and waved my hand lightly in front of my mouth so that the word which had just escaped it would disappear. Deep down, I don't know whether I was more excited or depressed at seeing him possess another woman. You always dream of having a man for yourself alone, but would this dream be as strong and vibrant if you didn't know that he might fall prey to the temptation to look elsewhere?

'Come on,' I concluded. 'So I've missed him. It's not so serious. I'm sure I'll catch up with him in the end. In the meantime, I might as well take advantage of the marvels this place seems to offer.' And I opened a door.

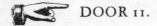 DOOR 11.

10

The Ghosts

The door opened onto the enormous lobby of an ancient hotel. I decided to leave straight away, in the hope of finding a more private place, for I was naked and very keen to avoid being seen in a public place. But the commissionaire, with a pretence of courteous deference, pushed me firmly inside.

Through the glass entrance door I could see that the lobby was crowded. Elegant people came and went, collected or deposited keys or messages at the desk, chatted or read newspapers at round tables. I wanted to turn back, but the commissionaire opened the glass door, took my arm again and, without a word, but with a look that brooked no argument, threw me into the middle of this busy throng.

I was sure everyone was looking at me. I didn't dare look up at anyone. For a while, I couldn't decide what pose to adopt, since I decided against the only reflex that came to me, to cross my hands over my sex. I'm sure this would have made me look more ridiculous. Without seeing anything around me, I walked with as much confidence as I could muster up to the desk, fixed my eyes on those of the receptionist and calmly asked him for a room. He gave me a cursory glance:

'Does Madam have no luggage?'

'Do you have a room, yes or no?' I insisted, impatient to get out of sight of everyone.

Around me people came and went, returned their keys, settled their bills ... I tried to forget how incongruous and out of place I must look, naked in such a civilized old establishment.

Finally he gave me a key, stating with some embarrassment that it was the last vacant room, and asking if I was sure I wanted it. I gave my name for the register, then I escaped, refusing to be accompanied, gripping the key tightly in my hand, as if it were my last hope of survival.

I decided not to take the lift, in order to avoid the lift attendant and the proximity of other hotel guests, which would be particularly difficult to deal with in that confined cage. I had been given room 413. But the staircase stopped at the first floor. I walked down the corridor, which opened onto a whole network of other corridors, at the corners of which were signs indicating the direction of the rooms. Occasionally, a sign pointing towards the ceiling announced the rooms on the upper floors, numbers 200 to 484, but I had great difficulty in finding another staircase in this maze. I met with the same difficulty on each floor. After a number of detours, from one corridor to another and from one flight of stairs to another, I finally reached my destination, on the top floor.

It was a spacious room, with bare floorboards, old furniture and two large beds, all plunged in darkness. I didn't switch on the light or open the shutters, happy at last to be somewhere private. I double-locked the door and sought refuge between the sheets. Alone. Alone and naked in the warmth of a large, comfortable bed, in silence, with time before me in which I was totally free to dream, sleep, think ... I gave myself up languorously to this delicious moment.

In my half-sleep, a throbbing erotic reverie took hold of me. I must have fallen deeply asleep, for I awoke with a start, feeling a mixture of fear and excitement. Lying in bed with my eyes wide open, it was some time before I accepted that these panting noises of love were really here in the room.

I sat up and peered into the dark all around me. Pressed

against the door, a couple were embracing passionately. Tangled up together, exchanging kisses, they touched each other feverishly, which seemed to take them to the edge of ecstasy.

I was violently shocked by this scene which, at that precise moment, set off a whole host of diverse and contradictory sensations and feelings in me, which I was unable to unravel. From this chaos in my mind and body only one question emerged: how had they been able to enter, since I had locked the door? And I put this question to them. They turned towards me, opened the door and, without saying a word, with perfect placidity and precision, they left.

I stood up, ran to the door, which I too opened, in order to look into the corridor. Nobody there. I double-locked it again and went back to bed. Now I regretted having chased them away with my harshness. When they had looked at me, for a moment only, I had seen in the dark two faces full of gentleness, and also, no doubt, a little melancholy. These two loved each other, that was certain. Why hadn't I been more understanding?

I tried to recover my calm, but the memory of their sighs and panting wouldn't leave me in peace. Lying in bed with my legs open, eyes closed, I began to caress myself gently, imitating their panting and imagining all the sensations they were experiencing when I had surprised them. I had a long climax, and then I sank back into sleep, my hands still clasped between my thighs.

This time I awoke peacefully, without anguish. I knew immediately that they had come back. I allowed myself to float in a half-awake state, lulled by the sounds of their love. They were right next to me, in the other bed. I opened my eyes and I saw them, naked, pale, in the lotus position, one inside the other. Their bodies undulated in harmony, and they never took their eyes off each other. Their bed was right under the window, and the faint night-time light fell on them through the gaps in the shutters.

He turned her over onto her back and lay on top of her. Then they both turned their heads slowly towards me and looked at me. I didn't dare move or speak, for fear of driving them away again. Suddenly I felt even more anxious than ever, and I didn't know the cause of my terror. But I did lock the door, I said to myself again. But something else was bothering me, something else which I didn't know.

The lovers reached out to me with their hands. I joined them and lay down next to the woman. She brought her lips to mine, put her tongue in my mouth and gave me a kiss which ignited my whole body, which had been frozen with fear. The man moved between my legs and penetrated me, while she continued, with her hands, her mouth and her breasts, to cover me in kisses and caresses. The two lovers made me come just once, but with an intense pleasure which simultaneously touched all the sensitive points of my sex and my body and vibrated and radiated to its very extremities.

After so perfect an orgasm I must have gone straight to sleep, for I have no memory of what we did afterwards. When I awoke the next morning in their bed, they had disappeared. On the ground lay the woman's flimsy little dress, which she had abandoned on the floor. Before leaving the room I slipped it on next to my skin.

Getting back to reception was again a complex operation. I had to find my way through the tangle of corridors and stair-cases before I reached the lobby, dressed in a less embarrassing way than when I had arrived. When I returned my key, the receptionist looked at my dress with a fearful expression and said:

'You saw them? Normally we don't let out this room ... it's the only haunted room in the hotel ... The only ...'

'What do you mean?' I said angrily, although I don't know why.

'Shush!' he continued in a low voice, trembling like a leaf. 'Please, we don't want any scandal! All right, we were wrong! Damn ghosts! You don't owe us anything, but let's not discuss this further, if you please! Let's not discuss it, let's not discuss it!'

'The man's mad,' I thought. I decided not to pursue it and I left the hotel. In the dark corridor, I hesitated between the two following doors:

 DOOR 11,

 DOOR 12.

The Black Knight

There was nothing in this room except an open book, a book which was taller than me. The black ink on the paper engraved gigantic characters, drew them in all their strangeness, their mysterious beauty. I took a few steps towards the work, my heart beating with enthusiasm and a vague apprehension, as if I expected to see the leaves close softly over me, to embrace me and lift me up. I entered the shadow of the pages.

I stood still among the columns of signs and I saw that these signs were secret armies of ants, busy building a sunshade to soften the midday-bright whiteness of the paper beaches. With a faint feeling of dizziness, I deciphered these lines of verse on the right-hand page:

> Alone like a serf, on adventure's quest,
> Full seven years have gone since, full dressed
> In armour as befits a noble knight
> I took a path which led me to the right.
> 'Twas a most treacherous forest road
> O'ergrown with bramble and with thorn
> And with much trouble all day I rode
> Until I reached the furthest borne
> Of this forest which was called Brocéliande.

I went closer to the page and took it in my hand to turn it. It swung like a door and I found myself in a forest, in the middle of an overgrown path. I started walking, in spite of the brambles which caught my dress and scratched my bare legs. Soon I came across a bush laden with large blackberries, which I feasted on.

At the end of the path a glimmer of light appeared through a gap, from which came the echo of some din. I went up to it and saw, in a cleared patch of land, a whole herd of bulls, as wild as bears or leopards, engaged in a combat of such sound and fury that I couldn't prevent myself from taking three steps back.

A swarthy bumpkin, inordinately ugly and hideous, was sitting on a tree stump, with a large club in his hand. As I approached the peasant, I noticed he had a head bigger than a carthorse's, a tangled mop of hair and a bald forehead the size of two hands, large, hairy ears like an elephant's, enormous eyebrows and a flat face, owl's eyes, a cat's nose, a slit of a mouth like a wolf's, boar's teeth, sharp and russet, a red beard, a twisted moustache, a chin planted in his breast and a long, hunched backbone. Leaning on his club, he wore a strange item of clothing, neither linen nor wool, which consisted of two freshly flayed skins, of two bulls or two cows, tied together round his neck.

The peasant leapt to his feet as soon as he saw me approach. I don't know whether he wanted to touch me, or what he wanted to do, and I stood ready to defend myself. He stood there quietly, without moving, on top of his tree trunk. He must have been at least five metres tall.

He looked at me, but didn't say a word, any more than a beast would have done. I thought he must be incapable of speech or reason. Nevertheless, I had the temerity to ask him:

'Tell me, are you or are you not a good creature?'

He replied that he was a man.

'What sort of man are you?'

'As you see. I am as I am, I haven't changed my form.'

'What are you doing here?'

'This is where I live, and I keep the animals of this wood.'

'You keep them? But by Saint Peter in Rome, they don't

know what a man is! I don't see how you can keep a wild beast, either in a field or a wood or anywhere else, if it is not tied up or locked up ...'

'Yet I do keep them. And I can guarantee that they will never leave here.'

'But how do you do this?'

'As soon as they see me coming, not one of them will move. For if I catch hold of one, I take it by the horns with these two fists you see before you which are hard and strong. Immediately the others tremble with fear and gather round me, as if to ask my pardon. But no one save I could do this. Anyone else who went among them would be killed on the spot ... I am thus the lord of my beasts, and you would do well now to say who you are and what you want.'

'My lord,' I said, hoping to win his benevolence through flattery, 'I came into this forest in search of some adventure. What its nature is, I cannot say, for I do not know why I walk among the beasts of the wood, such as yourself, kind lord, and these wild bulls of yours, who look ready to gore me.'

The mighty giant, as he listened to me, rolled his eyes beneath his eyebrows and I thought that to these eyes I must look as strange as he did to mine.

'What sort of woman are you?' he said.

'As you see. I am as I am, I haven't changed my form ...'

The tall peasant gave me another odd look, then he sat down on his stump.

'If you are looking for adventure,' he said, 'go to the fountain. Near here you will find a path that will lead you to it. Keep heading in a straight line, ignore all the other ways. Go to the end and you will see a fountain where the water boils, even though it is colder than marble. Shade is given it by the most beautiful trees ever created by nature. Their leaves last through all seasons and never fall in winter. Hanging there is an iron basin, on the end of a very long chain, which falls into the fountain. And there, nearby, you will find a block of stone, the like of which you have never seen, and beside that a chapel, which is small but most beautiful. If you so will, take water from the basin and spread it on the stone and there will be such a storm that from these woods all the beasts, deer and stags, boars and even birds will flee. For you will see so much lightning, wind and cracking of trees, rain, thunder and sparks that, if you can escape it without great trouble or damage, you will be luckier than those who came before you.'

With his finger the peasant pointed the way. He kept his beasts near him and I skirted round them and headed into the forest. It must have been nearly midday when I saw the tree and the fountain. This tree was the most beautiful ever to grow on earth, and so bushy that even in a heavy rain not one drop could ever penetrate its foliage. I saw the basin hanging from a branch: it was made of the finest gold. As for the fountain, it was boiling like hot water. The stone was an emerald, hollowed out like a vase and resting on four rubies of a brighter, more blazing red than the morning sun when it appears in the orient.

I bent over the emerald fountain and took some water in my hands. It was cold and pure. I dampened my lips and drank great mouthfuls. Then I sat down on the precious stone, at the edge of the fountain and in the bubbling ice-water washed the scratches which the brambles of the forest had made on my legs. The clearing was plunged in silence, as if the wildfowl were all at rest at that hour.

Suddenly the branches of the pine began to rustle with the beating of wings and the cries of birds. Immediately a knight appeared before me, in a full suit of armour and mounted on a brown steed. He climbed to the ground and, taking off his helmet, revealed the most charming man's face a woman could ever see.

'Fair lady,' he said, bowing, 'will you allow me to approach your fountain? An arrow in the thigh has so wounded me that I believe I will never recover from it.'

I saw that he had knotted his shirt around the wound under his hauberk, and that it was quite bloodstained.

'Noble sire,' I replied, as I headed towards him, 'I will gladly give you aid.'

And I led him to the fountain, where I sat him down and helped him out of his armour. When he was free of his heavy coat of chainmail, I undid the shirt knotted around his wounded thigh and soaked it in the fountain, which grew redder than its stand of rubies. His britches were torn at the spot where the arrow had pierced his flesh and I carefully bathed his wound.

As I was tending him, he told me his name was Gawain, that he was a knight of King Arthur and he would tell me, if I so wished, how he had been wounded thus. I encouraged him to speak and he told me this story:

'Yesterday evening,' he said, 'I was taken by the desire to go hunting. I alerted my knights and my huntsmen and my valets. And as there is great pleasure to be had, early in the morning, I went into the forest. On the trail of a large deer, we soon released the dogs. The huntsmen ran ahead, but I remained at the rear.

'Nevertheless, before leaving the forest, I wanted the chance to fire off a shot. That is when I saw a doe with its fawn, in a bush. The animal was completely white, with antlers on its head. The dog barked and leaped forward. I bent my bow and loosed an arrow. Hit in the hoof, it fell immediately. But the arrow rebounded, went through my thigh and made me fall into the dense grass, next to the doe. And she, wounded and anguished, moaned:

'"Ah! Coward! I am slain! But you, vassal, who have wounded me, such is your fate: never, by any medicine, any herb, any root, any doctor, any poison, will you find a cure for that wound in your thigh, unless she who cures you will suffer one day for your love as much pain as a woman has ever suffered. And you will suffer too, for love of her; and all who love, have loved and will love will marvel at it. Now go! Leave me in peace!"'

When he had finished his story, he looked into my eyes and added:

'That is how, dear fair lady, I found myself abandoned by destiny in your hands.'

From his look I felt that I myself had been wounded by an arrow, that arrow from the eyes which strikes the heart of lovers. And he had undoubtedly been struck by the same arrow himself, for, as I finished dressing his wound, I noticed that, beneath his tight britches, his pine cone of love was growing hard.

'Lady,' he said, 'I am dying for you. My heart is suffering a million torments. If you do not cure me of it, I will have to die. I ask you for your love, fair one, do not refuse me!'

'My friend,' I said with a smile, 'we would be proceeding with great haste were I to accede to your request. And that is not my wont.'

'Sweet fair lady, I ask you not to be angry when I say that a flighty courtesan needs much persuading, so that she might appear worthy and so that no one believes her to be accustomed to a lover's game. But the lady whose thoughts are honest, who has value and good sense within her, if she meets a man who pleases her, will not strain too greatly his desir. She will love him without hesitation and will find her joy in this. Before anyone knows, they will have given each other great happiness. Fair lady, I beg you, let us put an end to this debate!'

We ceased parleying to exchanged sweet looks.

Beside me, I felt him burning while my heart panted for him. He took me in his arms and began to kiss my face, to cherish me, to hold me tightly. I reached out my hand and grabbed that thick, warm love cone that swelled beneath his britches. Beneath my fingers I could feel his genitals so full and his dagger so stiff that, fainting with desire, I thought of nothing else than feeling him pound against my arse.

He pulled me back into the grass with him, at the foot of the fountain, and fondled at my shell. Pulling at his britches I discovered a proud dart and two fair-haired balls which fanned my rage. I got down on all fours and, with one push, he fucked me. We quickly came together.

After this ardent, first, fully-clothed fuck, we took the time to get undressed. He had a handsome, lean, muscular body which I delighted in. And since he was hale and hearty and able, in honour of his lady, to stiffen at will, valiant as a knight, he inhabited me three times more, though not before having most deftly tongued my jewel and given the greatest joys.

At the fourth thrust of his épée, he stretched out between my breasts and splashed me in abundance, up to my chin. Enticed by the fragrance of his unguent I began to tongue the tip of his now flaccid dart, and then I took it in my mouth and gave him such bounty that once more, between my lips, it began to become inflamed. He yelled out loud when I extracted the last of his sap, which I swallowed with relish.

'Will you have mercy on me, my sweet?' my courteous friend said finally.

And I lay myself to rest between his arms, for I felt a great tiredness, in my mouth, my crack and my behind, and also my legs, my whole body. The air was clear, sharp and serene. Radiant and tired from our languorous lovemaking, we let ourselves drift into a tender slumber.

Beneath the green foliage of the pine, amongst which darted swallows, we exchanged gentle looks.

'Most lovely friend with the bright face,' says my gentle lord, 'by your pleasure and by your hand I wish to live and die. My heart has led me to this wish.'

'And who has led your heart, my fine, sweet friend?'

'Lady, my eyes.'

'And who your eyes?'

'The great beauty I see in you.'

My heart pants for him again, again, for from him will come good and ill fortune, and everything that gives me life. My brow blushes, and I bury it in his shoulder, that he should not see my joy and my emotion. I am enclosed in his arms and he embraces me ardently, I kiss his skin, where I lie, I laugh and hug my lover, yet also cry, for something else beside, for great torment within great joy does oft reside.

Suddenly, a sound of galloping horses gives us both a start. We gather up our clothes from the grass and get dressed. The shirt has fallen from his thigh, and nothing remains of his wound other than a well-healed scar.

'Tender friend, the doe cursed me but you have saved me.'

He has barely put his doublet back on when into the clearing there bursts a group of knights, dressed in armour and in a great hurry.

'My lord Gawain,' one of them says, 'we are greatly in need of you. As we were riding with Lancelot in search of you, a hunchbacked dwarf betrayed us. By his trickery he abducted Lancelot, and we must free him.'

'How is the Queen?' asks Gawain.

'Queen Guinevere awaits you both, Lancelot and yourself, before returning to Arthur's side. But she would be heartbroken were she to learn that her friend has been abducted.'

'Sweet fair friend,' Gawain says, as he turns towards me, 'Lancelot is dear to me and I cannot abandon him. Will you grant me a week? In a week's time I will be here by the fountain, waiting for you. For, to this day, my heart has never been struck by such a love as I feel for you. At this moment, when duty and friendship are in conflict with the burning desire I have to stay by your side, I feel full of anguish. But I am at your command, my lady, and I will do as you say.'

'Noble lord,' I say, as I hold his hands, 'thus it is that lovers experience joy and pain in turn. Go with your knights in search of Lancelot. In one week, in this very place, if you keep your promise, you will return to kiss me.'

At the edge of the fountain my ardent friend bade me adieu and embraced me with a sigh.

'The body departs but the heart remains,' he adds.

Then he put on his armour and climbed onto his horse. With his companions he disappeared into the forest.

When he had gone, my heart began to swoon, and I felt the pain of love. Around me everything was silent. I sat down on the stone of the fountain and bathed my face in the cold, boiling water in order to wash away my tears.

'My lord Gawain, fine, gentle friend,' I said, looking at the grass where we had made love, 'see how lonely and depressed I am since you left me. And you, tender grasses, will you bear the remembrance of our love when we come to lie here one week from now?'

My eyes fell by chance on the gold basin which was hanging into the fountain from the tree and I remembered the words of the keeper of the bulls. I preferred to face any storm than remain in the despond in which I found myself. I sprinkled water from the fountain onto the large, hollow emerald.

But I must have poured too much, perhaps. For such a storm came up that from more than forty leagues away the lightning struck my eyes. And the clouds threw down a confusion of rain, snow and hail. And the storm was so strong that many times I thought I would die, from the thunderbolts falling and trees cracking all round. And I remained in this state of alarm for as long as the weather remained stormy. But soon God reassured me and it began to abate. Soon the winds died down and, on his order, no longer dared blow. Once I saw the clear, pure air, I felt safe again. For pleasure, once taken, makes you forget all concerns.

When the storm had passed, I saw massed on the pine tree so many birds that the branches and leaves could not be seen. It was completely covered with birds and was even more beautiful because of it. And softly they all began to sing, prettily in tune. Each sang its own song. I rejoiced in their joy and never wearied of their melodies or their concert which were so enchanting that nowhere else would you hear so great a celebration and so fine a chorus.

Suddenly I heard the din of a whole band of knights. At first I thought that Gawain and his companions had returned. But there appeared a single knight, a stranger, who advanced so noisily that you would have thought he was eight people. Aggressively he bore down upon me, faster than an eagle and more enraged than a lion.

I remained motionless beside the fountain, watching him approach, giving no sign either of defiance or fear. He stopped before me and cried:

'Who are you? Are you an alien?'

'Yes,' I said, 'I am a stranger.'

'How did you come here?'

'Not far from here, in the forest, a keeper of bulls showed me the way to the fountain.'

'Do you know what you have done? You have provoked such a storm over my lands that many trees have fallen, animals have fled, even my castle shook. And now you must make amends.'

Without giving me time to respond, he leant over me, lifted me from the ground and put me over the rump of his horse, which he urged away at a gallop. I hung onto his chain-mail, for he too was covered in armour. I still hadn't seen his face.

He took me thus on his black steed to a mighty castle, surrounded by high walls and a deep moat. A drawbridge was lowered to let us in. As soon as we climbed down, the knight held my arm in his fist, which was hard and strong, and led me through a vast hall and several beautiful rooms to the highest room in the keep. And I saw not one other man or woman in this manor. Then he left me alone in this room, not forgetting to turn the key in the door behind him.

I found myself locked in a large, flagstoned room. In the

middle, a bed was made up with two embroidered silk covers and fine sheets. I went over to the window.

Night was falling, and it was raining, a soft, fine drizzle. 'Alas,' I said, 'who will free me from this keep if not death itself one day?' Down below, far below, the dark bottomless moat surrounded me. The day was losing its light and the forest all around was disappearing. Fine gentle friend, my heart is drowning, sounds are fading and, in the wood, all life is drifting away with the night. Tonight no moon will shine. And the night and the wood trouble me greatly, and more than the night and the wood, the rain.

I lay down between the sheets. Soon the door opened and the sinister knight appeared.

'My lord,' I said, 'what will you do with me? Will you hold me here captive, in anguish?'

He was now dressed in rich finery, a black tunic embroidered all over in gold, a scarlet coat trimmed with squirrel fur. He had a long face which was more disturbing than ever, even though he was affecting good humour. He greeted me in a most courteous fashion and offered me a chemise, a silk dress and a tunic in white ermine.

He invites me to go down to the hall and dine. He looks at me and his dark, unblinking eyes sparkle. 'This man loves you,' I say to myself. And I don't know whether I should be hopeful or afraid.

I put on the dress and the tunic, he helps me lace it tightly over my hips. When I see myself in my finery, so beautiful and so richly embroidered is the cloth, that a little joy returns to my heart. By his side, I descend as far as the threshold of the hall, whose doors are wide open. On a long, covered table I see dishes, candles in chandeliers and gilded silver goblets, a jug of dark wine and another of claret.

Around the table there are so many candles that the light is bright. But at the end of the room, many shadows. On a bench are two bowls of warm water, for washing your hands, and a snow-white embroidered towel for drying them. Together we eat, and drink the honeyed and spiced wines. Then he accompanies me to my prison.

Into my bed the knight climbs with me. He has taken off his britches and shirt, but I have no desire for him. And yet, he is most handsome. But my heart does not incline me towards him, for it remains entirely in the hands of my dear friend. When he sees me still dressed in my chemise, lying at the end of the bed, cold as marble, the knight leaves the room in a sombre mood and locks me in.

I hardly sleep all night. Dawn arrives and wipes away the rain. In the flat grey sky an eagle soars, I watch it through the window. Its strange cry strangely reassures me and I go back to my bed where finally I find sleep.

All day I remain locked up and alone. Only an old woman comes into the room to bring me food and drink and to attend to my toilet. That night the knight returns, he lies in my bed and holds me tenderly. He is most handsome and his black eyes burn with sadness.

'Alas, fine sir,' I say to him, 'I cannot give you this heart which my friend has already taken. Take my body if you wish but my love I will keep for him.'

The knight says not a word but rises and leaves.

The third night, he does not come, nor the next night, nor any of the following. My soul is racked with torment. The days are deathly pale, at night I stay by the window, listening to the stars, heaven's silent choirs. At dawn, when the dark eagle soars soundlessly in the air, my heart pants, for whom I know not. And I return to my bed in search of sleep and forgetfulness.

On the seventh night, I hear the key in the lock. The knight enters the room.

'Lady,' he says, 'you are free.'

Then he turns to go, leaving the door open.

'Sire!' I say, anguished with love.

Then he comes towards me and in his arms holds me,

cherishes me, caresses me. Together in the deep bed we are thrown by our eager, long-silent desire and with our mouths, our hands and our whole bodies we make love, with mad abandon. In this rage of passion I fall onto my hands on the stone floor. Kneeling behind me, my dark lord pierces my behind and raises a strange cry in my throat, which echoes from wall to wall, in the room, in the manor, and escapes through the window into the night, above the dark water of the moat, to the beasts of the forest.

All night and all day the dark lord and I spend in carnal coupling. Never needing to ask which delights we wish to feed on, we graze on all those ordered by our limbs and our heads, our hands and tongues, behinds and crack, balls and penis, legs and arms, bellies and breasts, fingers and hair, nails and teeth. The one perpetually stirred and envigorated by the other, we fornicate tirelessly, as if, in play, to kill each other.

At nightfall, in the room scented by our torments and our joy, my body sore and exhausted by amorous combat, I fall into a faint.

'Am I alive or dead? Did I live this or merely dream it?' I thought as I returned to consciousness. It was the eighth night and I was alone in the shadows. The clothes I had been given, chemise, dress and richly embroidered tunic, lay in tatters all around. I put my little stranger's dress back on and left by the large open door. I walked through the rooms and the hall without meeting a soul. I left the castle by the lowered drawbridge and went into the forest.

I walked for a long time in the dark, but could not find our fountain. Dawn returned and I saw the eagle circling in the sky. 'Eagle,' I wept, 'why do you circle alone in this sky so vast? Have you lost your two friends?'

I found a tree and embraced it with all my strength, my eyes closed.

Gently the tree swings over and carries me to the other bank, the other side of the book. On the cover I read the words

Chrétien de Troyes, Marie de France. I close the big book, open the door and leave.

 DOOR 14,

 DOOR 12.

12

The Chimney Sweep

It was an attic, jam-packed with old objects. This bric-à-brac was gaily illuminated by the light falling through the gable window. Through the opening you could see the deep blue, transparent sky. On a pedestal table I found a charming parasol, slightly faded but in good condition. I decided to go and get a bit of sun.

I stepped out through the window and found myself on a tiled roof facing a forest of other roofs, at once similar and different, with their gentle slopes, their pink tiles, their grey zinc, their chimneys of all shapes and sizes, their aerials, their gutters, their glass windows, their projections, their more or less overlapping angles ... The roofs of the town, stretching away out of view, with ne sky above, a spring sky occasionally streaked with the sudden, darting flights of swifts, whose cries scratched the light reflected everywhere.

I started walking on the tiles, up above the large city, of which I could hear only a dull, confused rumble and see only this magnificent, joyous, disordered band of roofs. Every now and again I saw, through an open window, one or two silhouettes moving in an attic room like Chinese shadows.

I sat down against a large chimney to contemplate the sky and the town at greater ease. Everything was vast and beautiful, open and secret. The dark, pointed swifts cried and ripped through the air in a flash in all directions, then flew in flocks from one roof to another. My gaze was drawn to an attic room just a little below my observation post as two people, a man and a woman, entered. They undressed and started making love on the bed. I said to myself that, if it were I, I would do it standing up at the window, with the man behind me, so that at the same time I could enjoy the view of the rooftops.

I turned round when I heard a refrain from a well-known musical. A chimney sweep was stepping lightly from chimney to chimney, his long brush in his hand. Slim and agile, completely black with soot, he was humming cheerfully. He came towards me, greeted me and pushed his brush-head into the funnel and swept it carefully.

I moved away from my chimney to watch him work. He had a pretty little face and his blue eyes lit up with happiness. I bent over to look down the black hole.

'Nice job, isn't it?' he said, amused by my curiosity, and he broke into song: 'All day long I wander above the town, up with the clouds and the cats and the birds ... From chimney to chimney I wander and I sweep, I merrily sweep...'

He reached out his arms and we began to dance on the tiles, singing his song together. Then he pressed me against the chimney, lifted up my dress, opened the flies of his overalls, and took out his nice tool, which he pushed into my funnel and wiggled with the same dexterity and vigour which he had demonstrated with his brush. We continued singing.

Still embracing, we stretched out on the gentle slope of the roof, where we continued our work, still singing, though in an increasingly syncopated rhythm. My back against the tiles, my head tilted back in the sky, I came at the same time as him.

We remained lying on the roof, side by side, for the light was fading and it would soon be time to watch the sunset. When the sun had set, leaving nothing but large red streaks in the sky, I got up, opened my parasol, walked to the edge of the roof and jumped. I descended slowly through the air down to the street, where I found an exit.

In the corridor, ghosts darker than my chimney sweep surrounded me and kept me company with their whispers and breathing on my neck. Once again, I couldn't resist trying to see them. But once again, they disappeared into the shadow as soon as I turned round. Perhaps they were nothing but patches of shadow themselves? Sometimes their invisible presence terrified me. But, at this moment, I considered them more benevolently, like that dark spider in the corner of the ceiling, which you dread at first but which eventually becomes so familiar that you think he is listening when you speak to him . . .

I was in an excellent mood. Spontaneously I stopped walking and opened a new door.

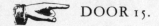 DOOR 15.

13

The Moon

I entered a conservatory, built over a verandah. There was no light on. Only the light of the moon, which I couldn't see from where I was, helped me distinguish in the dark some wicker chairs, a table with a number of glasses reflecting the light and a large green plant. I slipped between the furniture, feeling my way a little, to the french window.

It opened onto a neglected garden. On each side of a path bordered with stones, bunches of large yellow flowers blossomed in the tall grass. A washing line hung with pegs stretched between two trees. A light breeze rustled the leaves, and on their tips played a silver gleam. An owl hooted.

Standing motionless behind one of the tall clusters of yellow flowers, directly beneath the full moon, was a young man in a cream-coloured raincoat.

I opened the door and went out into the garden. The sky was laden with stars and crossed by the compact white band of the Milky Way. The moon, huge and creamy, rested in a broad halo, reddening like a wound. There was no sound but the rustling of the breeze in the leaves, the intermittent hooting of the owl and the imperceptible breathing of the garden and the man. I went towards him.

He was looking at an undefined point in front of him and didn't turn his eyes towards me, even though he must have heard me coming.

When I arrived in front of him, he very slowly opened his raincoat, beneath which he was naked. I knelt down in the grass, among the flowers, which brushed my shoulders and face. They gave off a strong, slightly acrid smell. I took the man's penis in my mouth.

I sucked it, slowly. When he came, I withdrew, to see his white substance spurt out, iridescent in the moonlight. Large beads of it dripped down my face and in my hair. I licked them. They tasted like vegetal sap.

The young man left and disappeared into the darkness of the garden. I went back to the verandah. I heard the owl again.

I could feel the traces of fresh, crushed grass on my knees. I walked across the room and went out.

In the corridor, I opened the following door.

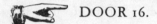 DOOR 16.

14

The Wild Animals

I found myself in a corridor as dark as the one I had just left but much more narrow and full of the echo of animal roars, which swirled round this narrow passage like a maelstrom. I stood still a moment, gripped by amazement and fear.

Then I carried on. At the end of the corridor, which was only three or four paces away, I could make out a curtain and was curious to find out what went on behind it.

When I pulled back the curtain, the roars, which had fallen silent, sounded out anew. In a large cage in the middle of an empty circus ring two lions were circling round their trainer, their mouths open and their lips drawn back to let out their raucous sounds. The trainer shouted out an order and the animals climbed slowly onto their stools and sat down.

They were magnificent beasts. I approached the cage the better to admire them.

The trainer looked at me, opened the cage door and waited, without saying a word or taking his eyes off me. I approached him slowly, my stomach knotted with fear, and entered the cage.

The animals watched me and roared again. One of them leapt down from its stool and took a step towards us. I was paralysed with terror. The trainer spoke to it gently in a language I didn't recognize and pointed to the stool. The lion went back and sat down.

The man took my hand and led me to the back of the cage. I didn't take my eyes off the animals, who returned my gaze. The man pushed my back against the bars and pressed himself against me. His vest revealed his muscular torso and arms, which emitted a strong smell. Through his tights I could feel his iron-hard penis against my thigh.

He unbuttoned my dress, opened it fully, lowered his tights and stuck his rod between my thighs. My legs apart, my arms open above my head, I hung onto the bars while he ravaged me with powerful thrusts.

The cage began to shake and rattle. I saw the animals leave their stools and start pacing round in the sand again. In a panic – and as if I thought it would shorten my terror – with my fists closed tight around the bars of the cage, which I shook violently in my spasm, I suddenly let myself go in an orgasm, my cries making a din with the rattling of the much manhandled cage, the groans of the trainer, who was coming also, and the roars of the agitated lions.

When I came to my senses, I stood petrified with fear. The trainer had returned to his beasts and was having great trouble calming them down. At least he had regained their attention. But instead of obeying his orders they defied him, open-mouthed. Finally, he managed to make them lie down. With a wave of his hand he signalled to me that the time had come to make a getaway.

Slowly, my back against the bars, without taking my eyes off the beasts, I inched my way to the door of the cage. The trainer kept talking to his animals, for they were still agitated and itching to get up. Very carefully, I opened the door, slipped through . . . Finally, I was outside.

I would have liked to say goodbye to my lover, but he was busy trying to get his lions back onto their stools and had completely lost interest in me. To be honest, I had paid him no more regard than he had paid me. We hadn't even exchanged a word. He had spoken only to his animals and I had looked only at them.

I glanced up at the benches and imagined the noise of an excited crowd watching the lions' routine. I went through the dark little passage to the corridors.

I realized that my legs were shaking and that I was exhausted. I opened another door, hoping to find a nice bed.

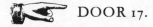 DOOR 17.

15

The Golden Phallus

I entered a huge gaming room, which was so large I couldn't see the other end. The pitiless artificial lights made everything shine brightly, especially the golden, neoclassical-kitsch décor. As far as the eye could see there were dozens of rows of one-armed bandits lined up in all directions.

The casino staff who patrolled the alleys were all men, handsome young men, entirely naked except for headbands in their hair and laced-up leather sandals on their feet. And the clients were all female, women of all ages, sitting on stools in front of their one-armed bandits, gripping in their hands the long, thick golden phalluses which served as handles.

The machines rang, spat out coins here and there and, when the jackpot was sufficiently large, one of the naked croupiers would run up to the winner to congratulate her and help her stack her dollars in a rack.

This was all rather exciting but I didn't have any change in my pocket with which to to try my luck. I crossed the room, looking for the hotel desk, for this casino undoubtedly belonged to one. It was probably the twin of a similar room reserved for men, with female lovelies on hand to provide the service.

I found the lobby of the hotel; it was vast and gaudy. These establishments are always flashily luxurious, but offer modestly priced rooms, in order to seduce the mugs into the gaming rooms. I located a lift, in front of which a fat man was waiting. I entered the lift with him.

As soon as the doors closed, I said to him:

'I would like to play, but I haven't any money for my first stake.'

And he looked me straight in the eyes. He seemed to have got the message. So I added:

'Twenty dollars for a blow-job.'

He took the notes out of his pocket and undid his buttons. I did the deed next to the lift buttons, so that I only had to reach out a hand to get the lift to move up or down. So we went up and down like that for as long as it took, which wasn't very long, for I thought it was more fun to do it on the move, rather than block the lift, which might have brought on my claustrophobia, even if it was only for a couple of minutes. Also, we ran the risk of being discovered, which added a little spice to the proceedings.

With my twenty dollars in my hand I went back to the gaming room, found a free machine and held fast to the golden phallus, which I lowered and raised vigorously with every coin I slipped into the slot. A nicely built waiter came to offer me a drink and I looked at him with interest but didn't stare, out of shyness. Then I noticed that the other women had no qualms about exchanging compliments and pleasantries with the members of the staff, and even fondling them a bit. When the waiter returned with my drink, without hesitation I flashed him a pleasing smile while gently weighing up his balls in my hand.

At one point I won a dozen or so dollars, then I lost the lot. So I had to go back to the lifts. Once again, I chose my prey well, for my proposition was warmly received, even though I had doubled my fee. I was particularly lucky, for another guy stepped into the lift on the eighteenth floor and caught us at it. I paused only long enough to tell him:

'I'm working, sir.'

So he undid his buttons as well and awaited his turn.

So I had eighty dollars in my pocket when I returned to my assault on the one-armed bandits and their golden phalluses.

This trick lasted all night, or perhaps all day, or all night and all day, for it was impossible to keep track of time in this place where there was no other life but the game and no other light but the neon.

I won the jackpot several times: the machine continually coughed out dollars and immediately the croupier would appear and, in my enthusiasm, I couldn't resist fondling him before offering him a large tip.

When I felt thirsty, I called a waiter; when I felt hungry, I went to the restaurant, where they served everything at every hour; when I ran out of funds, I went to the lifts; and, when I won, I played again until I lost everything.

When I had exhausted all the joys the place had to offer, I signalled to the croupier that I thought was the best looking, drew him to the end of my row and made him a present of the whole of my last winnings. He took my face in his hands and kissed me on my mouth, a long, real cinema kiss. As I left him, I had the pleasure of ascertaining that his member was as proudly erect as the golden phalluses. I would gladly have given him a blow-job, but my jaws were beginning to ache. We gave each other a little wave and went our separate ways.

I found the door back to the corridors and set off. Immediately the sinister ghosts came and breathed in my ears. To get away from the nuisance I opened the following door.

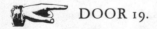 DOOR 19.

16

The Man at the Window

'Will I find him again one day?' I thought, as I opened a new door. Already I was unsure who this man was for whom I was searching. Wasn't he one of those I had made love to here? By following in the steps of the man who had entered the little circus, who must be wandering like me through this strange kingdom and making love to other women, was I not pursuing an illusion? Or, on the contrary, were the men I had loved here no more than mere phantasms? Would I find true love only once I had completed this quest, so full of desires, joys and pains?

How we would all like to be lucid all the time, to know what we are doing and why we are doing it! But, just as the more we gather knowledge the more we see the depth of our ignorance, so the more we progress in our understanding of ourselves and of the world the more the mystery, within us and around us, deepens. That is why, cast out in these dark corridors, we find ourselves at the mercy of fantasies which rule us more than we rule them, yet which are our allies, a sort of army which swells and accompanies us on our adventures.

I had entered a small, simple room. I went to the window which was covered by light white curtains. It faced directly into the window of another building, separated from mine by a narrow alley. And in this room, which was similar to mine, a man sat in an armchair, reading.

He was tall, well-built, mature, obviously handsome and athletic in his youth, but now grown a bit heavy with age. Was it the act of observing him through a window? Straight away I felt a strong curiosity about him.

Strangely for a man reading quietly in his room he was wearing a dark, elegant suit, a white shirt and a narrow, sober tie which he had loosened around his open collar. His hair, cut short on his thick neck, was greying, and, even though he had an intellectual look about him, his heavy head could almost be that of a boxer, with his lumpy nose, his low brow, his prominent cheekbones and square chin. The bottom of his right trouser leg had ridden up as he sat cross-legged and I could see his sock, a fine, grey cotton sock snug over his ankle. I wasn't able to make out the title of the book he was reading.

The man didn't move, yet the fact that I was spying on him without his knowledge excited me considerably. I felt that, by observing him, I was going to penetrate inside him, pierce his secrecy. It was like a rape without violence, something which filled me with a very soft, very sharp sensation.

I looked at him and wondered what his life must be like; I imagined his naked body, his way of making love, his way of life ... What was on his mind at this exact moment? What type of woman did he like? Was he sensuous, loving and sexual? Free? Capable of fantasy? Intelligent? Fun-loving? Shadowy? Mysterious?

The man got up, went to his window and stopped, directly opposite me. I don't know whether he could see me behind my curtains. We stood motionless for a while and soon I knew, from the expression on his face, that he was looking at me. I started slowly to undo the buttons down the front of my dress.

Once I had opened my dress, I opened the curtains. He looked at my body, looked at me. I knelt down at the window and placed my mouth against the glass at the height of his penis on the other side of the alley. With my lips against the pane I started sucking, staring into his eyes, imploring him to respond to my desire. He undid his flies and took out his penis. He was erect.

I closed my eyes for a moment in sheer happiness. He was magnificent. I devoured him with my gaze, again and again. Those balls and that thick cock sticking out of his elegant suit, beneath his tie, were magnificent. I got up, took off my dress and turned around slowly, wiggling my hips to allow him to examine my anatomy at his leisure.

I pressed my breasts against the window and fondled them. He took his cock in his hand and slid it up and down. Then I pulled the chair up to the window, sat down with my legs spread over the armrests and started wanking right in front of him, without taking my eyes off him. I came as I watched him rub himself, faster and faster. At the moment when my hips convulsed and lifted from the chair, at the moment when I cried out, with my head back, I was aware that he was watching me eagerly and that I excited him as much as he excited me. I opened my eyes in time to see him ejaculate, shooting his lovely semen all over the window, where it began dripping down slowly.

Then he left the room and didn't reappear. I went to lie down and fell asleep immediately. I woke up at dusk. In bed, my first action was to look out the window. At that precise moment I saw the light go on and the man come into the room accompanied by a woman.

She was a tall, strong woman wearing lots of make-up. 'A whore,' I thought. She took off her coat, beneath which she was wearing a basque and stockings, her shoes had excessively long and pointed heels. Her large bosom swelled out like a pigeon's breast.

I left the light off in my room. They started making love and I told myself that he had deliberately brought her back to fuck her in a fully lit room before my eyes. She knelt down in front of him, as I had done in front of the window, and began sucking him off. Then he took her to the bed and began to grope and chew her large tits. How I wished I were in her place! How stiff he must be! I wanted him to have pleasure, even if I couldn't give it to him myself. Yet, he soon lost interest. With the help of the girl he got undressed, lay on top of her and took her.

The girl's ankles, with their pointed heels, were wrapped around the neck of my loved-one, and his broad back moved up and down steadily between her thighs. I felt both very excited and very sad to see him making love with another woman. And I wasn't sure whether it was the flame of jealousy or lust that was keeping me there behind this window in the dark, my chest tight, breathing in short gasps, making sure I caught every single detail of their copulation.

The man made the girl go down on all fours in front of the window and, kneeling behind her, he buggered her, directly opposite me. I peered intensely at his face which was contorted with pleasure. I wanted to cry out 'No, no!' and 'Yes, yes!', for I wanted to be her, I wanted to be him, I wanted him, I wanted this to be happening in my body ... At the last minute he withdrew from the girl and ejaculated in the air, towards me. 'That's for me,' I thought, 'it's my present, he did it for me.' I came at the same time as him, my mouth open, as if I could swallow the come he was sending me.

I left the room, feeling a little lost. I was never able to touch the man. He had given me nothing but the sight of him, and he would never give me anything else. Yet, if I had been able to meet him, he might have been the man I could have loved most in the world...

I walked for a long time in the corridors, constantly seeing the same cruel and fascinating images. Was I right to expose myself like that in front of him? It was so ridiculous ... but it would have been even worse if I hadn't been able to express my desire. What had he thought of me? Had he loved me a little? Now that I had lost this man, this man I had never had, I had no appetite for anything else.

The ghosts followed me, whispering behind my back and disappearing each time I turned round to try to see them. In the end they preoccupied me more than the memory of the man at the window. To escape from their tormenting games I decided to open another door.

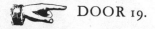 DOOR 19.

17

The Kilts

It was a quiet, grey street, grey as the mist which enveloped everything and lent it a slightly disturbing, very romantic character. There was no sound, nor shape, nor any sign of life, and I stood for a moment peering into the mist, incapable of action. Then I decided to walk, in any direction, since in any case it was impossible to know where I was going.

I had taken no more than three steps when I had the impression I had unwittingly set off some alarm or given some starting signal. For music began in the distance, or muffled in the mist, and people started appearing out of nowhere and gathering into a compact, excited crowd on the pavement, as if waiting for a procession to come past. I waited too, as I was caught up among them and it was very difficult to walk.

The music approached. Now I recognized a traditional Scottish melody and the sound of bagpipes. Finally we could make out the first row of the pipers marching up the street. I tried to slip out through the crowd to find a better vantage point. I had just reached the edge of the pavement when there was a huge surge and I found myself lying on my back with my head in the gutter.

At that moment the bandsmen drew level me. What luck! For the other people only had eyes for them and forgot all about me. I, too, was watching the spectacle with the greatest excitement.

I'm sure that no one in this crowd got as much pleasure from it as I. For I alone had the evidence in front of my eyes: the bandsmen were wearing nothing under their kilts.

Oh! What a lovely parade of pipes and drums was I privileged to witness! I saw so many at the same time, all different and all similar, fleshy and hugely appetizing, and bouncing nicely as they marched. I forgot about the crowd all around me and put my hands down between my legs, just for a few moments, just long enough to experience a heavenly spasm as the last rows paraded their divine charms above my ecstatic face.

As soon as they had gone past I got up and made myself scarce, fearing that someone might have noticed my little trick and desirous to know where this gracious regiment of men was heading. I followed them:

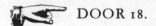 DOOR 18.

18

The Pissers

Finally the band of pipers went into a pub. I dived in after them, with no plan in mind, simply because they excited me. They put down their instruments and sat at the bar and merrily ordered some beer. I asked for one as well, sitting at the only remaining place, at one end of the bar.

Some of them who had perched on stools hadn't tucked their skirts under their bottoms. And I enjoyed the thought of their equipment resting softly against the synthetic leather seats, unbeknown to the other customers in the pub except me. I looked at their ankles and calves in their thick socks, the line where they ended, just below the knee and the small amount of flesh on display, muscular and hairy, before the hem of the kilt. Ah, how I would have loved to put my hands and face up those skirts!

I kept looking, I looked at everything, everything I could see, and I imagined everything, all the rest ... And I was so on fire between my legs that I decided to go and relieve myself in the toilets.

I didn't do it deliberately, or at least not consciously, but I realized I was following one of the pipers who was going to the same place as me. I was staring at his legs and couldn't detach myself from him and I followed him into the gents.

We had both had a few too many beers. I looked at him without shame and lifted up my dress in front of him, sat down on the seat and pissed.

'Your turn,' I said.

And I put my hand under his skirt to grab his cock and lead him to the bowl. Then I held it for him as he pissed. My aim wasn't good, and I sprayed it all over, laughing a great deal.

When he had finished I fell to my knees in front of him and started to suck him off. He hardened a little, grabbed me by the shoulders to stand me up against the wall and wanted to take me. But he had obviously had too much to drink. I started wanking him to get enough life into his thing. What a wonderful experience it is, wanking a man under his skirt! At the same time he fiddled with my pussy the best he could with his large thick fingers. I was in such a state that I came almost immediately, shouting out and banging my head against the tiled wall.

My enthusiasm seemed to give him the final spur he needed. He penetrated me with one thrust, just as another piper came into the toilet, which we hadn't bothered to lock. He went around us to go and piss in the bowl, right next to me, then he started wanking as he watched us.

When my partner had come and made me come several times, the second piper took his place. This time I bent over the bowl, holding on to the sides which were covered with piss, and he took me from behind.

When I finally left the toilet I felt calm for a while. I went out into the muffled softness of the street, as far as the exit. Once back in the corridors, I continued my quest through the doors.

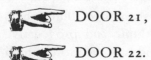 DOOR 21,

DOOR 22.

19

The Mud

It was raining, a dense, warm rain which dripped heavily between the trees, onto the sodden earth of the path. About thirty metres in front of me, on the same path, walked a man in khaki shirt and trousers. The wet cloth stuck to his small, round, firm bum and to the muscles of his back on each side of the supple groove of his spine. His hair was close-cropped on his thick neck, his shoulders were broad, his hips narrow, his legs long, and he wore cowboy boots. I started following him.

Before long my hair and my dress were also soaked and sticking to my skin. The forest gave off a strong smell of humus and sap. I abandoned my shoes to walk barefoot in the muddy earth. The sound of the rain seemed to fill the whole space, even inside my body.

'I'm going to have you,' I thought, my eyes riveted on the guy I was stalking, on that fine animal shape, that bum which flexed supply with each step, in a rhythmic and provocative movement. And the more I walked behind him the more turned on I became.

The mud kissed the soles of my feet and I pushed my toes into it. My damp dress rode up between my thighs and took on the warmth of my sex, where it turned into boiling water. 'Now,' I said to myself. And I walked more quickly to catch up with him. My desire had driven all thoughts from my mind, I felt feverish and superhumanly strong, as if under the influence of a drug.

I advanced with quick, rhythmic, confident steps straight towards my goal. The man turned round, looked at me for a moment with his small brown eyes, and a slight smile spread slowly across his tough guy's face, which was nonetheless still chubby. Then he continued on his way. I followed in his steps, breathing hard, until I was right up behind him. I walked for a while like this, almost touching him, smelling his scent. He was very athletic and virile, but emanated something fleshy, round and deeply sensual. You only needed to follow this man as I was doing, vibrant and receptive, to realize that he could just as easily be fragile as dangerous. In a quick, spontaneous gesture I slipped my hand between his legs and grabbed hold of his balls through his trousers. He stopped.

I held them firmly in my hand. Without letting go, I felt my way up a bit to get hold of his prick as well. I found it and began massaging it through the damp cloth. We were still standing motionless, me behind him. He had raised his head a little and opened his legs, and his penis swelled at my touch. His trunk expanded with each breath, he was slightly breathless, like me. I continued to fondle his cock, my forearm stuck between his thighs, against his firm buttocks.

He was thirty centimetres taller and forty kilos heavier than me, but, still standing behind him, I dragged him to the ground. We lay on our sides in the mire. I passed a hand under his hip, undid his belt and the buttons of his bulging flies. Then, together, I pulled his trousers and his pants to his knees.

I was already filthy with clay, and so was he. The sodden earth made a smelly, elastic paste which stuck to our clothes, our hair, our nails, our skin, and which felt delicious enough to eat. I filled my hands with it and rubbed it into his buttocks, pulling them wide apart. Then I licked them, smeared them with saliva with long strokes of the tongue until they were clean.

Once again I passed my hand between his thighs, took hold of his engorged cock and pulled it back down under his arse and made him close his legs to hold it there. I pushed my face into the dark, warm, fleshy triangle and sucked its tip. At the same time I grabbed one of his legs between my thighs and rubbed myself against it. I came against his trousers, my nose between his buttocks.

It was still raining, and the filth we were wallowing in became more and more slimy. It stuck to everything, making our bodies exceptionally soft, dirty and slippery. Alongside his pubis I dug a hole in the ground with my fingers. Then I made him lie on his stomach and stick his prick into the hole. I lay against him and nibbled his neck.

Straddled over him, with my dress raised, my clitoris rubbing against the ridge of his behind, my hands up his shirt and clamped over his chest, I started beating him with thrusts of the hips, rhythmically, while he was busy fucking the earth, the soft, sucking mud which enveloped his prick. When I felt my pleasure mounting I grabbed hold of his hips to control him better and, with a few fuller, firmer, more precise movements, I came, right in his mud-stained bum.

With my last groan I realized that he was about to come himself. So I went back to licking his arsehole and fondling his buttocks, where my juice was intermingled with the earth. His hips jerked and he ejaculated, held by the mud hole.

He fell back, laying his cheek on the sodden ground. I held my hands out in the rain to wash them, then I ran them over my mouth and over his forehead, where I planted a kiss. I got up and left him lying stretched out in the welcoming mud, his shirt pulled up his back, his trousers down around his knees, his bum softly smacked by the warm rain.

I went back up the path and gathered up my shoes. Before leaving I found a grassy spot in the forest where I managed to clean myself up. Then I went back out into the corridors, fully, absolutely and magnificently happy.

   DOOR 20.

20

The Corridors

My dress was still wet and stuck to my body. In the corridors I started walking quickly, my arms crossed over my bosom. The cold penetrated my bones, I shivered. Behind me, very close to me, I felt the breath of the two ghosts who were following me. I still smelled of mud and sex, my hair was still dripping large cold drops which ran down my neck and back.

I wanted to return to the path where I had left the man lying on his stomach, his trousers round his knees, I wanted to smear his bottom and his balls with mud and mount him from behind, as if I were a man, a man having it off with another man. It had been such a great and beautiful moment. I had wanted to believe I had achieved perfection. But I had to recognize that I hadn't really penetrated this man or been penetrated by him.

I carried on my way through the dark labyrinth, scorning the doors along the walls. Sometimes I thought I heard the ghosts talking, but I could make no sense of their whisperings.

Now I was beginning to feel tired of this voyage of sex and love and I wanted to find the man I had come looking for and then leave this place of wandering. For all the great pleasures I had found here, I also felt gripped by a nameless fear which manifested itself in the increasingly insistent presence of the ghosts. I didn't know the real cause of this fear and the mystery troubled me even more. Something decisive was going to happen to me eventually and that was just as likely to be something bad as something good.

I lay down on the ground in one of the corridors, against a wall, and tried to sleep. But as soon as I closed my eyes the ghosts began to spin around me, making the air swirl in all directions, as if tormenting me into continuing on my way.

I tried to resist, with my hands between my legs. Again, already, I wanted a man, to feel a man in me and next to me, to give myself up to him and to rule him, to draw out of him and give him joy and pleasure, to be rescued by him from fear, from myself and from the world. 'Men,' I said, 'I swear to love you and be faithful to you for ever.' And my hands gently pushed and undulated in my hot vagina, and I began panting and moaning, still lying curled up against the wall with the ghosts making a racket around me, cursing my passion for men, without whom I would have been carried away by death long ago.

When I had achieved orgasm, I realized that it was calm again around me. The ghosts had departed, or at least they had stopped harrying me. I felt a little sad but also peaceful and ready to continue my quest. I got up, rearranged my dress and my hair, which were still wet, and opened the following door.

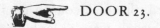 DOOR 23.

21

The Secret

I found myself in the middle of a happy crowd of men and women in extravagant evening dress walking hand-in-hand on a beautiful illuminated terrace on a fine summer evening. At first no one paid me any attention.

I weaved my way between the people till I reached the edge of the swimming pool. That's when a small group of four or five girls and boys seemed to recognize me and descended upon me with cries of 'Ah, there she is!'

They seemed slightly the worse for drink.

'Will you look at the state of her!' they added, laughing.

I thought that I wasn't particularly presentable in my little white dress and I felt a little embarrassed. But how could I get away now that that this whole crowd of people were all looking at me? At least, I presumed they were, given the fuss these weird jokers were making around me. But perhaps no one was heeding their performance. Whatever, I was beginning to feel stifled by the crowd. And it was almost a relief when the little group grabbed me by the arms and legs and threw me into the water.

I took my time coming to the surface, then I went under again. The second time I surfaced my eyes met those of a man who was standing at the edge of the pool staring at me. He was lean, of average build and very ugly. He was the only one wearing a more or less classic suit, one with a very nice cut. His ill-favoured face, tinged blue by several days' worth of stubble, was fascinating because of his piercing gaze. I swam to the edge of the pool and climbed out.

'Do forgive them,' he said as he came to meet me.

Then he introduced himself. He was called Hans, this was his place, and he was throwing a little party. He expressed himself with perfect distinction, poise and ease, which quickly cast an impressive aura of charm around his ugliness. He took me by the arm and I let him lead me inside the large, luxurious house where he entrusted me to a young member of his staff before disappearing. I watched him leave with regret.

The maid took me upstairs and showed me to a bedroom with en-suite bathroom and, in a very wide, mirrored closet which ran the whole length of one wall of the large room, a whole woman's wardrobe.

'This is your size, isn't it?' she said. 'Take whatever you want. These clothes belonged to Mr Hans's former wife. As you see, some of them haven't even been worn.'

'Why not? Is she dead?'

'No, she left.'

'Leaving all her things behind?'

'You will find Mr Hans on the terrace or in the large drawing-room. He is waiting for you. Do you need anything else, madam?'

'No, thank you.'

The young woman left, with an impertinent smile on her lips. I took a bath, perfumed myself and chose from the wardrobe a sleeveless, PVC body, with a zip down the front, over which I pulled on some silk hot pants with a thick metal belt. I had fun finishing off my outfit with self-supporting stockings, lace-up boots with high rounded heels, thin, silken gloves, cut off at the fingers like mittens and reaching to just above the elbow, and a string of grey pearls which dipped to my cleavage. I pulled my hair back and pushed it under a black silk and felt headdress which was trimmed with pearls and sat on my head like a wig. I carefully made up my face and hands and checked how I looked in the mirrors. I was quite beautiful.

I went back down to the drawing-room. This time my clothes were more in tune with those of the guests, who were all trying to outdo each other by being more dandyish and decadent. It was almost the end of the night. The D J slid his records on to the turntables, people danced to house music, others canoodled on the sofas and in every nook and cranny. I was making my way to the bar when I saw my host, Hans, coming to meet me.

He complimented me on my change of appearance and we had a drink. As I looked at him I had the unpleasant thought that his wife must have left in quite a hurry if she hadn't even taken the time to pack her bags ... What could have been the reason for this? Yet Hans was perfectly courteous and even a little touching, for behind his mask of dry humour one could see a certain sadness, perhaps a broken heart.

We weren't able to talk much, because of the noise. But we sat side by side, as if it were the most normal thing in the world, as if he had been expecting me, as if we were two old lovers or two beings irresistibly attracted to each other. I had another drink, and a third, and maybe a fourth. Through the window I saw the stars disappear and the sky start to turn grey. And, I don't know why, this spectacle, this moment, suddenly seemed unbearable to me. I leaped up to make my escape and went onto the dance floor, where I started dancing with all my soul.

I was surrounded by eccentric, charming girls and boys. One of the cuter ones never took his eyes off me and made sure he was always dancing in front of me, but I didn't notice for ages, for I was oblivious of everything except the rhythm of the music inside my body. Every now and again I went to quench my thirst with another glass of alcohol and then returned to the dancing. Finally I ended up in the arms of my pretty partner and we kissed with open mouths as we danced.

Then there was no one left on the floor and the music

stopped. It was completely light. I staggered through the mess of the drawing-room back out onto the terrace which was already basking in the fine morning sun. Lying down on the edge of the pool I dipped my finger in the water and stirred it to watch the reflections. Now I knew that Hans, his beard as blue as the water in the pool, would come back and take me. I waited for him.

I lay on my back and no longer thought about anything except breathing the morning air and feeling its still cool touch against my skin, losing my gaze in the foliage of the garden. In the silence softly embroidered by birdsong I heard him coming.

He knelt down between my legs, undid my belt and ripped my shorts; the silk seemed to scream in his hands. Then he undid the press studs on my body. I opened my legs wide, bent my knees and slightly stretched out my pelvis, hoping to feel his mouth, his kiss. But nothing happened.

I looked down at him and saw that he was still kneeling, motionless and lost in contemplation of my wide-open vulva. I was a bit surprised, but I decided to let him look as long as he wished, since it seemed to give him pleasure.

Time passed and nothing changed. Then he lay down on his stomach, his head between my legs, and I thought he had finally made his mind up. I had had enough time to imagine the sensations his beard would give me, to wait for the first contact of his tongue in my impatient little pussy, to hope that his would be the most skilful of tongues and that it would give me a delicious orgasm, as so few men's tongues are able to do . . .

But it seems that he only wanted to move his face closer to my gaping sex. He was so close I could feel his breath, but still no contact. I waited some more, thinking he would be doing the honours any moment now.

After a while I started moving my pelvis a bit and giving out little moans of pleasure to make him realize that it was time he put an end to his reverie or his examination. And, to make it obvious, I grabbed him by the hair and tried to force his mouth into my vagina, which he had so admired. But he pulled away without having touched me.

I sat upright, highly annoyed and frustrated.

'Excuse me,' he said. 'I am called away urgently, very urgently.'

He had a strange look about him, which frightened me. All of a sudden I wanted nothing but to see him leave.

'Here are the keys to the house,' he continued, handing me a bunch of keys. 'As you see, written on each one is the name of the room it opens. Go and rest in your room, get yourself something to eat, look round the garden and the house . . . Make yourself at home . . .'

He spoke in a flat voice, panting a bit, as if he were very excited. So why was he leaving me? I took off my body, beneath which I was naked, because I was too hot, and also perhaps in a last attempt to tempt him. But he only said, almost feverishly:

'I implore you, stay. I will be back this evening and . . . we will have all the time we need . . .'

And he left. After walking a few steps, he turned and shouted:

'Among the keys . . . must also be the key to the cellar . . . Open all the doors you want to, but not that one. Definitely not that one, it's very important . . . I will explain . . .'

I was exhausted. 'Bloody time-waster,' I thought. 'It takes all sorts . . .' I stopped thinking about him and got up to go to my room. I wanted only to sleep.

On the stairs I bumped into another maid, older but just as attractive as the one from the night before. She offered to bring me some breakfast in my room. I accepted gladly. While I was waiting for my coffee, I soaked in the bath. I came out to find a laden tray, which I polished off heartily. Then I went to bed and slept.

When I awoke, in the middle of the afternoon, I saw through the window that it was still fine outside, and I decided to go for a walk in the garden. From the wardrobe I picked out a cool, flowing summer dress, a pair of white tennis shoes and a straw hat and I went out. As soon as I closed the door I remembered the keys and went back to get them from the bedside table.

I didn't stay out in the garden long. This bunch of keys, even though it was small, was an encumbrance. I had no pocket to put them in, I had to carry them in my hand; I was afraid of losing them, I was thinking only about him. Why had he given me the keys? The rooms in the house didn't seem to be locked. The doors to some of the rooms on the landing upstairs were even open or ajar.

I suddenly felt a strong desire to look round the house. I walked back towards it quickly, even breaking into a run, reproaching myself sharply for not having thought of it sooner. And yet I could not have said what gave rise to such a strong desire, other than a dark foreboding which could not be expressed more precisely.

Instead of exploring the house, which was what I thought I wanted to do, I began feverishly searching for the entrance to the cellar. I was suffering, as if someone inside me were taking pleasure in torturing me by scratching my brain. I had lost control of myself.

When I finally turned the key in the cellar lock, I knew I was no longer driven by curiosity, but by a sort of foul jealousy. And I felt this jealousy, which burned me like the fires of hell, because my host, the man I had desired in vain, had let me suspect how much he was hiding and what a pit of lies and secrets he had allowed to open up between us, like the most demoralizing of barriers.

The door opened onto a steep, narrow staircase. I closed it quietly and began to descend in silence, without turning on the light. I thought I could hear the sound of a voice coming from down below. After the last step, I walked a short distance on what seemed to be a floor of beaten earth and my hands, which I was holding out in front of me to find my way, touched a curtain.

I didn't recognize it at first. The voice I could hear was my own. It wasn't saying anything, just sighing. I found the edge of the curtain and drew it aside. And the truth burst upon me. What I had thought I had kept private, secret, for myself alone, was being displayed on a screen. In bed, I was giving myself pleasure with the objects I had found on the bedside table. The pleasure my host had denied me I took with the aid of various instruments. And the man who had filmed me without my knowledge was sitting on a sofa facing the screen with a zapper in his hand, playing with these images of me, while the little dark-haired girl who had accompanied me to my room the previous evening was sucking him off.

I thought I would faint with shame. Was that the sum total of our relationship? Solitary or hidden pleasures, deceitful tricks? My heart filled with hatred, for myself, for him, for us, and for myself again.

The door to the cellar opened. I pressed myself into a recess in the wall. The light came on and the other maid, apparently quite used to the steep descent, strode quickly and lightly down the steps. I didn't move. After all, it didn't much matter whether I was discovered or not. The woman went past without seeing me, opened the curtain and disappeared behind it.

I wanted to leave. But in spite of the repugnance it caused me, I couldn't resist spying on my host one last time. While these unbearable, obscene images of me played on the screen, no one paid them any attention. All three were making love together. Everything he could have done to me he did without thinking to both these women. I fled, without even taking care not to make a noise. But they were probably so absorbed in their pleasure that they didn't notice.

I wanted to leave this house, go back to the dark corridors of the little circus. But I couldn't find the door I had come in through. I scoured the house from top to bottom, looked around the terrace several times, in vain. The exit wasn't there any more.

I went into the garden. I would have liked to disappear, efface myself from my own memory. I lay down under a tree and sought escape in a sleep full of bad dreams.

I was awoken by pleasure. There was a head stuffed between my legs. Hans was giving me what he had refused me that very morning, through the cloth of my knickers. He raised me up and I abandoned myself to his delicious kiss which I had awaited so long. He was just as skilful as I had dreamed he would be, his tongue transformed me into flows of lava on the slope of a volcano, into streams of cream, into open, ecstatic flesh, his tongue licked me, dug into me, sucked me, imprinted in my hot slit ever more frequent and electrifying wave patterns. I came in his mouth, arching my back as if I had suddenly been shot out of the ground.

He made me lie on my stomach. Kneeling behind me, he took me by the hips, made me raise my pelvis and arch my back, and penetrated me. I felt his hard, velvety cock rubbing along the length of my sheath, right to the end, where it knocked with muffled blows before pulling slowly back in the opposite direction, unfolding rings of pleasure all along its course. The orgasmic contractions went in a chain reaction from the inside to the outside of my sex, and so deeply into my belly that I felt my stomach heave, almost to the point of nausea.

He lay down on his back and I mounted him in turn, with my legs folded back and my hand stretched out behind me to scratch him under his balls while impaling myself on him with long, powerful thrusts of my hips. Again I attained a pleasure which rose like a hiccup to my throat.

I lay on top of him for a while, to rest, then I started again, squatting down on my feet this time, my thighs wide apart over his vertical shaft, riding up and down its whole length. I came again, at the same time as him.

I collapsed on his body, exhausted. When I came to, I remembered what had happened that morning next to the swimming pool and especially later in the afternoon. At first, I thought I would forget all that. After the pleasure we had had together, the rest wasn't important.

But little by little the poisons of distrust and rancour seeped into my veins. I saw again the painful sights of the cellar, that hidden side of reality which I suspected was the whole of reality, reality itself. 'He tricked me,' I thought. 'And he is still tricking me. If he came to make love to me, it was only to use me, to turn me into a cog in his secret machine, to which he will never grant me access.'

I freed myself from his embrace and sat bad-temperedly with my back to him, my head in my hands.

'What's wrong?' he asked.

'Nothing.'

'Nothing? Of course there's something wrong ... And you will tell me what it is immediately ...'

I didn't need to turn round to sense that he had suddenly changed. There was nothing but hate in his voice, as if he wanted to kill me.

'What is it?' he repeated, with a suppressed anger that froze me to the spot. 'What have I done?'

As if he didn't know! He knew very well the harm he had done me. That's what was making him mad. He must suspect that I had discovered him, he had done everything to make me discover him by forbidding me to use the key to his cellar. The harm he had done was in not letting me enter into his game, in betraying me and, above all, in showing me so cruelly how far we were from being partners ... All this churned inside me and tortured me, but I was unable to tell him. For to admit that I knew meant admitting how I knew.

He took me by the arm and looked into my eyes, trying to force me to speak. The desire to hear the truth blaze out caused his pupils to dilate, but he was just as terrified as I was that the unspeakable might be said. He was like the assassin who seeks to hear himself accused to lighten the weight of his guilt but, once accused, can only deny it vehemently or even kill his accuser.

At this moment I almost pitied him.

'What terrible crime has he committed?' I asked myself. 'Except to be himself, that is, different from me? Why is he trying so hard, perhaps without intending to, to be unmasked? Because he doesn't know himself what is behind his mask? Because he wants to push me into taking off the mask I am wearing without realizing it?

'I think I am playing the same game as he is: I am showing him, by my attitude, that I used the key to the cellar and intruded on his privacy, but I refuse to admit it.'

He started insisting more and more grimly, squeezing my arm and hurting me. Then I was seized by an attack of hateful anger. And since I couldn't say anything else, I accused him of having raped me when I was asleep.

'Do you think I would have fucked with you if I were fully conscious?' I screamed. 'When I woke up it was already too late, you had started raping me. Your stupid head up my dress ... What could I do? Struggle? What good would that have done? It was already too late. You took advantage of my weakness, you bastard! You are a bastard and a filthy pig and you disgust me!'

He sniggered and reminded me of the details of my part in our frolics. I wanted to kill him. I gave him a punch in the face, which he returned in the form of a slap. We started fighting. Anger increased my strength tenfold, but he soon bent my arm behind my back, forcing me to be still on pain of having it broken.

As soon as he let me go I ran off into the wood, without

bothering to get dressed. I soon realized that he was chasing after me, naked himself. As I ran I kept turning round to see his hate-filled face getting nearer to me. This time he would certainly kill me ... Crazy and breathless, I zigzaged between the trees.

Now I could feel him right behind me ... Then I stumbled over a large branch hidden in the grass and I crashed to the ground where I lost consciousness. As I came to I remembered the last image I had seen before my fall. Almost at the same time as me, Hans also tripped over the branch and hit the ground.

Now night had fallen. I felt pain in my hands, my head, all over my body, and I was cold. The moonlight penetrated through the gaps in the branches, just enough that I could see Hans's inanimate body lying by my side. His head, turned towards me, was lying on a stone. I reached out my hand towards him and touched his arm. He was cold. I moved my hand down to the inside of his wrist, searching for his pulse. Nothing.

I got up and went away into the darkness of the garden, constantly stumbling and making no attempt to orient myself. Finally I spotted the terrace, lit up as on the previous evening. I walked towards it.

There was no one about and everything was silent. Without its revellers, the space gave the impression of a dizzying void.

I dived into the swimming pool. At the bottom of the water I called out for Hans. But everything was dark and silent, and I almost suffocated. I reached the surface coughing and spitting. 'If we died side by side,' I thought, 'it is perhaps because we loved each other, in spite of everything.' And then I realized that I wasn't dead.

At the edge of the terrace, I found my dress and the door back into the corridors. I wandered there for a while before going through another door.

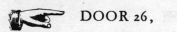 DOOR 26,

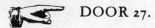 DOOR 27.

22

The Lake

The air was deliciously fresh and soft, the light like that of a summer morning, the silence merely fringed by the tiniest lapping of the waves against the shore. All around the lake was a warm forest of pines, its green line perceptible right round to the opposite shore, far away on the horizon.

I left my dress and shoes at the foot of a tree and walked to the water through the sand which was prickly with needles, stepping over a colony of large black ants.

The narrow beach formed a little cove, bordered by large bunches of reeds. It was completely deserted.

I went into the water, which gripped my ankles like two lover's hands. I walked straight ahead into the transparent lake, whose warm caress climbed slowly up my legs.

I was already several metres from the beach and the water only came up to my breasts. I dived in fully and swam. A little behind me to the left I looked at the bunches of reeds. Over there the water was like a huge black sheet. I swam towards it.

The water was deeper here. In the middle of the reeds, invisible from the shore, there was a tiny island of sand. I went towards it. I stood up when I reached the shallows and my feet got caught in something soft and sticky, a fine, abundant algae which covered the pebbles and made them slippery.

I lay down on the island in the sun. The reeds swayed gently as if they were inhabited by ghosts. I raised my head and saw a swimmer coming towards me. Doubtless he hadn't seen me behind my barrier of reeds. I lay down again and waited for him.

When he stepped onto the island I looked at him and reached out my hand. He pleased me. He was naked too, slim and bronzed. He fell down on the sand next to me and caressed me tenderly.

He penetrated me and playfully we rolled over together in the sand right down to the water, in the middle of the reeds. When the water became too deep he pulled out of me and we played at swimming one below the other in turn, giving each other caresses and kisses all over, particularly between our open legs, where our sexes resembled two aquatic animals.

As a few people were now arriving on the beach, we stayed among the reeds, near the island, where he penetrated me again. Our bodies had become a little oily, which lent a particular softness to our embrace. He was standing in the lake, which came up to his chest, and I was hanging round his neck, my knees wrapped round his back and my feet on his buttocks. It was all so easy and light thanks to the water. Our pleasure rose gradually and we climaxed together, with sighs and moans which were like the breath of the breeze in the reeds.

We rested a while on the island. When he dozed off I left him without a sound and went back to the beach where a few people had installed themselves. The magic hour had passed. I put my dress back on and went out through the exit.

In the corridor the whispers of the ghosts reminded me of the gentle noise of the wind blowing downstream and I smiled as I opened another door.

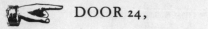 DOOR 24,

 DOOR 25.

23

The Old Woman

An old woman lying in a hospital bed watched me come in. In her thin, wrinkled, tired face her dark eyes, shining like two pearls, were strikingly vivacious. Two thistles in the middle of a desert.

She stared at me quite frankly and I myself was unable to take my eyes off her, for her features were painfully familiar to me. I had definitely met this woman somewhere before, and she reminded me of something bad, but my memory refused to relinquish the key to this mystery.

'Come nearer,' she said in a faint, trembling voice.

I obeyed, as if hypnotized.

Her bed smelled of death. I managed to take my eyes off her face to concentrate on the drip in her arm, attached to the plastic bottle over the bed. It was then, when I was no longer looking at her, that I remembered who she was.

When I turned to look at her face again, the truth which had dawned on me was confirmed in a flash by what I saw, what I had seen since the beginning without wanting to recognize it. Between this woman and myself there was only a short stretch of time, merely a few decades – in other words, little more than an instant, since this distance could not prevent our reuniting. This woman was me.

The sight of her now affected me so much that I was reluctant to look at her. But I was also very curious to see what I had become. So with my best efforts I started alternately to observe her, then, closing my eyes, to seek something of her in myself, in my body and soul as they are at present. *You cannot step twice into the same river.* If the body changes, does the soul remain identical to itself? Everything in this world is transient ... How I could believe that the little girl I was, the woman I am today and this old woman that I soon will be are exactly the same person?

The old woman opened her mouth, a mouth which on me was so fleshy and graceful, and said:

> You will have plenty of time to observe the stars
> when the worms are slowly eating you.

I recognized a poem by Garcia Lorca that I had read a few days earlier. 'Will I remember it, then, to the end of my days?' I thought.

'Lie down next to me,' said the old woman.

I slipped into bed next to her, her bony body against mine. I was torn between the desire to cherish her and bring her a little consolation and the desire to abandon her totally, to forget this repulsive sadness. 'Why has she forced me to meet her,' I thought angrily, 'against all the laws of nature?'

'Don't be stupid,' said the old woman. 'It's you who came to see me.'

I stiffened with apprehension as I felt her take my hand in hers under the covers, and she added:

'Lend it to me. It is softer than mine ...'

And she placed it between her withered thighs, on her scraggy, old, but still burning vulva. I almost screamed in horror.

I tried to free myself, but she held on to me with amazing strength. She started to masturbate, with *my* fingers.

I closed my eyes and saw myself, in my present skin, lying spreadeagled on a hospital bed. 'I've had enough of all this butchery,' I thought in my semi-dream. And I wanted to rest to escape the relentless fate of which I was a victim.

The old woman finally came. I could feel her body tremble and jerk by my side. She let her head fall back on the pillow and went to sleep.

My fingers were still held in hers, as in the claws of a predator. With my other hand I released them and got out of the bed.

I didn't resent her. 'You are right,' I said to her under my breath. 'You abused me but it was I who came to see you. Perhaps I disturbed you as much as you perturbed me.'

I went back to the corridors, where I walked for a long time. But the ghosts didn't show up at all.

I was in a huge void.

When this feeling had begun to make my head reel, when I felt near the edge of exhaustion, I opened another door, as if I were rushing out through an emergency exit.

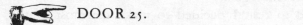 DOOR 25.

24

The Time-Waster

The light was out and the shutters were closed. When my eyes had got used to the dark I could see that I was in a comfortable room. A man was asleep in a large bed. I thought it must be the middle of the night, because it was particularly quiet in the room, which seemed to be part of an apartment. The man's breathing was light and regular.

I really wanted to rest. I decided to make the most of the bed, without waking up the sleeper. I undressed and slipped between the sheets. It was warm and soft and I sighed with a feeling of ease.

I lay right next to the man, for I felt a certain tenderness and it pleased me to drift off to sleep in the warmth of another body. But I soon had to admit that the more I sensed his presence, his smell, the more I realized he was within reach of my hand, the more the desire for sleep left me. I began tossing and turning in bed, trying to find some peace. I finally ended up facing him, curled up, a position which I thought would help me to concentrate on myself while keeping a slight distance between us. But as I curled my legs up, my knee inadvertently touched the man's sex.

It was hard, long and even wet at the tip. After such a marvellous surprise I no longer gave the slightest thought to sleep. Gently I closed my hand around his lovely erect cock.

The sleeper awoke and started kissing and caressing me without a great deal of passion. After a while, as we hadn't progressed beyond these elementary preliminaries, I decided to dive under the duvet to suck his cock. It was perfectly *al dente*, a real treat. But I wasn't ready to settle for that.

When I came back up he started to kiss me and caress me again. I didn't want to appear in too much of a hurry to get on to the serious stuff, but I was burning with desire. I clung to him eagerly, grinding my pelvis to let him know the time had come to penetrate me.

My manoeuvre succeeded, for he turned me over on my back so as to lie on top of me. I opened my legs wide, dying of impatience and excitement.

He was about to take me. Then there were two short rings of the doorbell.

'Excuse me,' he said.

He got up to go to the door. Another man came into the room. My almost-lover turned on the light and I could see that they were both quite charming, getting on a bit but still slim and cool, like two students, two perpetual adolescents. I thought this late-night visit was rather strange, and very bad timing, but then I reckoned it could be a bit of a windfall, if they both got into bed with me.

Instead, they invited me to come for a drink with them. Naturally I was very disappointed and frustrated. I tried to make light of it:

'Why move?' I said. 'I'm fine where I am ... Doesn't that say anything to you?'

But they seemed not to understand my offer and invited me again to accompany them. Resigned, I got up, quite naked, and slipped on my dress while my sleeper got dressed too.

We went out and ended up in a little, warm, simple bar sitting round a rustic wooden table. People came and went looking relaxed, and drank and talked like us. My two companions talked interminably and earnestly about everything and nothing.

In the beginning I joined in their conversation. Then, as time went by, my resentment took over. I got up brusquely and left the café without saying a word.

My almost-lover caught up with me in the street and asked me what was going on. By way of allusion to the fact that we hadn't finished making love, I replied bitterly:

'When you make a promise, you ought to keep it.'

He justified himself by setting off talking again like a tap in full flow, producing a stream of verbiage to the effect that, if you wish to educate yourself about life, you have to go out rather than stay locked up making love.

'I don't give a damn about educating myself!' I retorted violently. 'What I want is to have pleasure! Immediately! And constantly!'

Finally he seemed impressed by the strength of my desire. He took me by the arm and said that we would go back straight away.

When we got back to his place I found some female underwear in a chest of drawers next to the bathroom. Since I didn't want to blow it this time, I decided to give him the full works. I presented myself in his room dressed in a red basque, black stockings and high heels. I leaned over him and, while I scratched his chest, the inside of his thighs, and his balls, I ran my breasts, which were sticking out of the basque and were hard and inflated with desire, over his face. I made him suck them, one after the other, while my hand took care of his cock, which became as hard as a block of wood.

Now I was mad with impatience. I sat astride him and started to lower myself onto him.

At this precise moment, again, a bell rang. It felt as if I had been woken by a slap. Wearily I saw him leap out of bed to turn off the alarm clock and, without really understanding, I heard him explain that it was time to get up and that he couldn't be late under any circumstances.

He had already disappeared into the shower. I picked up my

underwear in a rage, calling him a bloody time-waster. I could have killed him. Before I reached that extreme, I got dressed and left, slamming the door behind me.

I strode through the corridors for a while before I opened another door.

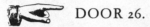 DOOR 26.

25

The Mask

It was a large, magnificent room in a stately home where a masked ball was taking place. I felt that I had landed in another era, for no one among the dozens of guests was wearing modern clothes, nor even clothes from the last century. An orchestra was playing refined music, to which the people were performing delicate, ordered, highly codified dances.

The men were all wearing wigs, doublets and tights which fitted snugly round their legs, bottoms and sexes. The women had beauty spots and wore long dresses with plunging necklines. They were all powdered and in masks, mainly large, richly ornate, Venetian masks in velvet.

As soon as I entered a lackey rushed up to me and led me into an adjoining room which served as a robing room. There a chambermaid provided me with some suitable attire, a corset which she laced up as tightly as she could, white silk stockings and beribboned garters, tiny satin slippers, a pink and white hooped dress which was staggeringly beautiful, hand-sewn in the finest fabrics, decorated with lace, embroidery and dozens of pearls, the finest I had ever seen.

After she had applied perfume, make-up and powder and dressed my hair, the chambermaid offered me a mask to match my outfit, embroidered in gold, decorated with pearls and white feathers. She spoke in a language I didn't understand, but which sounded a lot like Italian, although I didn't need words to express my satisfaction and gratitude.

The lackey accompanied me into the reception room, where the dancers integrated me into their group. By allowing myself to be led and by observing them, I managed to follow their steps quite well. Although they appeared as stiff as they were elegant, in practice their dances turned out to be as erotic and dynamic as any contemporary dance.

For you had to change partners constantly, passing from hand to hand and from arm to arm before finding your appointed partner. This created a sort of sexual maelstrom, which the masks rendered even more exciting. It was not unusual to see a partner approach you with a very visible erection in his tights, provoked by the fleeting but recurrent brushes against this great variety of women and dresses.

I danced for a long time and enjoyed myself greatly. Towards the end I always ended up with the same partner, a tall man in a black mask who was assiduous in his attentions. His eyes sparkled and his sex inflated a little more with each new dance, to the point where I feared he would come in his tights, and against my dress, during one of our dances.

At the end of one piece of music I slipped away to the back of the room. I was also very excited. I saw that my masked partner had also left the ball and was gradually making his way in my direction. I stared straight at him, then I left the room.

I waited for him out in the corridors of the house. When I saw his shape appear I lifted my dress and started running.

I heard him running after me. Every now and again I turned round, both to simulate fear and to throw him a challenge.

He trapped me at the end of a dark, silent corridor, a long way from the reception room. I yelled out stridently, which incited him to rough me up a bit. Just when he was least expecting it, as I was struggling, I placed my hand on his enormous cock through his tights.

He took me standing up first of all, dragging me savagely

from one wall to the other, then he lay me on the ground, where he made me undergo all sorts of atrocities. He came three times, and I so many times I wouldn't have been able to count them. I took advantage of the fact we were so far from everything to make lots of noise, bawling and groaning my fill. Since we didn't speak the same language, I sprayed him with every obscenity that came into my head, and he probably did the same, for he expressed himself quite noisily. Neither of us at any point took off our masks. And we separated without knowing a thing about each other, except the sexual rage we had experienced between us.

As my dress was now a bit torn, crumpled and dirty, and since I myself was exhausted, I walked back through the ballroom as discreetly as possible to go and get changed in the adjoining room. When I had collected my original clothes I left the house by the door I had come in and reentered the dark labyrinth, with its ghostly whispers and new doors to open.

 DOOR 27,

 DOOR 28.

26

The Lovely Talker

I entered a dark room and could make out nothing except the large bed. I was so tired I headed straight towards it, without turning on the light. I took off my dress and lay down.

I was half asleep when I heard a little voice calling out:

'Hey! Hey!'

I didn't react, as it was immediately quiet again and I thought I must have dreamed it. I turned over onto my other side, buried my head in the pillow and started to drift away into a good, sound sleep. Then the little voice piped up again:

'Hey! Hey! Please!'

This time I opened my eyes wide in the dark, on the look-out.

'Please! Don't go straight to sleep! I need you!' said the little voice.

The voice was soft and no louder than a whisper, but it was clearly audible and articulated distinctly. And even though I had never heard a voice like it, it sounded familiar. It was the voice of someone who needed me and I knew straight away that even if my tiredness, or anything else, made me want to close my eyes and ears, I would have found it impossible to resist its call and the compulsion I felt to afford the creature to whom it belonged the help it expected from me.

'Here I am!' said the little voice.

It seemed to be coming from inside the bed, under the sheets.

This gave me a bit of a start, as if I were expecting to feel a mouse running between my legs. 'Come on,' I told myself, 'rodents are intelligent animals but as far as I know they don't yet have the gift of speech.' And I threw the sheet and covers back and started feeling around on the bed.

'Over here! Lower! Higher! A bit more! Yes! There you are!' said the little voice.

My hand touched a soft, hard, warm cylinder which was damp at its tip.

'Ahhh!' said the little voice.

At this moment the moon came out from behind a cloud and cast its light over the bed through the window blinds. And I saw that there was a man lying asleep next to me and that I was holding his little willy. I let go immediately and looked at his face. He appeared to be fast asleep.

'Hey!' said the little voice.

The man's lips hadn't moved. I stared attentively at them, waiting for the little voice to pipe up again, which it did almost immediately,

'Don't worry,' it said. 'He's asleep. Please, come and see me ... There's no risk...'

The evidence was conclusive. The man was sleeping soundly and his mouth was as motionless as the rest of his body. He was lying on his back and was wearing nothing but a T-shirt. It was his dick that was calling out to me, standing up against his stomach and seeming to look at me with its one eye. His dick could talk.

I bent over it, aroused.

'It's you?' I said. 'It's you who was calling me?'

'Of course, my lovely. I know you are my friend...'

'How happy I am ... I've so often talked to ... to lovely cocks like you ... And none of them ever replied ... Oh yes, I'm your friend ... Your best friend...'

'All right, take me in your hand.'

'But ... what if he wakes up ...'

'Who, him? Rest easy, I'm in charge here. He won't wake up unless I alert him. But we can keep this just between the two of us, can't we? We don't need him.'

'Oh no, no ... The two of us, just the two of us ...'

'All right, hurry up, take me in your hand ... I can't hang around ... Ahhh ... Now wank me off ...'

I did everything it asked me to do, my heart beating fast, with all the dedication and love I was capable of, brimming over with happiness. The cock became harder and warmer, it filled my hand and moaned softly, giving me instructions every now and again:

'More slowly ... Go right to the base ... Yes, like that ... I love your soft little hand, my darling ... You're doing me good ... Oh, a bit faster now ...'

I wanked it, following its desires to the letter and, putting my mouth right next to the glans I murmured:

'I love you ... I love you ... You are so lovely ... And you will give me everything ... I'll do everything you ask of me ... Oh, I can feel your cream coming up ... It's so good ... You dirty little slut, I adore you, tell me you'll come right in my face ...'

'Ye-e-es ...' said the little voice.

And I got all its marvellous, creamy come all over my cheek, the corner of my mouth, my fingers and the joint of my thumb.

My darling cock detumesced slowly and didn't say anything else. I still held it in my hand, while I cleaned myself with my other hand and my mouth. Its sperm had an exquisite taste of hazelnut.

When it had shrunk like the ass's skin in the palm of my hand I let go of my true love, who then seemed to perk up.

'Forgive me,' it said, resting against the man's pubis. 'I was in that state too long, I had to relax as quickly as possible ...'

'No need to apologize. It was a real pleasure for me...'

'You see, he sleeps, he dreams, I don't know what he comes up with ... In any case, he excites me, and then there's no one to take care of me ... Not even him...'

'Don't think about it. I'm here now...'

'Yes, my angel ... And we can have some more fun, we two ... Do you want to?'

'It's my dream come true ... Playing with you ... Always, always...'

'All right, take me in your mouth. And then ... then do what you want with me ... I'm all yours...'

With flicks of my tongue I licked the tip of the glans, the edge of the foreskin, the whole length of the shaft ... Then I pushed it right into my mouth, to the back of my palate and, from one cheek to the other, I sucked it in and rolled it round ... Very gently, very slowly ... I was so stirred up I wanted to cry. Every now and again I stopped to stroke it and look at it, and I said to it:

'I love you so much ... I love you so much ... There's nothing in the world I love as much as you ... My treasure ... My darling ... My god ... I have never knelt down except before you ... My idol ... The goal, the soul, the spice of my life ... Oh, let me adore you ... You all alone, without the not altogether appealing body and person you are attached to ... You, my lovely, lovely at rest, with your little dangling tip, lovely when you're pissing, lovely when you're inflating, erecting, standing upright, quivering, lovely when you're ejaculating, lovely too when you're deflating ... My lovely one, my ever lovely one ... With your glans that looks so innocent, soft as a baby ... Your pretty line, like a seam, like a road ... Your skin so fine, so tender ... Your veins where the blood pounds through ... Your smell ... The magic of this shaft, which changes shape, expands and contracts, hardens and softens, vibrates and sprays and responds to caresses and often goes its own way, indomitable, reacts when you don't want it to, or doesn't respond when you sollicit its reaction ... For one needs to know how to handle you, isn't that true? You need to be loved, don't you? I love you, I love you more than anything ...'

My true love had finally swelled between my lips. I moved it all over my body, from the soles of my feet to my eyelids, via the back of my knees, my navel, my breasts, my armpits, my neck, my ears ... I caressed it, massaged it between my toes, breathed it in, twisted it, hit it against my skin, tickled it with the tips of my eyelashes, scratched it, licked it, pinched it, nibbled it, examined it, spoke to it, fondled it, tasted it, adored it ... And when it was quite stiff I sat astride it, facing the sleeper, then with my back to him, so that it would give me orgasm after orgasm, until I fell exhausted and tetanized. Then I whispered to it: 'Your turn now,' and, with a final effort, I jerked my hips a few times and made it come right into the depths of my belly, which contracted once more with the pleasure of it.

As I lay on the sleeper's body, I noticed through the blinds that it was almost daybreak. No doubt the man would be waking up soon. I leaned over to my sweet friend and said:

'Alas, I have to leave you now. If only I could take you with me ... But that's not possible and I'm not keen to make the acquaintance of this person you belong to ... Farewell, my love, I will never forget you.'

'Farewell,' it said. 'I too will keep you in my heart.'

I kissed it tenderly and turned away. After all, I had had my pleasure and didn't need it any more. I put my dress back on and left the room in silence.

In the corridor the ghosts returned to dog my steps. Rather than worrying about their invisible presence, I said out loud to them:

'Why don't I have one myself?'

And as no one replied I went through one of the first doors I found along the way.

 DOOR 29,

 DOOR 30.

27

The Bed of Roses

In the middle of a room with marble floor and columns, in a huge bed in the shape of a bath and filled with rose petals, lay a white-skinned ephebe, with a body as perfect as a Greek statue. He turned his beautiful, graceful head towards me and reached out his hand. I undressed and went to join him.

He moved his hands lazily over my body. I stroked his curly hair and embraced his chest. His flesh was tender and firm, his skin hairless and so soft that it seemed it had been bathed in milk.

The roses formed a soft, pithy bed, extremely velvety and with an exquisite scent. He took a petal between his plump white fingers and slid it between my lips. I bit it, savoured it and offered him one in turn, placing it in his fleshy mouth; he ate also while I gently sucked his middle finger. His pretty little member began to harden. I brushed it to disengage its pink tip.

He climbed over me and penetrated me. I closed my legs around his back, pressed my heels into the furrow of his backside and accompanied him in his up and down movements. He didn't rush it, but thrust his hips with consummate artistry, as if we were performing a ballet whose climax would certainly be a pleasure as total as it was refined. Indeed, the whole of my genital region was involved, for I could feel, at the same time as his member in my sheath, his balls beating a gentle rhythm underneath, at the edge of my buttocks, and his pubis rubbing against mine and exciting my clitoris.

He didn't forget to lean over me as well, to lick my earlobes and kiss my face, my throat, my collarbones, my arms and my breasts. For my part I scratched his chest, caressed his stomach or his balls, gripped him by his hair or his buttocks. Our pleasure rose so smoothly, and in such harmony, that we didn't even feel the need to change position. We achieved orgasm together, with a duet of languorous moans.

He lay on top of me and I embraced him and felt happy. We rested for a while in each other's arms, with our eyes closed and a smile on our lips. Then he withdrew and we wiped our love juices in the rose petals.

I kissed him on the forehead, got out of bed and dressed. As I opened the door I turned back to him. He looked at me, still lying nonchalantly among the roses, and blew me a kiss.

I went back into the corridor, filled with a sweet joy, and walked for a bit, before I opened the following door.

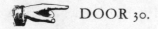 DOOR 30.

28

Ali Baba

It was a vast sandy beach, whipped by a warm ocean wind full of iodine. I could hear the waves but the sea remained out of sight, closed off by a barrier of dunes. I took off my shoes and started walking towards it.

The sand beneath the soles of my feet was cool and prickly in parts because of the vegetation. But it was a delicious sensation to feel it wed itself to my muscles so perfectly, and accompany them with each of my movements, from my toes to my heels.

When I reached the crest I saw the immense ocean stretch out in front of me, its grey waves wrinkled with white beneath a sky overburdened with heavy clouds. The sound of the sea was deafening. I walked straight towards it, facing into the wind.

I wandered along the edge of the waves for a while, following their ebb and flow on the beach, playing with them by getting my feet wet and even raising my dress and getting splashed with foam right up to my thighs. From their wet fringe I collected small pebbles, put them in my mouth and sucked them until they lost their salty taste. I kept a few, as well as some shells whose shape, gloss and colour I found pleasing.

The ebbing tide uncovered a broad band of wet sand. I

knelt down facing the sea, opened my hand and deposited the small hoard I had gathered. Then I started building a castle.

I worked on it for a long time. I fashioned outer walls, towers, a keep, the ramparts, turrets and battlements. I dug a deep moat around it and let it fill up with the sea water that had soaked into the sand. Then with my nails and fingertips I started making slits and other openings in the wall.

When I had hollowed out the main gate I was amazed to see the sand continue to crumble away behind the little excavation I had just made, as if a large sand fly were carrying on with my work. And I was absolutely astonished to see a tiny little man emerge from this same door, naked as a worm.

I must have looked like some sort of female genie to him, a supernatural giant who had emerged from some bottle washed up by the sea. I lay down flat to be nearer to his level and to observe him better. When he saw my – for him – gigantic eyes fixed on him, he crossed his hands over his miniature sex. Then, despite the difference in size, he started to strut around and look me over in a macho little way, as if he expected me to be impressed and find him attractive.

I laid my hand out flat in front of him, above the moat, inviting him to climb on board. Which he did, having gallantly bowed to kiss my finger.

His little feet pleasantly tickled my palm. He grabbed hold of my thumb and, very gently so as not to unbalance him, I sat up in the sand. Then I raised my hand with its precious contents to the level of my face. He was as cute as anything. Well-built and virile, with well-defined little muscles, his dinky little sex and his pretty, tough-guy face, fine and distinctive, ringed with greased-back hair as dark as his eyes, with their enticing, velvety, albeit slightly idiotic look.

'So, doll,' he said, expanding his chest to the full, 'Wotcher think? Ever seen a body as fine . . . as manly as this?'

That's when I noticed that his mini-cocklet was standing up proudly under my nose. I prevented myself from bursting out laughing, so as not to annoy him and not to drop him. I modestly lowered my eyelids and looked shocked.

'Don't be shy,' he said in what he thought was a reassuring tone. 'Come on, take your dress off . . . Don't be afraid . . .'

I put him down on the sand, on the other side of the moat, in case he got it into his head to run away. For I had no intention of letting such an amusing marvel escape. Without taking my eyes off him, I got undressed in the manner of a clumsy virgin, but with the skill of a stripper, in order to make him foam at the mouth even more at my – for him – colossal charms. Then I lay on my back, closed my hand around him (in his entirety he was no bigger than the penis of an ordinary man) and placed him on my stomach.

On all fours he started crawling round this womanly landscape, crazy with lustful desires. At first he climbed up to my left breast and placed himself against it, arms and legs wide trying to embrace it. Opening his mouth wide he managed to get my boob into his mouth and he started sucking it. At the same time I saw his little bottom undulating against my flesh and I felt his little hard rod rubbing against my breast. Finally a large drop of sticky, warm liquid shot out against my skin.

I almost forgot the size of my partner. Wasn't the fact he was a man the most important thing? I was now quite wet between my legs. Thankfully he then had the good idea of venturing down there, to what was probably a real Ali Baba's cave for him, and doing the honours.

He hung onto my hair as he descended between my spread-eagled thighs. Then he started wiggling between my lips and right into my sheath. He touched me and titillated me absolutely everywhere, and his tiny limbs lent such precision to his caresses that he kept me in a state of acute pleasure. When he had brought me to the edge of ecstasy, he penetrated me with his whole body. Then I came, arching back in the sand and shouting out against the noise of the sea.

The little man climbed back up my belly where he lay down, dripping wet. We slept together, under the wind.

I was woken by a blade of cold water that had slid in under me. I sprang to my feet. It had almost destroyed the castle and the little man had disappeared. I went to collect my dress, which had been blown a few metres away by the wind, and set off in search of the little man. At first I looked in the ruins of the fortress, then all around it. Finally I went into the sea up to my knees, hoping to see him struggling to stay afloat somewhere in the swirling water. But all my efforts were in vain and finally I gave up.

The sea had completely consumed my castle now. The sky had turned dark grey, the deep, huge storm was coming towards me, menacingly, the wind was picking up, full of salt and noise and whiffs of death-like smells. I dragged myself away from the powerful, disturbing attraction of this gigantic mass of water and set off, leaving the ocean behind me. I went back through the barrier of dunes, behind which I soon recovered my shoes and found the exit.

Once I was back in the labyrinth of corridors I started thinking how nice it would have been to carry this little man around everywhere with me, discreetly, in the palm of my hand, in a pocket, in my bra between my breasts, or even in my knickers. I bitterly regretted having lost him.

But in the end I forgot about him as I tried to make sense of the whispers of the ghosts which had started walking just behind me. And although the meaning of their whispered words escaped me, I felt that they were calming me. At the corner of one corridor I opened one of the first doors I could make out in the dark.

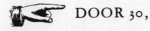 DOOR 30,

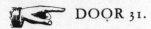 DOOR 31.

29

Adventure in Gotham City

I emerged in downtown Gotham City, in the heart of the dark blue city, in the jungle of gothic skyscrapers and busy streets, with their noisy, nervous, never-ending traffic, their crowded sidewalks displaying the whole gamut of types and oddities of the human species and human society, their drains belching out ghostly clouds of steam from their infernal depths, their subway entrances as dismal as rat traps, their spotlights sweeping the dark sky with their yellow beams ... Gotham City: vibrant, trembling, alive.

At the end of the street I came upon a square where a mob had gathered and was growing by the minute. People were shouting and raising their fists, protesting against one of the mayor's projects. I mingled with the crowd, trying to work out what was going on.

Then a group of hooligans steamed into us and panic began to spread. Sirens began to wail, people ran off in all directions to escape the blows raining down on all sides. Two men fell on me and started manhandling me. As I tried to escape I fell to the ground and they were getting ready to give me a good thrashing when, in the general mayhem, I just had time to notice a large, sophisticated car roll up, with two streamlined wings on the back; it was none other than the batmobile.

Batman himself emerged from it and, with a leap that caused

his dark cape to fly behind him, he rescued me from my aggressors.

On board the batmobile we quickly got back to the batcave, where the hero and his major-domo received me with every courtesy. Then the latter went away, leaving me alone with Batman.

I looked at him admiringly. He had the lot: his long, dark blue cape, his black boots and gloves, his grey tights and jersey, his black pants, his yellow belt, his mask with the bat cars and, on his chest, the famous black insignia on a yellow background. It was all there and already I wanted to know more, to get to know the man who was hiding beneath the hero's get-up.

'You saved me from those ruffians,' I said.

'They weren't ruffians, they were the police.'

'But...'

'The police disguised as a gang of ruffians ... You see, wherever you go, the police are just as dangerous as the hooligans...'

'I don't know how to thank you,' I said, modestly lowering my eyes (in fact I was taking a squint at his batpants which covered a very tasty looking bump).

'If you don't mind, I am going to rest for a while,' he said.

He went to the back of the cave where a deep precipice opened up, with only a natural stone bridge across it, narrow as a beam. Above the abyss a gym ladder was fixed to the wall. Batman suspended himself from it, head down, his cape with its black and blue shadows plunging down into the void.

I was reluctant to join him, not being part bat myself. But it was Batman, and I would always be annoyed with myself if I missed the chance to get close to him. Braving vertigo, I took a few steps on the narrow ledge above the abyss and reached the ladder.

I grabbed hold of the bars and began to climb up. When I reached the level of the black batpants, my heart began to beat twenty to the dozen. I gingerly reached out my hand, waiting apprehensively to see how Batman would react – he doesn't come across as a ladies' man. But he made no movement or protest. I merely noticed the batbump increasing in volume very nicely.

This was all the encouragement I needed. Forgetting my perilous position, with one hand I started pulling down the batpants, or rather pulling them up, with his tights, as far as his knees. The batdick appeared, flesh and bone, just as magnificent as the hero's other accessories and standing horizontally above the precipice, defying the void and the laws of gravity.

I climbed a bit further up the ladder, until my own sex was level with the batdick. Then I straddled it and, hanging from the top bar of the ladder, level with Batman's feet, I pushed it into my body.

I started moving up and down on the batdick, which was remarkably efficacious. I cried out several times and each cry echoed in the precipice, causing dozens of bats to take flight. Soon I could feel my lover was accompanying me in my orgasm and abundant spurts of batcream filled my belly.

When his next mission came along, Batman gallantly led me back to the exit via short-cuts, flitting first over the abyss and then over the furniture with the aid of ropes fired from a gun hanging from his belt, with grappling hooks on the end which could grip any ledge.

Gotham City was bathed in dark blue and we flew around in the night sky, occasionally passing through one of the yellow beams cast into the sky by the spotlights. Down below the city teemed with the complex lives of its inhabitants, in constant conflict with one another, and I watched it with fear and admiration, promising myself to come back to this fairy-tale world, where I still had to meet the Joker, the Scarecrow, the Penguin, False-Face, and many others besides...

After he dropped me off, I saw Batman fly away, soaring above Gotham City with the shadow of his cape spread out behind him. He reached the roof of a building and his lofty silhouette stood out against a large yellow moon. Then he disappeared.

After such an adventure I was rather dazed when I got back to the corridors. My head was still spinning when I opened the following door:

 DOOR 32,

 DOOR 33.

30

The Pirate

When I opened the door I was almost knocked over by a car, which mounted the pavement at full speed. I stepped back sharply and fell over backwards. The car continued on its mad course, spreading panic among the pedestrians and also among the other vehicles, who had to get out of the way of this strange, dangerous stunt by these two black racers, for there were two of them, and they were hearses, hurtling along at top speed trying to overtake and knock each other off the road by crashing side-on again and again.

'Have you hurt yourself?' said a voice.

Leaning over me was a young, dark, slim man, tanned and with curly hair, dressed in a white T-shirt and faded, ripped old jeans, which were a bit on the tight side and showed off his parts.

'I'm fine,' I said with a smile.

He reached out a hand and helped me to my feet.

He wasn't very tall and he looked a bit rough, but he was muscular, supple and well proportioned, with smooth, brown skin, a charming face, very dark eyes, high cheekbones, hollow cheeks and fleshy lips.

At the end of the street one of the hearses had managed to get slightly ahead of the other and disappeared inside a door in a long wall seemingly belonging to a cemetery. At the same moment the other one cannoned into its left rear wing, trying to trap it. The engines roared, the tyres rasped, the bodywork crashed noisily and, on top of all that, the two road hogs frantically sounded their horns and swore at each other through their open windows. The people in the street shook their heads disapprovingly, but without surprise, as if before a sad, but unfortunately all-too-familiar spectacle.

My friend looked at me, amused.

'Haven't you seen that before?' he said. 'It's always like this when the two sections have a funeral together.'

'Which sections?'

'The secular section and the religious section. The artisans put their bodies in free ground, the priests charge. So they call each other crooks and fight to get to the cemetery first, or stupid things like that...'

Not bothering with me any more, he set off in the direction of the cemetery. And without thinking I followed in his footsteps.

'What's your name?' I asked him.

I felt as if I were following him like a little dog. Or as if I had regressed to my childhood, to one of those occasions when you try to fit in with a larger group who aren't very interested in having you around.

'Don Juan,' he said, quite seriously.

He didn't ask me my name. I continued to follow him. We entered the cemetery, which the two hearses had finally got into, one in front of the other, and where they were now unloading their cargoes at opposite corners.

There was an enormous commotion in this cemetery. An odd mixture of people was milling around, noisy and disordered, among the various graves, tombs, sarcophagi and sepulchres. Along the alleyways between funeral monuments children ran, shouted or slalomed on skateboards or rollerskates, using stones and mounds as springboards for their leaps and their acrobatics. Students played ball games, joggers of all ages ran by in shorts and trainers, street hawkers plied their trade in ice cream, roast chestnuts, canned drinks, drugs, stolen goods, prostitutes of all three sexes waited for punters and led them inside the nearest chapel or mausoleum, mothers walked their babies...

Here and there drummers, singers, various musicians, preachers and militants were surrounded by little groups of people who danced, listened or argued. On some of the stones lovers, both gay and straight, embraced, often tightly and warmly. On other stones squatted tripping junkies or drunks sleeping it off. Behind the cypress trees it wasn't unusual to see a bare bum, for people went there to have a piss, or even a shit.

Dogs fought over near-rotten lumps of meat, a few chickens pecked at all sorts of leftovers, a goat pottered around grazing on whatever grass or poppies it could find, mainly on the wreaths and bunches of flowers, even artificial ones, that had been left on the graves. At a bend of an alleyway I was astonished to see some teenagers, boys and girls, bowling skulls at thighbones set up as skittles.

I caught up with Don Juan, who was walking a couple of paces in front of me, pulled him by the sleeve and asked him to explain.

'Come and see,' he said.

And he led me to the end of the cemetery where they were interring the body from one of the hearses that had recently arrived with such a din. The body was wrapped only in a shroud. The hired mourners threw it into a large common grave which was already full of a shapeless, pestilential pile of bodies. There were five people accompanying the corpse, among them an old woman who cried into her handkerchief.

Two workers started shovelling a pile of earth into the hole to fill it in. Since it was already full to the brim with human remains, the operation didn't take long. Then they started digging up the neighbouring plot. They soon started to turn up dozens of human bones, which they piled up in a large skip, and went on till the grave was empty.

'It's because of the earth rising,' said Don Juan. 'As time passed, the more bodies there were, the more the level of the ground rose. Haven't you noticed how low the doors of the chapels are? It's because they are half buried. If we hadn't done anything, the cemetery would have ended up spilling over the walls...'

'And how did you stop it?'

'They *think* they've stopped it ... But they've only slowed it down a bit ... They learned the trick of reclamation. They put the bodies all together in the graves. When a grave is full, they close it and open a more ancient one, where there's nothing left but bones. They recover the bones and no one really knows what they do with them. They used to put them in charnel-houses, but now there's no room any more, so ... Of course, there are leaks in the system ... Kids who reclaim bones to play with, dogs who tear the last bits of meat off bodies that are still a bit fresh...'

'But why are all these people here in the cemetery?'

'Because there's no room anywhere else ... During the day there's only enough room elsewhere for the people who are at work. In the evening and at night it's the opposite. You see that light in the middle of the cemetery? Soon, when the sun sets, it'll come on and everyone will leave. Because at night this is a car park, a supervised car park for all those who come for a night out in town. Because in the evening, in town, there isn't enough room to park all the cars...'

'And you? What do you do?'

'Come with me, you'll see...'

It was late afternoon. Gradually, as the light failed, the cemetery emptied. I followed Don Juan to a mausoleum, whose entrance was marked by a particularly dramatic sculpture. On top of a rock an impressive figure of death, skeletal, wrapped in a shroud, brandishing his scythe, stood proudly with empty eyes above a boat shipwrecked at the foot of the reef. Don Juan went inside the monument and reappeared with a lantern.

We were among the last to leave the cemetery. Some attendants had started patrolling to turf out the people lingering behind. A few streets on we saw the light come on, to signal to the living that this was resting place of the dead and also a safe place where they could park their cars.

Don Juan led me to a dark, open, deserted space. Even though there were no lights he refused to light his lamp. The moon came up, a dented moon, almost full, and a few stars managed to pierce the layers of pollution. In the middle of the space there stood a decaying wall, the last vestige of a building long since destroyed. From the foot of the wall, among the nettles, he picked up a ladder which he placed up to a window cavity in the ruin.

'You will climb up there,' he said. 'You will sit down on the window ledge, then you will put the lamp next to you, you will light it and you will not move until I come to get you.'

I took the lantern and did everything he said, without protest and without question. I felt no fear. Once I was sitting up there I felt as if I were floating between heaven and earth. I had rarely felt so good. Down below, everything was immersed in shadows, in spite of the moon, and Don Juan had disappeared. The air was cool, and I could hear the noise of the city. It was as if I were near to everything and far away at the same time. I waited for a while, but without feeling as if I were waiting, rather as if I were suspended in time.

Then I saw a car's headlights and heard the sound of an engine approaching. For a couple of seconds a part of the open space was luridly lit up, and I saw the shape of Don Juan running in this light. Almost at once everything was switched off, lights and engine, there were voices shouting, a door slamming. A short while later Don Juan reappeared at the foot of the wall and he asked me to put the lamp out and climb down.

When I reached the foot of the ladder he took me in his arms and carried me to the car.

'You're lucky,' he said. 'Tonight we've got a convertible.'

He put me down next to him on the back seat. He spoke in a light-hearted tone, but there was something in his voice I hadn't heard before, something serious which he was trying to hide and which worried me.

Sitting askew on the back seat, face to face, with our legs crossed, we began to kiss and caress each other enthusiastically, as if gripped by some sudden, pressing hunger. He had a long, agile tongue and pulpy lips which gave tasty, penetrating kisses. My breasts were taut, my belly was on fire, my thighs damp. Fortunately I wasn't wearing any underwear, so his fingers could wander freely under my dress, with a sure knowledge and instinct.

I slid my hand under his T-shirt, appreciated the rounded palm of his shoulder, ran my fingers through the sparse hair on his chest, pinched his nipples, then descended over his abdominal muscles, passed his navel, and reached his abdomen by sliding my fingers under the waistband of his jeans. I could feel the warm, wet tip of his cock straining against the cloth and realized that he too was naked beneath his jeans.

I undid his flies impatiently and his cock sprang up, magnificently free and stiff. I also felt his balls, which were firm and full. His cock was quite long and elegant. I closed my hand over this bone-hard bar and, as he had slid his fingers into my pussy, where he caressed me with great skill, I came, still holding on to his gantry.

As I came I fell back against the car seat. He moved over on top of me and penetrated me. He fucked with a mixture of artistic subtlety and rage, sometimes letting himself be carried away by the demanding force of his desire and his virility, sometimes taking control in a sort of playful spirit, with a lightness bordering on humour. As soon as I reached an orgasm he changed rhythm or position, despite the discomfort of our situation.

We made love without saying a word. The night was full of

our moans and our breathing and, in the narrow confines of our back seat, we were the most eager and unified lovers in the world. He came, and when I felt in my burning cunt the palpitations of his cock, quivering with the rising spurts of semen, I came with him.

We started to make love again, naked this time, and beginning by slowly sucking each other. He was extremely tender and refined during the foreplay, but became more radical during the act itself, abandoning himself totally this time to the violence of his desire, and pumping me with strong thrusts of the hips, with no thought to my pleasure, which came anyway, so savagely and with such force that it was accompanied by retching.

Then we smoked some cigarettes together and chatted quietly, staring into the sky.

'When you got me to sit up there with the lamp,' I said, 'was it to make it look like the cemetery light, to attract a car?'

'Got it in one.'

'So you're a pirate, then?'

'So are you ... The pirate's fiancée...'

'Where's the owner of the car?'

'Somewhere, where he wanted to go to...'

'Where's that?'

'I don't know. In town...'

'How did you make him leave his car?'

'Don't worry about it. It's no problem, everything's fine. The guy'll pick up his car tomorrow and no one will think any more about it.'

'Will you think no more about it? Will you think no more about me?'

He started to laugh and said I was silly. He jumped over the front seat and looked for a radio station playing heavy rock. He turned the sound up full blast and we leapt out onto the grass and started dancing wildly. Finally he took me standing up against the bonnet of the car, to the roar of the music.

Then we turned off the music and returned to the back seat

where we spent the rest of the night, swopping laughs and tender words and watching the shining stars disappear one by one.

Before the end of the night, Don Juan accompanied me back to where he had found me, on the pavement where I had nearly been knocked down. I could see it was time to part and I felt like crying.

'Do you do this every evening?' I asked, stupidly, unable to stop myself.

'What?'

'You know what I mean . . . The lantern . . . With a girl.'

'Yes,' he said.

And he seemed so sad I didn't say another word. Then he started laughing and making fun of me.

'Why the funny face?' he said, raising my chin. 'You know full well we are alone, you and I . . .'

He took my face in his hands and we looked at each other. I embraced him tightly, then I turned round, opened the door and left.

In the corridor I let the tears flow as I walked in the dark. I cried as much as I wanted, bawling and banging my head against the wall. When I had calmed down, I went through another door.

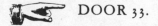 DOOR 33.

31

The Naked Soldier

I set off along a straight, paved path in the middle of a pine forest. The trees cracked in the heat and gave off a smell of resin. Flowers sprouted between the old, eroded concrete slabs.

At the end of the path I found an old, sinister, ruined blockhouse, with creepy black holes for windows. Behind the blockhouse was a disused water trough, made out of the same concrete and covered with moss. And lying motionless beside the trough, on a carpet of pine needles, was a soldier in uniform.

I crouched down beside him and tried to wake him up. He was breathing but remained completely unconscious. I examined him to make sure he wasn't wounded. He had a handsome, innocent, boyish face and an athletic body which filled his uniform.

As there was nothing on the front of his body I rolled him onto his stomach to check his back. Everything was fine here as well. He had a nice, little, round, muscular bum, which I refrained from feeling, even through his clothes. I rolled him onto his back.

I tried to wake him up again, but in vain. 'Perhaps he has some wound which is hidden by his uniform,' I said to myself. And I decided that I had the right, and even the duty, to undress him.

As I took off his clothes one by one, I felt as if I were back in my childhood and was playing with my doll. When he was completely naked I could establish that his body bore no trace of any injury. On the other hand, he was as firm as he was soft, and very well proportioned. I planted a kiss on his shoulder, for it was a shame to see him so lifeless.

Now that he was completely naked, I told myself that the pine needles might irritate his skin. The best thing would be to put him in the trough, which was lined with moss and sprinkled with the slanting rays of the sun and would make a soft, warm bed for him. I placed myself behind his head, held him under his arms, lifted him and started to drag him across. He was heavy and I had to stop several times before I got him to the foot of the trough.

Hoisting him inside was another thing entirely. After a while my efforts had made me so warm that I, too, had to strip naked in order to continue my work. Unfortunately I dropped him several times, through exhaustion or clumsiness, often just when I had almost managed it, when I had already succeeded in getting one of his shoulders over the rim.

But I wasn't discouraged. Each time, after a short pause, I went back to pick him up and deployed all my strength once more to lift him up and transport him to the bed I had found for him. And finally my perseverance was rewarded and I was able to look down on my fine, naked soldier stretched out in his bowl of moss, like a jewel in its box.

'You owe me a little thank you,' I said to him.

And I rubbed my nose against his, an inoffensive but powerful pleasure that men often consider childish or a bit ridiculous and which they only give you for a few seconds. Nostril to nostril, one after the other, I indulged in this game for as long as I wanted, with all the refinements it pleased me to bring to it. I found it hugely satisfying.

Then I turned my mind once more to my soldier's state of health. I had no doubt roughed him up a bit by dragging him over, particularly on his back, which had been scraped along the concrete edge of the trough. I was worried and turned him onto his stomach.

And indeed his back was covered with a horrible variety of bruises, cuts and scratches, which were already scabbing. Fearful that his wounds might get infected, I decided to clean them.

I flipped off his scabs with my nails. Beads of blood appeared. I licked him carefully, on each wound, for I remembered someone telling me that saliva made an excellent antiseptic.

When I had finished I pulled his buttocks apart to see if he had been damaged there as well. At first I saw nothing. Then I thought I could see a splinter stuck in his skin, near to his anus. I picked up a pointed piece of wood, with which I tried to rid him of this little thorn, which could turn out to be quite painful and get infected itself. But I only succeeded in ripping off a patch of skin, where a little blood appeared.

I didn't think that I had got the splinter out. Not wanting to hurt him any more, I decided to try to suck it out. And so I stuck my mouth between his buttocks, holding them apart with my hands. Despite my long and repeated efforts I didn't do any better, and I finally gave up. At least he had been well cleaned.

The blood on his back had congealed again. So I decided it was all right to turn him over. There were virtually no scratches on the front of his body, but I decided to clean it too. I began licking with great application, with little darts of the tongue, from head to toe.

When I saw that, in spite of all my ministrations, the soldier still did not wake up, I started to feel angry. Maybe he needed a slightly more energetic remedy. I raised my hand and gave him a resounding slap. No reaction. So I hit him again and again, all over his body, with all my strength. He didn't move.

Finally I fell over him and asked his forgiveness. I went down to his sex, which I fondled and sucked, which I thought would console him. But in spite of my passion, it remained soft and cool, appetizing but ridiculously amorphous. It was maddening.

Once again I felt an excessive anger filling my limbs and

clouding my head. I looked at the poor devil whose cock I was yanking and on whom I was about to wreak my vengeance. Then with a last prick of conscience I was afraid of myself and picked up my dress and ran off at top speed, far from the sinister blockhouse, far from the ruined trough, as far and as quickly as possible, along the paved path to the exit.

Once I was in the corridor I got dressed. I would gladly have forgotten the whole thing immediately, or be tormented by the ghosts, but I remained alone with my distress and my incomprehension. I didn't dare move on elsewhere. However, in the end I opened another door, for I had to go on.

 DOOR 32,

 DOOR 33.

32

The King

I took my place in the long queue of women waiting in front of the king's throne. He was a fat man, decked out in pompous clothes. He struck me as both unpleasant and attractive at the same time. His long penis rose vertically from his diamond-embroidered pants, and at this very moment the first woman in line had just stuck it in her mouth; it only went part-way in. On each side of the throne were two giant hourglasses, which two valets in full livery turned over at the exact moment that the woman set to work.

She sucked the royal phallus with energy born of despair. But when the sand had run out, she got up and left the room in tears. The following woman took her place immediately.

The king seemed impervious to everything that was done to him. He allowed himself to be manipulated without losing one jot of his majesty or his sang-froid. I saw several women take their place at his member; some of them wanked him, some of them sucked him, some of them mounted him. But he preserved his equanimity and lost none of his substance or vigour and, when the sand stopped flowing, the women who had serviced him so passionately left in tears.

I asked the woman in front of me in the queue for an explanation.

'He is the king of Time,' she said. 'He has promised that the woman who makes him come will live for ever. But as you see, no one ever manages to get anything out of him. They cry because they have failed, like all the others. And yet, who wouldn't give it a try?'

Soon her turn came and, in spite of her efforts, the king remained as stiff and cold as when I had first come into the room. She left in tears.

I approached the king, but stayed at a respectful distance. Even reaching out my hand I wouldn't have been able to touch him. I remembered one of the most erotic moments I had experienced behind the doors of this little circus and I started to recount it to him, stressing certain details. When the hourglass was two-thirds empty, I stopped talking.

'Well?' said the king after a moment.

'Well what, Sire?' I said ingenuously.

'Well, what happened next? How did it end?'

'Will you agree to come if I tell it to you?' I promise you won't be disappointed . . .'

'Very well. But get on with it.'

I continued my story, putting my heart into it to make it as arousing as possible. The king was panting. At the moment when I reached my conclusion an abundant fountain of shiny. white sperm shot out of his member. There was a flurry of excitement in the audience. The sand finally ran out on each side of the throne.

'Will I live for ever, Sire?' I asked.

'Well . . . Come back tomorrow, tell me another story and we will give it some consideration.'

'But . . . you promised whoever . . .'

'You don't argue with the king of Time,' he said in a sharp tone.

I bowed and returned to the back of the room. 'This king's nothing but a fraud, I should have known,' I thought. And, with a shrug of the shoulders, I returned to the corridors where I opened another door.

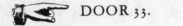 DOOR 33.

33

The Exchange

The fog clung to the windows, a fog as thick and grey as hair, which encircled all the openings hollowed out of the thick stone walls of the house. In the corners of the single large room stood the woodstore, the fireplace, the fridge and a window – more or less all the necessities of life.

Beside the pile of wood a large rock jutted out of the mountainside into the house. And on this rock, in the middle of a few twigs and bits of dried branches, someone had put a thick, shabby, pink dressing gown, on which lay a cat and her kitten. She was lying on her side, suckling her new born, which from a distance looked like a slightly darker ball of fur.

I approached them. She was a gorgeous little cat, with very long ginger, white and black fur and an adorably graceful, feminine face. She purred as she clawed at the cloth, allowing herself to be stroked with the greatest pleasure. The kitten, which still had its eyes closed, was also in three colours, but was a darker brown.

I climbed up an old wooden ladder to the attic. The eaves had been arranged into three little rooms, marked out only by the different levels of their floors and some curtains tacked onto the beams. Facing the large window, in a vast bed with a white iron bedstead, a woman lay on some cushions, writing.

'Hello,' I said.

'Oh, my word! I'll be late!' she said between her teeth, seemingly in a big hurry.

She looked just like the March Hare in *Alice*, but, instead of running, she remained lying on her pillows, spreading blue ink over the page of white paper that rested on a cardboard folder, which itself rested on her lap. It seemed there wasn't actually anything to get worked up about. I wanted to laugh, but I refrained, for she seemed seriously perturbed.

I sat down on the edge of the bed. As she seemed to be working flat out under her quilt and didn't even have time to raise her eyes to me, I looked elsewhere. A bunch of fresh mint had been stuck between a stone and a beam. Beside the large oval mirror, on a small table, her beauty products looked like a display of trinkets. And outside the glass door the constant fog, like a giant cotton rag.

I got up and decided to leave. Then, still without interrupting her writing, the young woman deigned to look at me.

'Please stay,' she said. 'Forgive me ... This meeting is not easy for me ...'

I didn't know what she meant by that, and no doubt she was embarrassed herself, for she added immediately, as if to change the subject:

'Have you seen Dinah?'

'Dinah?'

'The cat ...'

'Oh yes! I've seen her. She's very cute ... She's had a kitten?'

'She's had three.' It's my neighbour's cat, the farmers who live in the meadow in the summer. In winter they take their cows and go back to live in their other house, lower down the valley. For we're very high up here. Dinah had gone off into the wilds when they left. She lived on her own for a few weeks, and then she turned up here on Christmas Eve ... She's cute, don't you think?'

'Very pretty.'

'We had to get rid of two of the kittens, a brown one and a white one. I don't think she noticed. But I dreamed about these two kittens during the night. They were two fat, hairy spiders, spiders in the shape of cats, one white and one black, on their webs, looking at me. I felt so anguished I woke up. It was still early for me, I hadn't slept much, but I got up. I am so late . . .'

'She's raving again,' I thought.

'Is there always this much fog?' I said to change the subject again.

'Yesterday the sun was shining. I sat outside, on a stone, to write. Where the snow has melted there is a nice smell of herbs . . .'

'What are you writing?'

'Your adventure. Everything you experience, as you experience it. Right now, for example.'

I leaned over her sheet of paper, which she had just turned over, and I saw that she had noted down our exact dialogue and at this very moment was finishing a sentence describing how I was leaning over her shoulder reading.

'You write down everything I do?' I asked, rather bad-temperedly. 'Is this some sort of report? Are you spying on me?'

'I'm inventing you. It's a novel.'

'You're trying to tell me I don't exist? I'm just dreaming, perhaps. Or rather I'm just someone else's dream?'

'You are the dream of a whole host of people. But that doesn't mean you don't exist, quite the contrary.'

She continued writing. We sat there a moment without saying a word. I refused to ask her for any further explanation. What I understood about my situation and hers was worth anything she could tell me.

'I don't particularly look like you,' I said finally.

'You are much more beautiful . . . I'd have loved to be like you . . . And the motorbike? Do you like it?'

She looked at me dreamily, enviously perhaps. Then she seemed intimidated.

'I am often more at ease with boys than with girls,' she said. 'I hope you've had as much fun as me in this little circus...'

'What bothers me is that I've forgotten about the man I was looking for. Will I find him?'

'Come.'

She got out of bed and I followed her downstairs. She opened the door and we stepped out into the corridor. Then, for the first time, I finally saw the ghosts who had been pursuing me for so long. As it was quite dark I could only make out their silhouettes, one pale and the other dark.

'Meet the Ghost of Yourself,' said the woman, indicating the dark ghost. 'And the Ghost of Lost Love,' she continued, pointing to the pale ghost.

'Come,' said the ghosts in turn as they took hold of my arms.

I heard the door creak behind me.

'And the Man?' I asked just before the woman closed the door on me.

'Outside!' she said. 'You will find him outside!'

And she disappeared.

At the end of the corridor a feeble illuminated sign indicated the exit. I looked at the ghosts, one after the other, and wondered whether I should:

– follow the Ghost of Myself:

 DOOR 35;

– or follow the Ghost of Lost Love:

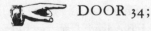 DOOR 34;

– or, in spite of the curiosity I felt about these two ghosts, leave the little circus immediately to find the Man without any more delay, on the outside:

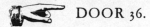   DOOR 36.

34

The Ghost of Lost Love

Only a few steps ahead of me the little green neon light indicated the exit. There was nothing else in this corridor but two doors, one facing the other. Soon I would be outside and I would find the Man I had been seeking for so long.

I turned to the pale silhouette of the Ghost of Lost Love, whose features I couldn't make out, but who appeared in the dark like a long streak of phantom-like, almost phosphorescent whiteness. Once again he reached out his hand to me and in his warm, melancholic voice repeated:

'Come . . .'

I looked at the Ghost of Myself, who was also inviting me to follow him, but I couldn't resist the sad, amorous appeal of this pale ghost, who seemed to need me so much.

I followed him to the left-hand door and we entered a small, circular room with a high ceiling, like a cylinder, which had no furniture except an unmade bed, whose satin sheets glistened in the filtered light of the lamps hanging all round the room.

The Ghost of Lost Love was wrapped in a billowing white cape and wore a roughly made hood over his head, like a bag made of white cloth, from which three round holes had been cut in the places where the eyes and mouth were. He came towards me, took me by the hand, and, after looking deep into my eyes with his dark, fiery gaze, slowly bent down to my mouth and gave me the softest, most passionate, most languorous kiss anyone had ever given me. Then he took off his cape and let it fall to the ground.

He was magnificent. Tall, slim, muscular, his body had a rare grace and harmony, as if it had been imagined and fashioned by an artist rather than born as flesh. As a sort of loincloth he had wrapped several ropes around his waist, letting their ends fall down between his legs.

His hood was also held tight around his neck by a rope. I reached out my hands to undo the knot and uncover his face. But he recoiled sharply.

'Don't do that,' he said. 'You mustn't see me.'

'Why not?'

'Please don't ask questions. Everything would be finished if you saw me.'

I looked at him, incredulous. Was he really going to keep that hood on? Was I supposed to love a man without a face?'

'Please . . .,' he added gently, stroking my hair.

Through the two round holes his dark eyes shone. He took hold of my hands and placed them on the ropes coiled around his waist. I started to undo them, dropping my head to hide my desire to cry, my disappointment at not being able to see his face. A desire which eventually gave way to excitement as I undid the ropes around his abdomen.

When I had finally freed his sex, as fresh and arousing as a fruit-dish full of fine pearls, he took me to the bed, inside the satin sheets. The ropes had left some marks on his flesh. I tenderly kissed his arms, his shoulders, his chest, his stomach and then, on his hips and around his pubis, his bruised flesh.

His sex had inflated a little, but I was so moved I was afraid to take it in my mouth. I moved around it, admiring and intimidated, unable to make up my mind. Finally he took hold of my hair and guided my lips towards it.

When I had his member in my mouth, I felt as if I had entered eternity. I sucked it and nothing else existed but this hard, thick, warm, tasty piece of flesh against my cheeks, my tongue, my throat and my palate. I sucked it, I milked it, and his dug made me forget, his fat dug concentrated the world, which existed solely between my lips in order to give me its nourishment and make me come.

I could have stayed there for hours, attached to his cock, perhaps until I died of lassitude. My mouth was directly attached to my belly, to my sex, which contracted to the rhythm of my lips, as if it too were sucking. When he ejaculated, I felt an orgasm at the same time, without having touched myself. I swallowed it as I came.

He turned over on his side and I kept him in my mouth; I felt deliciously tired and infinitely grateful. I closed my eyes, ready to go to sleep. And I probably dozed a little, before I noticed that it had started to get erect again and was blocking up my mouth once more. Once again he took hold of my hair and brought me up to his face.

He lay me on my back, took my legs between his hands and penetrated me. At first I tried to concentrate on his chest, or closed my eyes so as not to be affected by the sight of his hooded face and that rope he wore round his neck like a hanged man.

'Do you still love me?' he asked.

'Oh yes,' I replied with passion.

For, although he himself was lost in my memory, I had retained the strong, painful memory of the love I had felt for him, long ago, and of the infinite length of time I had awaited his return.

'I love you so much ...,' I said, pulling him towards me so that I could bury my head in his shoulder. 'I have never stopped loving you ... My love ... My beautiful lost love ... Do you remember? One day, you said: "The moon stealer will return to gather the stars ..." I thought you were talking about us ... Why did you not come back to find me, my beautful love?'

And as I said these words of love to him, I came.

He stayed inside me for a long time, exhausting me with pleasure. I was no longer afraid of his hood, in fact I stared straight at it each time I felt an orgasm approach and then I flew off like an arrow, as if I were being sucked by this sinister object towards an irresistible void.

Perhaps hours passed before he came in turn. Then he let himself drop on the pillow and went to sleep.

I contemplated him, full of feeling. I was in love with every part of his body, I was in love with him in his entirety, even with what he hid from me, even, and perhaps above all, with his mystery. Soon I could see he had started dreaming. His eyes moved under his eyelids and his breathing changed. What was going on in his head? What did he see, what was he experiencing that I couldn't see or experience with him? Kneeling above him, quite gently, I started to undo the knot which fastened the rope around his neck.

He didn't wake up. I delicately tugged on the hood. And where I was expecting to see a face disfigured by some misfortune or defect, I in fact found a beautifully oval-shaped face with pure, fine, very distinguished features, high cheekbones and slightly hollow cheeks, and perfectly smooth, fresh skin.

He was so handsome I felt quite bewildered, I didn't dare touch him or even look at him any more. I forgot that he had forbidden me to see him and I didn't even think to replace the hood to cover my wrongdoing. On the contrary, I allowed myself to plant a kiss on his lips, a kiss I wanted to be the last. Then he woke up.

When he saw that he had been discovered, he flew into a mad, desperate rage and started sobbing and crying. He started to hit me with the cord I had taken from round his neck. I let him do it, for I was desperate with sadness myself and I could see that I had betrayed him.

When I fell to the ground under his blows, he took me in his arms and we cried together, with our faces pressed together, drenched in tears. We wept convulsively in each other's arms and I felt the inside of my thighs go damp and his member harden against my navel. And finally he wet my stomach also, without having moved, simply because of the tears which united us.

I crawled away to pick up my dress and I ran off, confused and unhappy. Once I was in the corridor, I got dressed and wiped the tears from my cheeks.

The Ghost of Myself opened his door and loomed up out of the shadows. Through the window in his room I could see mountains soaring into the sky.

'Here,' said the dark ghost.

And he handed me a small handful of coloured pebbles.

'Keep them,' he went on. 'They will help you.'

I felt that he could have helped me, but that it was too late. I gripped the fine stones in my hand. Now I had to leave.

I thought about the Ghost of Lost Love. I didn't want to abandon him. I wondered whether I should:

– try to take the Ghost of Lost Love with me:

 DOOR 38;

– take the hand of the Ghost of Myself, to whom I felt irresistibly attracted, and take him with me to the exit.

 DOOR 39.

35

The Ghost of Myself

'It's the last lap,' I thought as I looked at the white letters of the word EXIT standing out feebly against the green background of the illuminated sign at the end of the corridor. There were only two doors left and I was under no obligation to open them. But the Ghost of Myself, whom I could just make out in the dark, filled me with curiosity.

I looked too at the Ghost of Lost Love, who seemed more feverish and full of expectation. But the dark ghost attracted me like a magnet and I knew immediately that I would not be able to resist his silent appeal. Without another word or gesture he walked away and I followed him.

I followed him into a light, square-shaped cell. Next to the window, on a table, a large book lay open at the middle. On the other side, a second table had been laid for two people and a steaming dish was waiting to be served. The rest of the furniture consisted of two chairs, a small iron bed and a narrow wardrobe. Oddly, the austere simplicity of this place inspired great joy in me.

The ghost was a mature man in a long, dark tunic, with piercing eyes of an extremely light green, and resembled some oriental high priest. The moral strength which emanated from his whole person would have set an unbridgeable gap between him and others were it not counterbalanced by his natural kindness, quite lacking in affectation or curtness. I felt happy to be in his company, in his gaze which displayed perspicacity and goodness, with a hint of cruelty.

I went to the window and saw that we were perched on top of a rocky peak, surrounded by arid, deserted mountains. In front of the cell a tiny garden, surrounded by a low stone wall, occupied the rest of the narrow summit. A couple of birds of prey hovered in the morning light. Far away in the valley I could see a village.

The Ghost invited me to share his meal. I was starving. We sat down at the table to eat our meal, which was simple and frugal, but made of excellent ingredients.

'Why have you been following me through the corridors?' I asked him.

'I didn't follow you. I was with you. As always...'

'But you weren't with me behind the doors...'

'Of course I was ... You were too occupied to notice, but I was there ... How could I leave you? I am the Ghost of Yourself, don't forget...'

I lowered my eyes to my plate, for I could feel myself blushing. So he could see everything, he knew everything about me. I felt like fainting. In a semi-conscious state I fell at his feet, under the table, and with both hands gripped his bare ankles beneath the hem of his monastic tunic. His large, slightly twisted feet were bound in the thongs of his leather sandals.

'I am yours,' I whispered.

'You are mine, as I am yours. The time has come for us to know each other physically.'

I placed my head under his tunic, kissed his strong, hairy calves and breathed in the shade and warmth of his body. I clamped my head between his knees, slowly moved my hands up his thighs and then stayed a while without moving, my fingers halted at the edge of his pubis, my eyes closed, so as to savour fully this suspended moment, the impatience at the tips of my fingernails. Then, quite gently, I pushed my head up along his thighs beneath the dark tunic.

Until the moment when my lips met his large, full balls and his hard cock hit against my forehead.

I felt myself swooning with happiness. Losing all reserve, I rubbed my hands and face wildly against his whole engorged cluster, groping, kissing, chewing, in an uncontrollable erotic frenzy, a desire to guzzle, to extract, to devour, a desire whose savagery I had to contain, to channel into furious lovemaking, without the violent impulses which might have caused me to hurt him.

I felt as if I had been awoken with a start when he lifted up his tunic, took my head between his hands and made me stand up. He undressed me and took off his own tunic, beneath which his huge, powerful body was naked.

'First we must know what we are and in what world we are,' he said.

He put a finger in my behind and forced my middle finger into his. We poked about in each other's anuses. When we withdrew our fingers he had us sniff them and said:

'This is what we are: creatures who transform good fare into shit, in a world which constantly transforms itself into shit and is reborn from its shit.'

Then he sat me on the edge of the table and took me with quick, deep thrusts.

Gripping the edge of the table with both hands, my thighs wide apart, I felt him touch right to the end of my vagina, and rub along its whole length, in a persistent, regular movement, until my flesh took light and started to vibrate, until I was overcome by orgasm, and then by a series of orgasms.

Then he started alternating between orifices, penetrating me in turn in my arse, my cunt and my mouth, without respite, as vigorously as ever. My head spun and I lost consciousness, totally offered up and seized by a series of convulsions which wouldn't end, thrown out of the world and myself by an uninterrupted ecstasy, which made me cry out and grunt and moan like an animal copulating or being slaughtered, for when your senses are exacerbated to this degree they turn your body into an infernal chaos as well as a field of ecstasy.

Towards the end I held on to the hairs on his chest and on his head, on to his neck, which I clawed, I held on to him as to a lifebuoy, and also to hurt him and to gain his favour. Then I felt his large cock quiver in my behind and he ejaculated in long jerks.

Still stuck inside me he dragged me to the floor and we rested, in each other's arms, in each other's bodies.

Later he lay me on my back on the bed. As I floated off to sleep, exhausted, he opened my legs, pushed his head between them and started touching and licking me for what seemed like an infinity. Sometimes I came softly and sometimes we both allowed ourselves to drowse deliciously, his mouth or his fingers remaining clamped between my thighs the while.

Then I asked him to sit on my face and wank himself off. His large balls swung before my eyes, I fondled them and licked them without taking my eyes off his hand sliding up his dick and shaking it. He released spurts of shining white come which, on contact with my skin, turned into coloured pebbles which rolled over my breasts.

I was stunned by this marvellous spectacle. He gathered up the handful of fine stones, placed them in my hand and recommended that I should keep them always.

'Have you got any scissors?' I asked.

And I asked him to cut my hair to neck length. I sat down in a chair, he stood next to me and the scissors began to rasp. When all my long locks had fallen to the floor, I picked them up and offered them to him.

At the moment I left him my heart tightened. I looked at him for a long time and wondered whether, on leaving the little circus, I should:

– find the Man I had come here to look for:

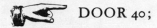 DOOR 40;

– leave alone:

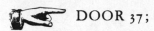 DOOR 37;

– or try to take the Ghost of Myself with me:

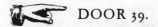 DOOR 39.

36

The Monster

The two ghosts, the one dressed in pale clothes, the other in dark, waited for me, without moving. I warmly shook their hands in the dark and then left them, for it was time for me to go back to my life outside and to find the Man I had come to look for in here.

I walked towards the illuminated sign and my heart was pounding. I was no more than three paces away from it when I heard a moan behind me. I turned round.

In the dark I could make out the shapes of the two ghosts embracing. It seemed as if they were kissing each other on the mouth. Then I saw them disappear together behind one of the two doors.

I began to wonder whether I wasn't making a mistake in leaving before I had met the two ghosts who had been following me during my journey through the labyrinth. Didn't they, too, have something to teach me? And would I have another opportunity to make their acquaintance? I turned back and opened the door I had seen them go through.

I entered a bright, square-shaped, simple monk's cell. They didn't seem to have heard me. Near the window, through which I could see an arid, deserted mountain landscape, the Ghost of Myself was undressing the other, that is, was taking off his ample white cape, beneath which he was naked. Then

I discovered that the Ghost of Lost Love was a very beautiful young man, at least his body was beautiful, for his face remained hidden under a white hood, a cloth bag with three holes cut in it around the eyes and mouth and tied around his neck with a rope. Oddly, he was also wearing ropes around his hips; their ends fell between his thighs as a sort of loincloth.

As for the Ghost of Myself, he kept on his long black tunic. His dress, his demeanour, his gaze and this cell which seemed to serve as his bedroom, seemed to suggest an oriental high priest or wise man. His gestures were calm and precise and you could see determination and moral strength in his face, as if he were preparing to perform some duty rather than abandon himself to lust. He was quite impressive.

He started to undo the ropes around the pelvis of the beautiful pale ghost. When he was free, the latter leaned on the window sill with his back to me and offered his behind to his companion, moaning.

Then the dark ghost turned to me and signalled me to come forward. When I came near to him I reached out my hand towards his arm but he pushed it away. So I approached the naked body of the pale ghost. But he pushed me away again.

'Don't touch us,' he said. 'Not me and especially not him. Whatever happens, make sure you don't touch. It would bring about a great misfortune for all three of us. But watch and wait, for we will have need of you before long.'

And he sat me down on a chair, next to the table, where two places had been laid.

The Ghost of Myself picked up one of the ropes that had been wrapped round the young man's waist and started to beat him with it. The Ghost of Lost Love moaned and complained, but he put up no resistance. He even started running round the room as his persecutor pursued him, whipping the rope against his flesh with all his might.

At first I was horrified by the cruelty of this scene and I wanted to intervene. Then I noticed that the pale ghost had an erection and, while going through the motions of running away, seemed to be exposing himself to the most painful blows, offering every part of his magnificent body to be beaten.

His member grew ever more stiff and purple. I slipped my hand under my dress, for, in spite of my discomfort at this spectacle, I was beginning to feel very excited.

The hooded young man fell to the ground, lay on his back and was being beaten on his chest as he writhed about, not making any effort to protect himself with his arms. His cock stood up and twitched above his stomach. Then I forgot what the dark ghost had told me. This man needed me and I had to help him.

I slid to the ground and went towards him on all fours. When I got close, I grasped his extremely hard and warm cock and wanked it vigorously. He let out a cry and came straight away in my hand.

The dark ghost recoiled, looking grave and troubled. I felt relieved, as if I had come myself. But the pale ghost leapt to his feet and pulled off his hood wildly. His face, which was also very beautiful, was twisted in anguish. He tottered, looking at each of us in turn with an expression of disbelief.

Suddenly he started to undergo a transformation, at lightning speed. His hair grew out and turned white, his back bent, his flesh turned flabby, his skin drooped, his face became covered in lines, his teeth fell out of his mouth, his nails grew extraordinarily long. He hurled himself at the Ghost of Myself and clawed at his neck.

The latter fell to the ground. His neck was striped by a long, deep gash, which began to bleed profusely; large drops of blood flowed to the floor.

The pale ghost lost his strength. His flesh hollowed out and turned blue, hanging off his bones. He too fell to the ground on his back, in the position in which, a moment earlier, I had grabbed his eager sex, which had now shrivelled up. His body gave off a smell of death, he didn't move or breathe.

Since the beginning of his transformation I had been standing with my back to the wall, my head in my hands, screaming, paralysed. The Ghost of Myself stood up and said:

'You have to kill him now.'

At the spot where he had lain there was a pool of blood on the floor. But his haemorrhage seemed to have stopped. I was still screaming. The Ghost of Myself silenced me with a slap and stuffed a pair of scissors into my hand, repeating:

'You have to kill him now.'

'But he's dead! Can't you see he's dead?' I sobbed.

'If you don't stick these scissors in his heart he will never be dead. You have to do it if you don't want him to suffer forever and return to torment you for the rest of your life.'

I approached the body and knelt in front of it. I was crying so much I could hardly see. I gripped the scissors in both hands, raised them over his emaciated chest and stabbed him several times, sobbing. Nothing came out of his body, as if he had been drained of his blood. I passed out.

When I came to I saw a rectangular hole gaping in the ground next to me.

'Help me,' said the Ghost of Myself.

We wrapped the body in the white cape and lay it in the grave. Then we replaced the floorboards. I was exhausted, but strangely calm.

'You intend to live on top of him?' I asked the dark ghost.

'We all live above the dead,' he said.

And he took me in his arms. I wept softly, my head lying against his chest.

'I love you,' I whispered.

'Remember,' he said, 'I am and will always be with you. Especially in your most intimate moments, in your dreams, in your pleasures and in your pain. If you are able to recognize my presence, listen to me and love me in those moments and everything will be all right.'

And he kissed me.

I washed the wound in his neck, which was scarring already. Of the spot where his blood had soaked into the floor there was no trace except a small pile of coloured pebbles. He picked them up, put them in the palm of my hand and recommended that I keep them with me. I kissed him again and left. I knew now he would never leave me.

In the corridor I walked slowly towards the exit, wondering whether, when I left the little circus, I would:

— find the Man I had come to look for in here:

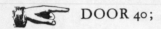 DOOR 40;

— or decide to leave alone:

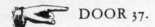 DOOR 37.

37

The Hermit

Ahmed came to see me this afternoon. I heard the sound of his engine way off. I knew straight away it was him. He said he was going to buy a motorbike. We stood admiring his machine for a while, then he asked if I wanted to give it a go. I told him I was too old for motorcross, but I agreed to ride behind him and we went for a long ride in the forest, on the road and, in the end, on the beach. I held on to his leather jacket, it all took me back . . .

Then we returned home, but Ahmed didn't stay long. I think he was impatient to get back on his bike. We smoked a cigarette and then he was off. I took off my dress and walked down to the beach.

I've lived here for years, in this hut in the middle of the forest. At first the people on the island thought I was mad. With the passage of time I think they came to see me simply as an eccentric. To be honest, I don't care. But, although no one ever comes this way, it soon became common knowledge: an old woman was living naked in the middle of the trees, in the old forester's wood hut.

Of course, whenever I have visitors or go shopping in the village I put my dress on. The rest of the time I see how I feel. And it's so good to feel the air and the sun all over you. I don't don't think a body which is naked and happy to be so is ever ugly. I feel good in this body which has lived through so many adventures with me. This body, my old friend, which still loves life so much, sometimes even more than I do...

The only thing I keep on is the bracelet made from the coloured stones given to me by the Ghost of Myself. He has followed me everywhere in my long and beautiful life, so full of loves, of apprenticeships, of movement. For that's how life is for me: never fixed and definitive, but in a state of constant evolution, as it was in the beginning, in childhood. And throughout this life only this bracelet of stones has remained constant, my rallying point.

Who can say what tomorrow holds? I am happy.

I already told the police. I'm sure it wasn't Ahmed that did it. It's not even certain the old woman was killed. Why would he kill 'er? They say she had some cash stashed away, but no one's ever seen it. If you ask me, she didn't have a penny. It's not 'er style. Anyway, she could 've easily drowned herself. Just 'cos Ahmed disappeared the same day, it doesn't mean he killed 'er. Specially since he liked 'er. A mate of mine reckons he saw them both goin' off on a bike yesterday morning. And she was drivin'. I know it's hard to believe, since they were fishin' out her body at the same time. What I find really strange is, she went swimming in 'er clothes. That's not like her ... Anyway, she were a smashing lady. I liked her too. I went to see her with Ahmed, the first time, to invite 'er to a show. Eight shows, we did, on the island. One in each village. We'll miss Ahmed if 'e doesn't come back, that's for sure. In a little circus like ours, we haven't got tightrope walkers to spare. But we're travellers, us ... And whatever happens, we won't hang around forever...

38

The Mad Woman

I don't even want to talk about the little circus, no one understands. The stupid doctors leaned over me like ambulance men and asked me to talk. What did they want me to talk to them about? About what they've lost themselves and were trying to find by pecking around like vultures in other people's brains? Fuck off and sort out your problems yourselves, you useless bunch of wankers! I know I shouldn't have tried to bring the Ghost of Lost Love out with me, I don't need anyone to spell that out to me, I know I should have left him in his room, back there, in the pitch-black labyrinth. I held him by the hand, and with all my heart, but pouff! as soon as I stepped out into the sunlight,

no one there.

Just me, on my own. I didn't shout or cry or anything, for I didn't even realize what had happened. I didn't even remember that I had tried to bring Lost Love with me. Oh, oh, my beautiful lost love, how beautiful you were with your rope round your neck, how you beat me with your rope, how I loved you, how I loved you! I stood for a moment in the middle of the square, in the sun, with the feeling I had forgotten something,

but what?

For a long time I didn't remember, I knew I was looking for

something, but what? If I had wanted to remember, I would have, but I didn't want to, it's as simple as that. At first I didn't have time in my busy life and then I had affairs, I fell in love with all the men who looked at me, I took them by the hand but after a while they didn't even want to see me any more, it was always the same and I said it doesn't matter there are lots of other things

in life

and so I did other things, oh I knew how to go about fulfilling myself, I tried everything and tasted everything acting alcohol women gambling meditation and even philosophy rediscovering the source contemporary art parallel sciences charity and even celebrity I did great things don't laugh you poor cretins you think you've lost nothing you who lost the desire to live much longer ago than me because you are already dead and buried in your impoverished little

lives.

It's not you who will die in the sea one day one fine day after meeting your double in a hut in the middle of a wood your double who went off with a handsome young man on the motorbike of her youth while you went off into the waves to talk to your beautiful Lost Love. Oh, oh, my beautiful love, will you love me always?

39

The Dead Woman

Finally I had a visitor. A fine, upstanding policeman. He approached me with a bewildered expression and then he leaned over me and stared at me, reached slowly towards my breast ... and slipped two fingers between my ribs to grab the bank card, which he looked at more curiously than at my skeleton.

That's all that remained of me: my bones and my bank card. The crows had even eaten my shoes, unless they were swept away by the elements. I had been lying there all winter. Oh, they looked for me for ages! My heirs, obviously. Without proof of death, they were stymied. These months must have seemed very long to them, even longer than they seemed to me ... And now they will start squabbling over my remains ... Over my card as much as over my bones, of course ... Would that this pack of dogs could kill each other, that's the best gift they could make to the human race!

As for me, I don't regret anything. When I came here last autumn, it was to find the Ghost of Myself. I shouldn't have tried to make him leave the little circus. That's how I lost him. I ended up outside on my own. One moment I was holding his hand, the next he had gone. Disappeared, vanished. Just like the pebbles he had given me. After this I never took any pleasure, I never dreamed again.

At first I started collecting men. As none of them was able to give me what I had lost, I became bitter, then spiteful. I took everything I could from them and in return gave them the contempt which filled my hypocritical heart. In the middle of my social ascension I married the stupidest and most vain of the men I had got into my bed, so as to play cat and mouse with him, while I continued to be interested only in power and money.

I trampled over everything to pursue my career, friends, lovers, children, and when I reached the summit I saw that I was alone above the void and that suited me fine. For I hadn't lived any other way since I had left the little circus.

Then I had this dream, last autumn. It was my first dream in all these years, in which I met the Ghost of Myself. I saw him at the window of his cell, at the summit of his mountain peak, and he was holding out his arms, as if calling me. Several nights in a row I waited for him to return. I couldn't sleep. When I finally managed to drift off, my sleep was so deep and so dark that when I woke up I felt as if I was emerging from death. I had no more dreams.

One morning I took a plane, hired a car and set off, alone, into the mountains. The next day, around dawn, I was on an upland path, setting off on a long climb towards a summit. I had the confused idea that once I was up there, in an environment like his own, he might perhaps agree to reappear.

After a few hours a mist came down. They had warned me at the tourist information. But I don't usually listen to what people say to me. I could barely see the end of my arm. I came off the path and tumbled downhill. I managed to get up, in spite of a pain in my knee and zero visibility, and tried to continue upwards, feeling my way from stone to stone.

I don't know how long I was up there. It was cold and I had no point of reference. I lay down among the stones and let myself die.

I heard them looking for me, for days and days, with helicopters and dogs. Then the silence returned, the snow fell and held me in a long, white, dreamless sleep. In the end this policeman discovered me by chance, when he went off the path to have a piss, after the snows had melted. I was no longer living in my body.

It's months since I started to climb to this summit. A slow, difficult operation in my condition, as you can imagine. For strangely, my soul, freed of its body, has become much heavier and more clumsy. I'm afraid it will give up at any moment. But I continue to pull myself up the hill, for up there I still hope to meet the only being I have missed on this earth, the Ghost of Myself.

40

The Jugglers

How did I not recognize him as I left the little circus? It's a question I still ask myself. His convertible was still there, I looked around the square, I even had a look in the café. I thought he hadn't come out yet and I waited for him.

During this time he was outside too and was waiting for me. But we didn't see each other until the evening.

We both went to the circus show and that's where we met up. What followed was like a dream. After the show we made friends with the circus artistes and the jugglers, who lent us their caravan for the night.

It was midsummer's night. The shortest night, but also the longest. Everyone carried on partying in the square, we heard them dancing and laughing and shouting around the fire, with music, while we made love. And we had so much love to make.

Of course I was in love with him. Only it is sometimes difficult to say that after one night. The next morning we parted tenderly and exchanged phone numbers. And we set off, each in our own direction, back to our own lives.

That same evening I wanted to call him. I looked everywhere but realized I had lost his number. I had no means of finding it, as I didn't even know his name. I waited for his call.

The following year was a bad one. I felt as if something had been ripped out of me and my stomach had been left open. I didn't know he too had lost my phone number. And yet I had the feeling he was suffering also. I knew that we were bound to each other and I felt badly for him as well as me, because he was separated from me. I tried to distract myself with other flings, but they offered only temporary comfort and left me even sadder afterwards.

I made a bracelet with the coloured pebbles from the Ghost of Myself. When I felt troubled I held it in my hand and rolled the stones between my fingers.

The following summer, by chance, I came across the little circus as I was riding along. He was there too. By the same chance, if you can call that sort of coincidence chance. We stayed there a while. We wanted a new life. We learned to juggle and became travellers.

Then we left and did a whole host of other things. From the start, for us, life has been constantly new, the world always there to be discovered. Love also.

Of course we've had our arguments and separations and shied away from getting into habits, from shutting ourselves away. But we always catch all the balls, by juggling with them and throwing them back to each other with the increasing virtuosity we've learned. He is my lover, my brother, my companion, my friend, my partner. No me without him, or him without me, these are the words we juggle with.

behindcloseddoors

alina reyes

behind**closed**doors

translated by David Watson

Grove Press
New York

Originally published in France as *Derrière la Porte* by Editions Robert Laffont, Paris
This translation first published in Great Britain by Weidenfeld & Nicolson in 1995
First Grove Press edition published in May 1996

Printed in the United States of America

Library of Congress Cataloging-in-Publication Data

Reyes, Alina
  [Derrièrre la porte. English]
      p.   cm.
  ISBN 0-8021-1589-6
  I. Watson, David, 1959–   II. Title.
  PQ2678. E8896D4713   1996
843'.914—dc20   96-2103

Grove Press
841 Broadway
New York, NY 10003

10 9 8 7 6 5 4 3 2 1

behind**closed**doors
an adventure in which you are the hero

Contents

Welcome, man, to the lair of Eros. I, its humble servant, want to be with you everywhere your desire impels you as you enter the doors of this kingdom, for my ambition and my ecstasy will be to offer you all the pleasures you indulge in, to give myself to you as queen and subject, to experience with you all the ardour, all the excitement, to satisfy with you the most secret dreams and the most intimate impulses of our souls and our bodies.

Man, my joy and my torment, should I address you familiarly, as if touching, or more formally, with desire? At least know this, my dashing friend, that once we have passed through the doors of Eros, once we have been introduced to my master's labyrinth of fantasy, I will be your warmest accomplice, I will be the hand which guides your hand, and also all the leech-like kisses of silent mouths which will raise volcanoes of ash in your manhood.

So, if you are willing, let us play. For the only guide to losing yourself in this kingdom is the game, with its pleasures and its risks. At the entrance to the cave you will choose a thread, then another with each new adventure, these threads leading you through the maze according to the uncertain laws of your desire and of chance.

It is up to you to enter the labyrinth, to choose the doors you

want to open, so as to trace your own route, your own book, your own destiny.

Come, see how dark it is inside. Now everything is possible.

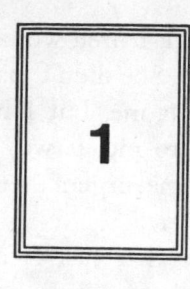

The Little Circus

It was summer, and I didn't want to end up stuck in a traffic jam on the motorway. I took the first exit and headed down the ribbon of asphalt, straight as a die through the forest. It was hot; the air, split open by the convertible, whipped against my skin. Not a soul. I put on a new cassette, turned up the volume, put my foot down. Only one captain on this ship. The car shifted, fast, docile, engine noise drowned out by the raging voice of Kurt Cobain.

Suddenly the road began to twist and turn, then there was a junction in the shape of a Y. I took the left fork. A bit further on I slowed down as I passed between some houses, crowded together on each side of the road; half the shutters were closed, as is normal in very hot weather at siesta time.

Now the air was stifling. I cut the music. In the centre of the village, perfectly silent, the cars and caravans of a little travelling circus were arranged in a circle in the deserted square. There was a red motorbike parked in front of the only bar. I parked next to it, with the intention of going in for a drink. But I never entered that café.

The moment I shut my door, a low growl drew my attention to the circus. Next to the tiger's cage there was a black caravan. Above the arched doorway was an unusual sign, painted in tall, slightly shaky gold letters: *The doors of Eros*. Inside the dark

doorway stood a small, dark-haired woman, in a tight, reflecting, moiré dress, her arms bare. She didn't make any gesture, perhaps she wasn't even looking at me, but I had the feeling that her shiny pupils were calling to me. It was at once an order and a petition, as if she had some urgent need of me. I crossed the circle of caravans to join her.

She smiled and I saw that her face, though showing the effects of time, was still attractive and expressed a certain candour. Despite her gipsy-like appearance her skin was white and her slender figure, small-boned but plump, seemingly naked under her tight dress, had a child-like quality. She named a price, and I thought she was referring to her body. At the same time, she turned round confidently and opened the curtain covering the entrance. I watched the material stretch taut across her bottom. It was so round I had to stop myself touching it. I paid and went inside.

The curtain closed behind me, and I was standing in the dark. I took a few steps, then turned round to wait for her. Since I saw and heard nothing, I called, 'Madame! Are you there?' I hated having to resort to calling out like this, but I didn't know her name, and the bitch had left me in the lurch. It had all the appearances of a trap, and I told myself I'd be better off leaving straight away. But she had succeeded in exciting me and now, alone in the dark, my imagination was overheating. One thing was certain, there was no way I was leaving here without getting what was due to me.

Perhaps the little whore had come in through another entrance and was already waiting for me on the bed of the caravan. In which case, I was bound to find her if I went on a bit further. Or else she was on the other side of the curtain, and I'd be better off going to find her instead of standing here in the dark, where – who knows? – I could be risking getting my throat cut by one of her accomplices. So I made my choice between:

– going forward in the dark

☞ DOOR 2;

– going back to look for the woman

☞ DOOR 3.

2

The Inspection

I decided to go forward a short way, and turn back if I couldn't find a way out of this dark corridor-type thing I seemed to be in. Holding my arms out in front of me because of the dark, I proceeded slowly. My hands hit a wall, and I pushed against it. A door opened.

I immediately closed my eyes because of the blinding light. An authoritarian voice summoned me to enter.

When I opened my eyes I saw that I was on the threshold of a small room like in a police station or perhaps a hospital administration. It was an old-fashioned office, with faded pictures on the walls and outmoded furniture. A table, a metal filing cabinet, a chair, the whole thing reeked of a shortage of money, including the ancient computer plumbed with a multitude of grey cables. Four photographer's spotlights placed in the upper corners of the room provided the harsh lighting.

Behind the table, in a well-worn imitation leather armchair, a fat woman in a uniform sat in state. She had salt and pepper hair, neatly tied in a chignon, and a full, unlined face, rather charming in spite of its extreme severity. A trace of deep red marked the line of her thin lips, her dark eyes were ringed in blue and decorated with false eyelashes, her cheekbones heavily highlighted with rouge. This make-up, applied on a white foundation, was simultaneously repulsive and fascinating.

However, my attention was grabbed by a little girl whom I hadn't previously seen, who took my hand and invited me to enter. She must have been between eight and ten years old, and she wore a short summer dress decorated with pink roses. She seemed lively and happy, with her bracelet of sweets around her wrist and a red ribbon in her chestnut curls. She held me firmly by the hand and led me to the table in the middle of the room.

The fat woman bade me welcome, with a kindness I wasn't expecting. She said that I had entered the kingdom of Eros where I would be able to realize all my desires. But first I had to complete a small questionnaire, 'in total confidence, of course, but you know how it is, for our records ...' Then she asked me to approach.

I went round the table to her side. She swivelled on her chair and, facing me, looked me over from top to bottom. She was wearing a uniform made of khaki cloth, with epaulettes and a row of medals worthy of a soviet general pinned to her ample bosom. Her legs, thick but shapely, were sheathed in flesh-coloured stockings, and her thighs completely filled her tight skirt.

The fat woman had adopted her severe tone again. Still sitting in front of me, she reached out and started undoing my belt. Something, I don't know what, made me want to acquiesce. 'A simple inspection,' she said. She calmly unbuttoned my flies, pulled down my trousers, then my pants, and wheeled her chair forward to come nearer to me.

Suddenly, I was aware that the little girl was still there on the other side of the office and was staring at my sex. The fat woman caught my movement of recoil and said, 'Don't worry, she's blind.' The little girl started to laugh. I looked at her eyes again, and I saw that they were turned up. Was it possible that I hadn't noticed anything before? The woman said, 'You won't be allowed to proceed if you don't pass the inspection,' and I let her get on with it.

With her chubby, red-taloned fingers, the fat woman took my

glans, pulled back the foreskin and bent over to check it closely. Then, with a kick, she propelled her chair back to the table and started typing something onto the computer.

With the same speed she returned to my sex and started weighing up my cock, then my balls, checking them in detail, from every angle, before making her report. She went back and forth several times between her computer and me. Her breasts, lifted high by a powerfully-boned bra, looked like two artillery shells. Her blouse, stretched to breaking point, gaped between the buttons. If you paid careful attention, as I did whenever she was busy examining my genitals, you could see through these gaps the place where these two parcels of soft, white flesh began. So voluminous were they that only a narrow furrow separated them, where, as the inspection advanced, tiny beads of sweat appeared.

I didn't dare look across at the little girl, to check whether her eyes, which I had thought at first were directed at my sex, were still turned up. I was sweating in the heat of the spotlights.

The fat woman announced that the inspection was over. I was beginning to enjoy being manhandled. Instead of getting dressed, I left my trousers round my ankles. I wouldn't ask her for anything, but I wanted her to know that my cock, now stiffened slightly, was still at her disposal, should she want to play with it some more.

And indeed she looked at me with a certain interest. Then she came over to me. But all she did was dress me, as if I were a little boy. She carefully arranged my cock inside my pants, tucked my shirt into my trousers, did up my flies and fastened my belt.

'And now you can go,' said the fat woman. 'In here you can experience things you have perhaps never dared dream about. But I suppose, before anything else, you would like to find her.'

'Who?'

'I was told she came in just after you. But that won't make your task any easier. You won't be able to recognize her. A very

beautiful girl, by all accounts, dressed in skintight black leathers. But you will meet so many beautiful girls ... And she has time to change her clothes a hundred times, women love that ...'

'Who are you talking about?'

'The Woman, of course, the Woman of your life. Let us see!'

She started to talk down to me:

'You're so awkward! Get a move on! She is already madly in love with you, and she's looking for you! She's looking for you! She's looking for you!'

The little girl was already in front of me and she was pulling me by the hand. I couldn't see her eyes. She slid open a door at the back of the room. I turned round to the woman who, with a movement of her head, signalled me to go. I would have liked to say goodbye to the child, but she kept her head and her eyes lowered. She squeezed her little hand in mine, then left me. When the door was closed behind me, I heard the little girl burst out laughing.

I found myself in a sort of circular corridor. The pale neon light was just strong enough that I could make out three doors. *She's looking for you! She's looking for you!* The inspector's words were probably mere derision. But I was excited now, I needed to know, to see and, if possible, to take whatever was awaiting me in this strange place.

The moment I opened one of these doors, I thought I felt a cold shadow fall over me. But, overcome with impatience, I didn't turn round, and I chose one of these exits:

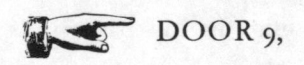 DOOR 9,

or

 DOOR 11.

3

The Nurses

I was starting back in the direction from which I had come, holding my arms in front of me in the darkness, when my hands encountered two mounds of warm flesh which I immediately recognized as two large breasts. I was so thrilled I didn't move, and I felt the nipples harden into the palms of my hands.

I began stroking the breasts. They were voluminous and on the heavy side, but firm, and they became even firmer and more swollen as I kneaded them. They were the most amazing tits I'd ever had the good fortune to lay hands on. I stuck my head right in between them. There was a nice female smell in there, reminding me of when I was a small boy and I found a way to press myself furtively against my mother's bosom.

In the dark I was like a blind child, and nothing in the world existed but these two large breasts in my hands and next to my nose. I closed my eyes and started to suck them, one after the other. Time passed, in the dark.

Above me I heard panting, then moaning. In my pants my prick was so tight it hurt.

Then two hands began undoing my belt and unbuttoning my flies. At first I thought they belonged to the creature whose two beauties I had been sucking, but I quickly realized that the hands were coming from behind me. There was another woman, and this other woman was now pulling down my trousers, lifting up my shirt and rubbing her breasts down my back.

I tried in turn to undress the two women, but they wouldn't let me. They seemed to be wearing long dresses which covered their whole bodies, leaving only their breasts bare. I was sorry I was unable to admire the sight of these two pairs of bare breasts sticking out of tight dresses. My eyes were getting used to the dark, but I could only make out two white masses which seemed to be free-floating in the dark.

I had the women stand side by side, so that I could touch all four breasts at once. They both giggled. They turned face to face to rub their breasts against each other. I got my mouth and hands in there as best I could. They began to sigh, louder and louder. Then they pulled me to the ground, which, to my surprise, was covered with a deep-pile carpet.

One of the women, on all fours behind me, dangled her breasts above my face, moving gently, sometimes to give me one or the other breast to suck, sometimes to smother me between the two. At the same time, the other, bending over my legs, squeezed my cock between her breasts.

At that rhythm, I couldn't hold back for long. My head stuffed between the two large breasts, I groaned and bit them as I came, my cock spurting semen in spasms into the bosom in which it was contained.

'Did you feel how warm and hard it was?' my companions said to each other as they amused themselves touching me a bit more.

I already felt ready to give them the benefit of my virility once more.

'But,' they added as they drew away from me, 'you probably want to carry on your way. You know, here you have the right to open any door you want, to experience all the adventures you desire. Then there is the woman, the one who is looking for you . . .'

'Who? The woman at the entrance?'

'Oh no, she's just the janitor . . .'

They laughed.

'Who then?'

'That woman from the outside, of course, the one who came in just after you ... The Woman, the Woman of your life,' they whispered together.

And they laughed again, quietly.

I tried again to find out who this woman was, but instead of answering me, my two friends started yawning and falling into each other's arms, saying they needed a bit of rest.

It seemed difficult to take them seriously, but this story intrigued me. If she really existed, was this woman someone I knew? Someone I had loved? I thought about different faces, and I tried to guess who, among these friends and lovers, past and present, might be harbouring a need to follow me into this place where I was promised an orgy of sex, and perhaps even love. Perhaps this woman was a total stranger, driven by some mysterious desire for me?

My two companions were still resting, wrapped together face to face, breast to breast. I could hardly make them out in the dark. Where was I? I suddenly felt the shadows were waiting for me, and I was torn between excitement, anxiety and curiosity, intense, contradictory desires all knotted together in the pit of my stomach:

– stay with the two women, whom I still wanted to undress:

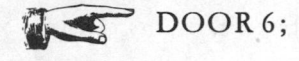 DOOR 6;

– continue to explore this marvellous kingdom, where apparently I was to meet many other women, and perhaps the Woman:

 DOOR 7;

– or get out of here while there was still time, for after all I could now say I had got my money's worth, and I didn't know

what was in store, and this story about a woman looking for me troubled me a bit.

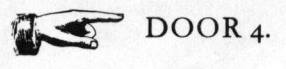   DOOR 4.

4

Too Late

Now it's all over. You think about it your whole life, or rather do everything you can not to think about it, and finally the moment arrives. In a few hours' time, I will be dead.

They say you see your life pass in front of your eyes at the moment you die. I don't know if I am seeing my whole life. How would I know? You can only see what your memory has preserved. And all my memory has retained is a regret. What I am seeing now is the moment I left the kingdom of Eros, only a few minutes after entering it. Simply because I thought I had had sufficient relief from fucking between the breasts of two women. Simply because, in all honesty, I was scared. I was about to say, I was dying of fear. But what in God's name was I afraid of? Pleasure? The woman who was looking for me? Myself?

Well it's too late now. Oh, I've had a few pleasures in my life, but why did I spurn so many? I've had a few women, and even one woman above all the others, but how can I be sure that it was really her, the woman of my life? How can I be sure that it wasn't the other one, the unknown woman who was looking for me and from whom I had fled?

Yes, it was definitely myself that I was afraid of. Of going to my own limits. Too late. I'll never have the opportunity again. It is as if my life were a book and I had only read the first few pages. I have been absent from my own life, and I have only one life to live. Too late, too late.

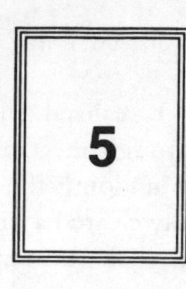

5

The Secretary

It was a deserted office. I sat behind the large desk and waited.

I opened a file which was lying close to hand and began to read it. It seemed to be about some international business transaction.

There was a knock. It was at a door at the side, different from the one by which I had arrived.

'Come in,' I said with some relief.

A charming young woman in a sky-blue outfit, her hair tied back, her green eyes behind a pair of tortoise-shell glasses, slim and dapper, varnished nails, fine gold jewellery, sheer stockings and pumps, made an appearance.

'I'm your new secretary, sir,' she said as she approached the desk.

She had a memo pad and a pen in her hand.

'If you have any instructions for the day ...' she added, ready to take my orders.

'Look, I think we will work well together,' I began, with the utmost seriousness. 'Very well indeed ...'

I was busy trying to take a peek at her legs, and I didn't know what else to say.

At that moment, she dropped her pen, which rolled under my desk. I was about to bend down to pick it up, but she was already squatting down, quick as a flash.

'Please don't disturb yourself,' she said as she disappeared under the table.

It wasn't long before I realized she was after a different implement altogether. Through my trousers I felt her hand on my balls, then her fingers undoing the buttons of my flies one by one. Once she had finally cleared a direct path to my privates, she unpacked the lot and took the object of her quest in her mouth. I lay back in the armchair, my head against the headrest, to savour this sweet experience in comfort.

I was really into it when the door opened. I sat up smartly in my chair, grabbed the file on my desk and pretended to read it, in as detached a way as possible. A young man in a suit burst in.

'Can't you knock?' I said with as much authority as I could muster.

'I'm sorry, sir,' he replied, 'but it's a matter of some urgency. I have been informed that a woman has infiltrated the company by passing herself off as your secretary. She is an imposter, she photocopies documents, she is a secret agent, in short, a spy, whose mission is to steal our files and pass them on to our competitors.'

'Well, well,' I thought as she continued to suck me off out of sight, 'she is one shady woman ...' But in her current position, what information could she be gathering that would be of any interest to our competitors?

Under the desk, she was unstinting in her ardour, and I was having some difficulty in following the intruder's alarmist announcement.

'I haven't seen anyone,' I said. 'You may go.'

'Very well,' he said, only half convinced. 'If you need anything ... Don't forget that I am your secretary ...'

And with some regret he headed for the door.

That was when, in her enthusiasm, my spy made a little sucking noise.

The secretary spun round and dived in turn under the table, shouting:

'I've uncovered her! I've uncovered her!'

Then there was a real commotion. Apparently, the beautiful spy had no intention of relinquishing her task. For, if she had been forced to free her mouth to provide an explanation, she was now holding my cock in her hand with the utmost firmness, determined not to let it get away.

They finally stopped squabbling and began to parley in a whisper. My sorely tested member again found the sweet comfort of a mouth.

The secretary had not reappeared, and the fellatio with which my spy was gratifying me was even more skilful and energetic. I thought that she must be excited at having a man under the table with her who must certainly be taking her while she was according me her favours. To be honest, I didn't think long or hard about it, for pleasure was getting the better of all other considerations. I felt I was being literally sucked in. I came, sprawling back in my chair.

Once I was free of the mouth I had come in, I pushed back my chair, finally curious to see what was going on down below. And I got quite a shock when I saw the secretary's face. For it was he who was now down on all fours in front of me.

But he saw nothing, for he was just coming himself. At the other end of the desk, lying underneath him, the girl was sucking him off.

So it was he who ... I had no complaints about his technique, but all the same ... This isn't normally my cup of tea. I did myself up and left without saying goodbye, annoyed.

In the corridor, two invisible shadows, whose presence I could sense just as much as any creature of flesh and blood, dogged my footsteps. I shook them off by opening a door.

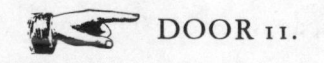 DOOR 11.

6

The Bath

'I think I'll stay with you a bit longer,' I said to my two friends.

They got up, with cries of joy which struck me as rather exaggerated, and took me by the hand, one on each side, to guide me down the dark corridor. After a few steps, we took a fork to the right and ended up at the entrance to a very long corridor, lined with doors and faintly illuminated by neon lights. I turned to my two companions to look at them, finally.

As I had been able to tell in the dark, they were wearing long, tight dresses of a very dark colour, a bit like those worn by classical musicians and choral singers at concerts. But in these dresses, with their very high collars, large, oval-shaped holes had been cut around the bosom with scissors. Thus their breasts protruded through the material, which had been cut so crudely that the edges frayed against their skin.

I felt like touching them again. I placed my hands on each of their bosoms and they laughed.

One of them was dark, with black skin, narrow hips, a large mouth and a smouldering look. This was Anna.

The other, blonde, a bit stouter, very white, with little pink lips and very pale blue, almost transparent eyes. This was Aurélie.

I told them they were beautiful, and I wanted them.

They opened a door in the corridor and ushered me into their

place – a room whose floor, walls and ceiling were completely covered with mirrors. With the exception of the bed and the gigantic bath, the furniture was made out of some sort of transparent plastic.

We were scarcely through the door when the two women took off their dresses, and, quite shamelessly, walked around the apartment, entirely naked. Anna had a slim, firm body, with long legs and high buttocks, admirable African buttocks. Aurélie was plumper, more curvaceous. They both had long hair which fell in a shining mass all the way down their backs, one as blonde as the other was dark. The mirrors reflected their bodies to infinity, vertiginous images of every aspect of their most intimate parts.

One after the other they sat on the toilet, which was also transparent, to have a long piss. I saw the powerful stream spurting out from under their clitorises, sparkling against the translucent side of the bowl, while their open thighs unveiled all the pink folds of their pussies. When she had finished pissing, Aurélie lifted her bottom and shook herself to dislodge the last little drop, then made way for Anna and started to run the bath.

'Come on! Get undressed!' said Anna, as I watched her pissing.

Neither of them was laughing now. Aurélie looked at me almost shyly from under her fringe of blonde eyelashes, as if she'd done something wrong. And Anna's voice sounded rather authoritarian, almost frightening.

I had barely time to lift a finger when they were all over me, Anna's black hands unbuttoning my shirt, Aurélie's white hands struggling with my flies. I had a massive hard-on, but they refused all my advances. What they wanted was to dive into the bath with me.

The grey marble bathtub resembled a coffin. It was now full of a heavy water, like diluted mud. I climbed in with them and we started to touch each other, all three of us in the warm liquid. I fondled their pussies, their arseholes, their breasts ...

They fought over my chest, my cock, my balls ... Fondled each other ... The oily water made their skins even softer, more slippery.

The girls began to get very excited. Anna, who seemed to have a certain ascendency over the gentle Aurélie, made her lie back in the bath, while she kept her head and shoulders above the water by hooking her arms under her armpits, and ordered her to masturbate.

Aurélie immediately thrust two fingers of her left hand into her cunt and moved them in and out and, with circular movements of her right hand on her clitoris, began frenziedly stimulating her blond pussy. Her large, white breasts floated on the surface of the water like two balloons, her hips undulated at the bottom of the tub. Sitting in front of her, I wanked off slowly, watching her face, which lay back in Anna's breasts and was tensed as she moved towards orgasm. Anna gave her little kisses on her hair and eyes, and encouraged her gently: 'Yes, my dear ... You are beautiful ... He's looking at you, and he thinks you're so beautiful he's doing it as well ... And me too, I find you exciting ... Show us how you will come, my lovely darling ...' Aurélie panted and bit her friend's breast. Suddenly her hips heaved convulsively in the water, she threw her head back and came with a screeching noise.

We got out of the bath to stretch out on the ground on the cold mirrors, now streaked with water and steam, but still reflecting the images of our bodies and our excited organs. I slid my hand between Anna's thighs, and this was enough to make her cry out. She was on fire. Unable to hold back, she mounted me and began vigorously bouncing up and down. She came almost immediately, with a long, throaty scream. I managed to hold back, long enough to roll over on top of her.

When Aurélie, who had started masturbating again as she watched us, saw her friend now lying on her back, she came and sat on her face, to be licked by the woman I was pillaging. While, in this position, Aurélie's fat bum was bouncing in front

of my face, I suddenly noticed that Anna's breasts, far from being voluminous as I had thought in the dark, were small and firm, quite delightful. At that precise moment I felt the ring of her sex tighten over mine, they began to cry out their pleasure together and I came with them, with deep thrusts of the hips.

We all three slept in each other's arms.

When I awoke, I hesitated for a long time between:

– staying longer with my adorable Aurélie and Anna:

 DOOR 10;

– or leaving this room to set off in search of the Woman, other women, other adventures:

 DOOR 9.

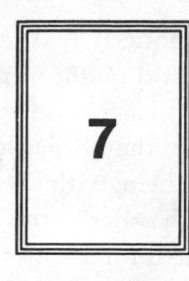

7

The Rape

I set off down the corridor, guiding myself by touching the left-hand wall. My eyes had had time to adjust to the darkness, and I proceeded without too much difficulty. However, I had the sudden feeling I was being followed. Light footsteps dovetailed into mine, a denser shadow pressed against my back. I turned round repeatedly. The first time, I thought I could make out a shape, but it vanished in an instant and did not reappear. In the end I convinced myself that it was merely an effect of my tiredness, and managed to put it out of my mind.

Soon, I reached an angle in the wall. Moving by touch, I made out two doors. I was about to open one of them, when I changed my mind and went for the other.

Behind the door, a little dancer in a tutu greeted me with a smile of relief. 'Ah! We've been waiting for you!' And she dragged me into what seemed to be the backstage of a theatre.

In her pink, silk ballet shoes she ran among the electric cables, saying, 'Come quickly! They are so impatient!' I strode after her. She showed me into a dressing room, where a stoutish old lady received me with the same relief and with the same haste. 'Ah! There you are! Quick, get those on!' And she handed me two pairs of pants, one of which was a tiny G-string.

I protested. But she insisted that we mustn't let them down, and there was no time to lose. In the face of this sense of

urgency displayed by my companions, I didn't pursue the matter further. As I lowered my jeans, the old woman observed me out of the corner of her eye. 'They'll like you a lot,' she said. I pulled on the two pairs of pants, one on top of the other, as I had been asked, then I put my trousers and shoes back on.

The dresser made me sit in front of the dressing table, picked up a puff, dipped it in powder and ran it over my forehead, my nose, the rest of my face. She took a lipstick, unscrewed the pale pink tip, rubbed a little brush on it and painted my lips. She did my hair, spraying on some lacquer and smoothing it back. While this was going on, the little dancer was showing signs of impatience. When I was ready, she dragged me back out into the backstage area, still running.

When we arrived behind the stage curtain, I opened it a little and saw an auditorium jam-packed with women, who were shouting and stamping their feet for the show to begin. Immediately, the heavy curtain opened and the little dancer led me by the hand to the centre of the stage. We were met by a barrage of tumultuous applause, shouts and whistles. The little dancer, who was carrying a microphone I hadn't seen before, silenced the audience with some authority and, stepping back to make a big intro, announced:

'And now, ladies and girls, the man you've all been waiting for, our fine, fearless and flawless knight, who is going to go all out to give you one red-hot striptease that you will remember for the rest of your lives. Ladies, put your hands together!'

The audience became more delirious than ever. I was a bit blinded by the footlights, but I could still see that it consisted of hundreds of women of all ages, young and old, beautiful and ugly, and they were all carried away with excitement.

'They haven't seen a man for years,' the little dancer yelled in my ear. 'Don't disappoint them or they will invade the stage and tear you into tiny pieces.'

She presented me once more to the audience, then she exited backstage dancing on her points.

Not knowing what to do, I went forward to the edge of the stage and bowed to the audience, several times, with my hand on my heart. Then the lights went down, the music started and some spotlights were turned on me. The audience fell silent again. I had the impression they were holding their breath.

Right. Since they hadn't seen a man for years, I would show them one. In one movement I turned my back on the audience and walked back to the centre of the stage to the rhythm of the music. The spotlights followed me.

I began by wiggling my bottom, as I had seen the professionals do on television, while unbuttoning my shirt. Then I turned to the audience, still swaying my hips, holding the two sides of my shirt tightly before yanking it open, sliding it slowly off my shoulders and throwing it away behind me. The women started screaming again, as if before some idol.

The thought that I alone was giving them so much pleasure encouraged me. With the same suggestive movements, I dropped my trousers. I was down to my pants, and I strutted slowly around the stage, exhibiting myself from every angle and flexing all my muscles. They had become so hysterical they were like a huge harem having a collective orgasm. I returned to the centre of the stage and, turning my back to them, removed the first pair of pants.

When I turned round, I saw some women climbing onto the boards brandishing large banknotes. Soon there were dozens of them, fighting to get near me, to touch me and slip their money inside my G-string.

Very quickly the crush became so strong that I found myself flat on my back on the ground. Dozens of hands felt my body, the notes were spilling out of my G-string and were fluttering all around me. I couldn't move a muscle. The more excited among them lifted up their skirts to show me their undies, opened their blouses to fondle their breasts. I could feel my pants being ripped and there were strident cries. It was the start of the rape.

They began by wanking me and sucking me and then, one by one they mounted me. Whenever one of them took too long, the others dragged her off me, pulling her by the hair, and the next one took her place. They had lost all restraint and were fighting to get ahead of each other in the queue, while others held me pinned to the ground. Those who had raped me without having time to come finished themselves off by hand before my eyes, or plonked themselves down on my face and rubbed themselves off until they reached orgasm. I ejaculated several times, mechanically, without even noticing whether the woman was fat or thin, dark or blonde, young or old. Each time, I hoped that my torture had finished, but each time they worked on my cock to get it hard again, in order to continue their demonic ritual.

Finally they must have abandoned me when they saw they couldn't get any more out of me; I must have slipped into unconsciousness, for, when I came to, I couldn't remember how it had all finished. I was still lying on the stage, naked, with bruises all over, and sore genitals. The little dancer was by my side.

'Come,' she said softly. 'I'll take care of you.'

She picked up my clothes, and the money scattered over the stage, which she stuffed into the pocket of my jacket. She was kind and maternal. Given the state I was in, I had no other choice than to follow her:

☛ DOOR 15.

8

The Amputee

I entered a hallway, where a friendly young man greeted me.

'If you wish to see Madame,' he said, 'I'm afraid you will have to wait a while . . .'

And he led me to a curtain, which he opened slightly.

'See,' he said, inviting me to take a look. 'Madame is at the back, behind the curtain. She has opened it a little, like us, and you can see her through the gap.'

I slid my head into the opening and I saw a stylish lounge, where two handsome, athletic, blond guys were fucking.

I turned to my companion with a quizzical look. But he insisted, pointing with his chin:

'There! There! Look through there!'

And indeed, on the other side of the room, behind an open curtain, a naked young woman was squatting down. She was gazing passionately at these two men making love and she was masturbating.

I burst out laughing.

'Ah, women!' I said to my companion. 'They see two guys doing it, it turns them on. But if they found out their own bloke was queer, then there'd be tears!'

I put my head through the curtain again. My companion came and joined me.

'At least she's able to wank herself off,' he whispered.

I laughed again.

'What's stopping you doing the same, if you feel like it?'

Then he showed me his gloved hands.

'I'm an amputee. This is all machinery,' he said, showing me his hands and arms. 'And machinery's no good for such a delicate operation . . .'

'Poor you,' I said, genuinely sorry for him.

He went back to looking through the curtain, and I followed suit, to take my mind off his misfortune. The two guys caressed, kissed, sucked and buggered each other like any eager lovers, while the woman, behind her curtain, continued to give herself a damn good session of solitary pleasure. What a shame! She was very pretty and she looked really hot . . .

I began to feel excited myself. I heard my companion panting. I turned to him. He seemed on the edge of apoplexy. There was a huge bump in his trousers and he couldn't touch himself.

'It's always like this,' he said, a bit worried. 'If I don't find anyone to help me get relief, the blood causes me so much pain that sometimes my heart stops and I pass out.'

I hesitated a little, embarrassed by his confession and the request that was implicit in it. But he had such a pained expression. And it really was a terrible misfortune to have lost your arms, for a boy of twenty, as handsome and full of life as he was.

'OK,' I said finally.

And, without looking, I undid his flies, freed his cock and took it in my hand. We looked through the curtain again, together. I tried to imagine that I was wanking myself, but his cock was huge in my hand, much bigger than mine.

I watched the woman as I stroked him, and I told myself that this would give her a lot of pleasure, if she could see it. That encouraged me. At the same time, I wouldn't want her to see me in this position. For the more I wanked him, the more she excited me. And I promised myself I would find her later and

gave her a taste of more elaborate pleasures than the unrestrained little wank she was indulging in now.

When I felt him coming, I let go, so that he would ejaculate into the curtain. Then I left the way I came. I was still erect, and there was no one to give me relief.

In the corridor, it felt as if shadows were harrying me, and I didn't need that. I pushed the first door I came to, determined not to allow the next beauty I came across to get away.

 DOOR 17.

9

The Widow

The moment I opened the door, a draught blew a whiff of sweet-smelling perfume against my face, a woman's perfume, with a hint of musk and violet. The door slammed behind me.

I found myself in a corridor similar to a narrow street, at the end of which an elegant woman dressed in black was just slipping out of sight. Without thinking, I followed in her footsteps.

Before she turned the corner to the left I had just enough time to glimpse her tall, slim figure and hat, and yet I was forcibly struck by her voluptuous shape, accentuated by her outfit, which clung tightly to the curves of her hips, her bottom, her waist, its knee-length skirt split up the middle, wonderfully following the scissor-movements of her very shapely legs, sheathed in black stockings whose seams formed a triangular shape above the cambred heel of her shoes and ran in a straight line up the curvature of her calves, into the hollow behind her knees, finally losing themselves high up on her thighs, in the split in the material which stretched open as she walked.

I started running to catch up with her, trying not to make a noise, for I didn't want to startle her or risk making her run away. But when I reached the corner of the corridor, I found her only a few metres ahead of me, as if she had been waiting for me slightly, and she turned towards me. The movement was

over in an instant. Through her veil, her eyes were fixed on mine, dark, shining. Then she started walking more quickly.

I didn't know whether that look had been an invitation, a challenge, or whether she wanted to order me to leave her alone. But even if my mind had requested that of me, my body, my whole being would have refused to give her up. This woman attracted me as surely as if we were magnetized.

My heart was thumping in my chest, and when my eyes rode up from her pointed heels to the split in her skirt, then above this split where, with each step she took, I could see the dark strip of her stockings, when my eyes slid up the sheer nylon of these stockings, from the darker, triangular bit where the seam started, shooting like an arrow from between her ankles up beyond the hollows of the knees, when my eyes, with each step she took, embraced her swinging hips and bottom, I felt as if my heart were beating down below my stomach.

I was obliged to walk faster and faster in order to keep up with her. The clicking of her heels on the ground formed a rhythm, and the sound echoed against the walls, I was no more than three strides behind her, in three strides I could catch her, grab her by the hips ... Perhaps she would struggle, perhaps I would see fear in her eyes, and then all the desire I felt for her would transform itself into the desire to protect her from me, perhaps she would see that, my wish to reassure her, to excuse myself, and then she would no longer resist, she would suddenly fall into my arms, as soft as a rag doll, available, and then I would raise her veil a little to place my lips on hers, open her mouth with my tongue, and at the same time slide my hands up her skirt, forage with both hands in her knickers, then she herself would fall at my feet, open my flies with her fingers sheathed in black lace, my erect cock would surge up between her long nails, and then she would give a little moan of joy and through her veil her lovely, red-painted lips would gobble my fat sword. Or else, rather than struggle, as soon as she felt my hands on her, she would lift up her skirt over her bottom, take

down her knickers and bend over, standing up, mad with impatience.

After taking several turnings in a maze of corridors, she finally pushed open a door and disappeared inside. The rhythmic clicking of her heels, that mincing bottom a few metres ahead of me, the hypnotic movement of her legs, the fascinating seam of her stockings, like a line to follow, had put me in a trance. Nothing else mattered than those legs and that bottom, nothing else mattered but walking behind this woman, waiting for the right moment to seize her.

She had left the door open, which was all the invitation I needed to follow her. I entered slowly behind her, certain that I had my prey now. I found her kneeling in what seemed to be a sanctuary, a sort of church with tall, burning candles. Still with her back to me, she was meditating in front of a tomb. As I drew near, I heard her reciting prayers in a low voice. In this position, her heels were pointing towards me horizontally, and her black dress was so taut it seemed ready to give way at any moment.

I placed myself right behind her, grabbed each side of her skirt in my hands and ripped it apart along the split right up to her waist. Thus her wonderful bottom was revealed, its whiteness enhanced by her little, transparent, black panties, which I slid down to her knees. I had never seen such a magnificent sight. I quickly lowered my trousers, knelt down in turn behind her and penetrated her with a single thrust.

I felt so happy I almost came on the spot. But the widow also seemed to be enjoying the exercise, and I wanted to give her a bit more. Still reciting her prayers, which she interrupted with increasingly piercing sighs, she fell onto her stomach on the granite flagstone and, grasping the edge of the tomb with both hands, began energetically grinding her hips. Before I lay on her I noticed that, under the clip of her suspender, there was a hole in the seam of the stocking which was strangely evocative of the female sex. She was definitely the most gorgeous slut I had ever

met and when she began to cry out her pleasure on the tomb of the man who had also once made her cry out this way, I contained myself no longer and came with her, in long jerks.

Now I was exhausted. The widow lay on the tomb on her stomach, her skirt split in two along its whole length, her knickers round her knees, her arms in the shape of a cross, her cheek against the stone. She let out a deep sigh of satisfaction, closed her eyes and smiled. I pulled up my trousers and left that place.

 DOOR 5.

10

The Three Accomplices

We were lying with our knees curled up, all three of us wrapped together. Aurélie's white bosom was crushed against my back, her little blond tuft slotted between my buttocks, while I held Anna's small, firm breasts in both hands and my member was snug and warm, embedded in the African's splendid rump. I told myself I would make love to them once more, take better, more thorough advantage of them than just now, but I had probably given a bit too much, for I fell asleep again, the happiest sandwich-man in the world, between their voluptuous bodies.

I was dragged from sleep by sounds of love. I was alone in the middle of the bed, my arms and legs in a cross shape, firmly tied to the bars of the bed by cords of silk knotted around my wrists and ankles. I tried to get up, but I could hardly move. How had those two bitches been able to tie me up like this without waking me up? Either they were fiendishly skilful or, more likely, they had administered some soporific drug without my knowledge. But then they must also have injected a powerful aphrodisiac straight after, for my sex was more erect than ever — and the scene which was taking place before my eyes was unlikely to relax it.

Lying on the ground, and still naked, Aurélie and Anna were kissing with open mouths, their breasts pressed together, their

hands thrust down between their entangled thighs. Standing above them, and also naked, a tall, athletic black man in his forties was slowly tugging his impressively large tool and urging my two friends on, occasionally even giving them orders which they eagerly carried out.

'And now', he said, 'do me a nice 69. I want to see you come.'

'Yes, master,' they replied, more docile than trained dogs.

And they rolled over, one on top of the other, head to toe, their legs wide open, and moaned more than ever as they licked each other greedily.

The man continued to wank himself slowly, his eyes riveted on his prey. I couldn't stand it any longer. I begged to be released but the black man only laughed and, seeming to see me for the first time, gave me a mocking look, running his tongue over his lips and grinding his pelvis in the most obscene manner, and rubbing his balls with his spare hand to wank himself more obviously before my helpless gaze.

As for the girls, my cries of anger and my supplications only served to excite them, and they climaxed noisily, while I struggled to try to free myself, or at least turn myself over, to have a chance of rubbing myself against the sheet, which, in the state I was in, would have been enough to release my pleasure.

As soon as the two girls had reached orgasm, the man ordered them to walk on their knees up to his cock and to suck it. Their two mouths attacked his monstrous member, gobbling it up in turn (though neither of them managed to swallow more than a quarter of it), one licking the glans, the other the shaft . . . The large penis leaped up, causing them to giggle and shriek with fright.

While Anna now sucked him without interruption, Aurélie placed herself under the man's legs and began licking and nibbling his balls and his anus, craning her neck in her gluttony. When she sensed it was the right moment, she rejoined Anna in front of his cock and pushed her middle finger into the man's bum. He threw his head back and let out short, jerky gasps.

Straight away, Anna freed his cock, which ejaculated long, powerful spurts of sperm onto their two adoring faces.

I began to struggle again, desperately trying to free myself. Still on their knees, they licked off the streams of come running down each other's cheeks into the corners of their mouths, in their hair, trickling heavily down their throats to the tips of their upright breasts. My cock was harder than a tree trunk and was hurting me; I wanted to scream, to kill, to sob with desire. Then the man, seeming to take pity on me, harshly asked the women whether they weren't ashamed to leave me in such a state and dragged them unceremoniously to the bed.

I felt simultaneously full of hope and full of apprehension, since it was quite possible that the colossus had something even worse in mind for me. But the awful desire that was torturing me made me forget all fear – unless fear made the desire even more unbearable. I felt so wretched, tied to this bed, spread-eagled with a hard-on, at the mercy of these three accomplices. Perhaps they would free me, the man would let me take the two women, in any way and as often as I wanted, for I felt capable of fucking them a dozen times before being satisfied.

They all climbed onto the bed, but no one untied me. Aurélie sat over my face, and the man as well, behind her. He was erect again, already. She stretched out her bottom and, delicately at first, then vigorously, he buggered her. The blonde, glistening with moisture down the inside of her thighs, must have been used to this practice, since she didn't bat an eyelid and, despite its width, his tool penetrated easily into her tight orifice by sliding in in stages. It was nice work – and I was well placed to judge.

At the same time – at last! – I felt my cock taken in Anna's large mouth. I came almost immediately into the back of her throat, with a cry that was a mixture of relief, pain and pleasure.

Anna swallowed the lot and she continued to suck me softly. Above my face, almost touching me, the man's balls were shaking, his cock was moving in and out of Aurélie's dilated

rosette as she wiggled her white, slightly fat buttocks between the large black hands which were holding them tight. The round, hard balls swung in the same rhythm as the enormous prick moved in and out, methodically, as if he were trying to break down a door with a battering ram. With one hand Aurélie fondled her breasts, then her pussy, pushing first one finger in then another. They were almost on top of me, the movement of their private parts filled my field of vision, their mating smells went to my head and all this time Anna's mouth sucked, licked and rubbed my cock. When the man began to accelerate his to-ing and fro-ing, she took my balls in her hands and began to suck me ardently, keeping time with the thrusts of her accomplice. Suddenly, Aurélie seemed to lose her head, screaming and flailing about like a woman possessed. After one last violent thrust of his cock, the man withdrew sharply and let his come spurt over her buttocks, also splashing my face. At the same time I ejaculated again directly into the back of the deep throat.

Aurélie and the man let themselves fall by my side on the bed, Anna came and cleaned my face with little dabs of her tongue and then undid my cords. I was now free to:

– stay longer with the three accomplices:

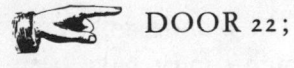 DOOR 22;

– or take my chances elsewhere:

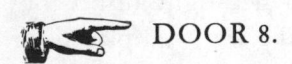 DOOR 8.

11

Sleeping Beauty

I recognized her. She was the Beauty of the sleeping wood. She rested on a tall, ancient bed, richly dressed, serene and lovelier than the day was long. Had I been chosen as the one to wake her? I approached her and sat by her side on the edge of the bed.

The room and the whole castle were immersed in silence. All I heard was the creaking of the beams and, as I leaned over her, the low, regular sound of her light breathing.

Her face was gorgeous, haloed in light and framed by the long locks of her golden hair. The purety of her brow and the paleness of her skin were enhanced by the fine crown of little white flowers which wreathed her head. Her peach-coloured silk dress flared out from her waist and fell to her tiny feet which were shod in satin slippers with square heels and ribbons. Very low-cut, in the old style, it revealed an adorable throat, a slender neck and two round breasts, palpitating like a pigeon's heart, which rose softly with each intake of breath.

I leaned over her face and planted a kiss on her pink lips. She showed no reaction. I waited a moment and then tried again, more forcefully.

She still didn't wake up. This was obviously something the stories never made clear: perhaps it needed a deeper kiss. You don't emerge from a hundred-year sleep as easily as that. As

delicately as possible I opened her mouth with my tongue and gave her a long kiss.

Beauty continued to sleep. I renewed my kissing and also fondled her breasts for good measure. Her skin was like a peach, incredibly soft. Her bosom emerged fully from her dress, almost in spite of me. I kissed her all over her face, her neck, her throat ... Until finally I could no longer resist the temptation to kiss her greedily on her breasts, which sprouted from her dress like two lovely, fresh, firm fruits.

I calmed down, examined her face, held her hand, tried to talk to her. But she remained frozen in the same serene, languid expression, except that her mouth was now open, which sullied her pure features with a slight hint of obscenity.

Her slippers were truly charming, with their ribbons tied in a bow over the instep. And she seemed to be wearing silk stockings.

I raised the hem of her dress a little. She was wearing several petticoats underneath. I permitted myself to raise them to her knees, just in order to see her legs. What pretty legs! I let go of both dress and petticoats. I was finding it harder and harder to control my excitement.

Once again I kissed her with my tongue. In vain.

I couldn't stop myself. I pulled her dress right up to her waist.

I only wanted to look. After all, it couldn't do any harm, since she was asleep.

And I saw. She wasn't wearing knickers. Her silk stockings went as far as mid-thigh, where they were held up by ribbons, and thereafter the white surfaces of her body lay exposed to the open air. A fine, blond down barely concealed her pretty, chubby little slit.

I took her thighs in my hands and opened them gently. The lips of her vagina were as pink and tender as those of her mouth. I leaned over and gave them a long, lingering kiss, so soft and juicy and sweet-smelling were they.

When I went back up to her I found that even these kisses hadn't managed to rouse her from her torpor. I was almost getting cross. Her stupid, gaping mouth was getting on my nerves.

I took off my trousers and stuck my cock into it. I rubbed it in and out against her palate and her cheeks. But that made her face look deformed and I felt a little ashamed.

I went back down between her thighs and penetrated her, kneading her breasts at the same time. It felt so good that I no longer even wanted to see her wake up. It was a rare pleasure when I came inside her motionless body.

I must have lain beside her for several hours. I undressed her completely, amused myself by taking her stockings off and putting them back on, turned her over every which way, kissed her, caressed her, took her, everywhere and in every way imaginable. Nothing I did succeeded in waking her up. I took advantage of her to the same degree as she had excited me and I came as much and more.

When I was worn out, I put her clothes back on, remade the bed, laid her carefully back in it, arranged her hair and closed her mouth so that when her Prince Charming arrived he would find it as beautiful as I had.

I went off whistling into the dark corridor, where I felt as if I were being followed by two scolding shadows, which didn't bother me too much.

I decided on a change of scene. After walking down several different passages and corridors, I climbed a small flight of stairs, at the top of which I found two doors.

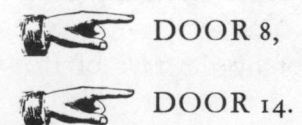 DOOR 8,

DOOR 14.

12

The Bride

What a strange place, I thought, as I pursued my course through the dark corridor. Already I had virtually forgotten why I had come in here but my curiosity compelled me to remain. Curiosity and desire, yes, but also something resembling fear, for, from the moment I first found myself cast out in these corridors, I had felt a vague menace weighing on my shoulders, as if I were being followed by someone or something I couldn't see.

I had already known lots of women. But up to this point neither my amorous aspirations nor my sexual appetites had been fully satisfied. Women always hold something back. Or else they want to give too much and then they start to suffocate you. The woman of my life, if she really existed, would be simultaneously loving and mean, submissive and brazen, mysterious and beautiful. In the dark I thought of the things I might do to such a woman and I started to get an erection. 'That's enough dreaming,' I said to myself. 'Find this woman, then you can have all the pleasure you wish.' And I pushed open the door which I found in front of me.

It was a completely white room, swept by the rays of the morning sun.

'Is that you, my love?' I heard someone say.

I squinted, as I was still dazzled by so much light. Sitting at a dressing table, her face thrust towards the mirror, a young

woman was applying make-up to her eyes.

'I'll be right there,' she added, without turning round.

She was wearing a wedding dress in white lace, which was tight around her nice, neat bosom and flowed from the waist into an ample petticoat. From her chignon, which was threaded with flowers, locks of chestnut-coloured hair fell down her graceful neck.

'Excuse me,' I said as I turned to leave.

When she noticed her mistake, she turned her head towards me and gave a little cry. I was about to repeat my apologies and exit but she rushed madly towards me and grabbed my arm.

'No, wait,' she said, scanning the room as if she were looking for something.

There was the sound of footsteps and I began to understand what was making her afraid.

'My husband,' she said. 'If he were to find you here . . .'

She didn't even finish her sentence. In desperation she lifted up her large petticoat and, with an authority surprising in a woman so young and so fresh and fragile in appearance, made me hide underneath it.

A moment later, beneath her vast nuptial gown, I heard her repeat her little phrase like an echo:

'Is that you, my love?'

'How lovely you are,' a man's voice replied.

And his footsteps approached, right to the edge of the petticoat under which I was crouching.

Although my position was uncomfortable, to say the least, it was not entirely lacking in attractions. For greater discretion, no doubt, the bride had hidden me under the rear part of her dress, in the train. I couldn't move a muscle, paralysed both by the fear of being discovered and the joy of having my nose practically jammed between her lovely buttocks, right up against her tiny silk knickers.

Then the bride's body began to move, I saw a man's shoe, black and polished, slide between the white slippers and I

realized that he had taken her into his arms to kiss her. In doing so, he had caused the woman's legs to part a little. They were sheathed in white stockings held up by suspenders of a lacey basque and, on one side, by a traditional bride's garter decorated with a pink rose. Her whole underwear was white, pearly, delicate.

As she parted her thighs, I ventured gently between them, to be able to look at the gusset of her knickers. The man was still kissing her. I heard them laughing and exchanging silly remarks. I placed my hands on her calves. She trembled. I ran them slowly up her legs, above her stockings, my eyes still fixed on her knickers. Then I experienced one of the most delicious emotions of my life: while I was there, stuck under the dress of a young bride being kissed by her future husband, while I caressed her legs, on the fine silk of her tiny knickers, only a few millimetres in front of my eyes, there appeared a small patch of moisture.

Since she had had the good sense not to perfume herself, the only smell under this petticoat was that of this woman's desire. I took deep breaths of it, it made my head spin. With one hand I pulled aside the strip of silk to reveal a gorgeous, shiny pink pussy, its hair carefully cut and shaved to form a trim little bush of just the right thickness. I moved my face closer again and gave it its first lick.

The outer lips parted completely, revealing two burning inner lips, themselves open, and an eager little button, which immediately came in search of its share of the favours. I held back, so as not to moan with pleasure, but she let go a long sigh, which her jealous fiancé must have attributed to the effect of his kisses. But my own mouth kissed the better mouth of his intended. I felt so bold that I undid my flies, took out my already very hard cock and started wanking while, with my other hand, I held her knickers away from her lovely cunt, which I licked without sparing any effort.

My little bride grew bold herself, moaning more than ever

and risking some movements of her hips, so as to achieve greater pleasure from my tongue. I didn't want to, but the tension was too much: I ejaculated in her lace petticoats, with such long spasms that I couldn't stop myself groaning, which was fortunately covered by a deeper sigh from her, accompanied by a jerk which signalled her own climax.

Then I was terrified to see the dress being raised on one side and the husband's hand, obviously encouraged by his fiancée's passion, slide up her leg. Luckily her reactions were quick and she asked him, in a suggestive whisper, to go and shut the door. As soon as I heard him move away I took the opportunity to slip out, without further thought, through another door which stood open at the back of the room. Before finally disappearing I couldn't resist one last look at them. When her future husband returned to her, the bride went to meet him, knelt down in front of him and started to undo his flies. As much, no doubt, with the intention of seeking pardon for a crime of which he knew nothing as to satisfy the appetites I had aroused in her. On this her wedding day, I had been the first to make her come and to starch her petticoats with semen.

I went out into a corridor, still deep in shadow but different from the one I had come from. I had to continue my search and the only means available to me was to open one of the doors in this corridor, behind which I would no doubt experience new encounters.

☞ DOOR 13,

☞ DOOR 16.

13

The Turkish Bath

I was submerged in a wave of humid heat. The door closed on its own, heavily and silently.

In spite of myself, I ran down the steps of a broad, greyish-yellow stone staircase made slippery by the steam. The staircase narrowed and ended on a circular landing. The whole thing had the appearance of a giant lock, and I was a very small key for it. But I was already passing through the lock and, even though I didn't know what was waiting for me on the other side, my heart was beating with hope and desire for that woman who had been promised to me and who, no doubt, was also searching for me.

In the centre of the little round place, itself paved with large, glistening stones, stood a sort of toll-booth with a pointed roof, a closed-up, wooden sentry box from which you might expect to see a guard emerge at any moment. Painted in ridiculously bright, gaudy colours, decorated with geometric designs drawn with a felt pen – eyes, mouths, flowers, hearts pierced by arrows, penises, skulls and crossbones, sentimental or obscene graffiti – it was pierced halfway up by a barred aperture with wooden slats, like a confessional grille. I pushed my face towards it and the flagstone I was standing on, which was really a trapdoor, went from under my feet. I fell a few metres, straight into a deep basin of warm water, from which I emerged half-drowned.

I pulled myself up onto the side of a narrow, round swimming pool. I was in the middle of a vast, vaulted, oval-shaped white marble room. There were wooden benches all round the walls, their damp slats covered in men's and women's clothes. I particularly noticed the women's underwear, knickers and bras of all sizes. It was very warm. I took off my soaking clothes and left them on a bench. From the only opening, a porthole at the end of the room, came a continuous murmur of light laughs, moans and sounds of lovemaking.

I went to the porthole and wiped away the steam with my hand. On the other side of the glass stretched a Turkish bath which was so large that, from where I was standing, I couldn't make out its shape. On the flags of stone, inside and on the edge of the pools, around the marble columns, dozens of men and women, entirely naked, abandoned themselves to the pleasures of water and love. At that moment, their happiness seemed so perfect and I felt so keenly the desire to join them that I forgot all my former life and the reason, if there ever had been a reason, why I had entered the kingdom promised by the little circus, which was turning out to be richer and more marvellous than I could ever have imagined.

I unbolted the porthole, which worked like the door on the front of a washing-machine, and slid through the opening into the bathhouse. The murmur which had penetrated through to the changing room now grew into a vibrant noise of love, where the nearest sounds seemed to catch the echo of thousands of others lost in the distant and uncertain bounds of the room. Everywhere bodies combined in twos, threes, fours or more, their sexes intermingled; they seemed to form mythical animals with a multitude of limbs, writhing in successive, uninterrupted waves of orgasm. The warm, damp air was suffused with the smell of human juices which, just as it is sometimes enough simply to inhale a drug being smoked by someone next to you, was almost enough in itself to intoxicate me to the point of ecstasy.

I walked round one couple who were lying head to toe and indulging in languorous oral pleasures, wondered whether to accept the invitation of a splendid redhead, who was already sandwiched between two men, and, feeling too hungry to share, finally chose a group of six girls, piled one on top of the other and busy kissing and licking passionately and greedily. A heart-rending stream of moans emerged from this pile of flesh softened and whitened by the steam.

As they seemed to be completely absorbed in their games, I stood motionless above them for a moment, my cock erect, not quite sure how to join in. They were a delicious mixture of small and large, plump and slim, blonde and brunette, breasts like pears, apples or bullets, bums which were round, fat or small, pussies more or less shaved, more or less bulging, faces of whores or angels.

I placed my hand on a pretty white rump and that was enough for them to know what to do with me. A woman with short, blonde hair and clear eyes stopped sucking the enormous breast of her friend, took hold of my cock, which she placed between her thick, pink lips, and began sucking with renewed gluttony, while a dozen hands touched my body, fondling it eagerly, their fingers opened my buttocks, their tongues licked my balls and my bum, their teeth gnawed my chest.

They had pulled me down amongst them and were taking it in turns at my cock, which they all wanted to taste. As I was trying to stay as cool as possible, I took the opportunity to squeeze the great confusion of bums and tits which came within reach. Despite my best intentions, the struggle was unequal and they soon got the better of me. With my nose stuffed into the blonde pussy of the youngest of the girls, who had plonked her fat behind on my face, I came in the mouth of the most skilful of the suckers, a little dark-haired girl with muscular cheeks, who swallowed the lot and kept me inside her mouth so that I was once again up and running.

As soon as my prick had become hard again, which didn't take long, given the intense excitement caused by the sight and touch of these women's bodies tangled up with mine, they all wanted to have me between their legs. I was more than happy to grant their desire. I lay them down on their backs in a line, side by side, knees raised, legs apart and I set about penetrating them methodically, one after the other, waiting for each of them to rear up in orgasm before mounting the next one. I ejaculated in the last one as she cried out and under my eyelids I ran the images of the other five girls at the moment when their faces contorted with ecstasy.

Almost immediately I found myself lifted up and hurled into the nearest pool like some obsolete object. As I lay calmly in the water with a smile on my lips, I saw the five women who had been deprived of my sperm take it in turns to taste it in the pussy of the one who had received it. Then they returned gently to their Sapphic games, as if nothing would ever make them tire of it.

Already my strength was returning. I contemplated the other groups of lovers around me and decided to explore further this place of delights where I was sure I would have no difficulty in finding more tasty partners and good companions of my own sex.

I was about to get out of the pool when I was violently tugged underwater. I tried to struggle against the force which was dragging me but I continued to descend at full speed. This damn pool seemed to be bottomless. I thought my number was up.

I must have lost consciousness, for, without knowing how, I found myself back where I started, in front of the sentry box at the entrance. This time there was a guard inside. He handed me my clothes, which had been dried and folded, with a remark that I didn't really appreciate.

'How was the water?' he said.

I gave him a black look but it was difficult to tell whether he

was just trying to be polite or whether he was taking the micky. I got dressed without a word, went back up the stairs and left.

I walked for a while through the corridors, trying to work out the layout of the place. But it was impossible not to get lost in this multitude of corridors, passages and flights of stairs which headed off in all directions. In the end, I opened a door at random.

 DOOR 19.

14

Fire!

I was greeted by a hubbub of men's voices and sounds of rattling. There were at least fifty men getting changed in this little room. One of them chucked me a uniform which I caught in mid-air and said to me:

'Get a move on, there's a fire!'

'Quick, quick,' the others joined in.

I realized they needed me. I quickly pulled on my fireman's uniform and, as I was adjusting my helmet, asked:

'Where? Where's the fire?'

'Up your bum,' they replied in a chorus, with great guffaws.

I felt disappointed, but I was immediately swept along in the mad rush to the exit.

I expected to find myself in a garage where we would climb into fire engines, our nozzles in our hands. Instead, I was propelled along with the others into a large, well-to-do salon, at the opposite end of which two women sat cross-legged on a long leather sofa, waiting for us. They were both dressed in all-red underwear, stockings, suspenders, knickers and bras. Their shoes were red, their nails and lips were red, and you could say they gave us a red-hot look when they saw us coming. One of them, who seemed to be in charge, made us line up against the wall. Then, standing in front of us, she gave the order:

'Present arms!'

There followed immediately a disciplined rattle of belts being undone as my comrades dropped their trousers to present their manly clusters to the lady who had given the order. I followed suit, eager not to stand out. I was only afraid that she might call out: 'Attention!' for I would have had difficulty obeying that order as quickly.

The lady walked among us, as if inspecting the troops, and divided us into two equal groups. I had my eye mainly on the other woman, the one who stayed sitting on the sofa. I found her beautiful and thought I'd seen her somewhere before.

The chief rejoined her friend and they sat one at each end of the sofa. I saw the men in the first row start wanking, and I realized why: they had to be ready to extinguish the fires of these two ladies.

The first two in each group moved towards the two women and took them, each at one end of the sofa. When they had finished, they made way for the next man, and so on. We had to run to take our turns, our feet shackled by our trousers.

We were each granted complete freedom to take the woman allocated to our group in whatever position we chose. Most didn't get bogged down in fantasies and adopted the classic position, with legs in the air on the sofa. Some preferred to be sucked off, or to do it on the floor, with their partner on all fours, or to have her on top . . .

When my turn approached, I began to prepare myself so I would arrive in a sufficiently erect state. Not that that was too difficult, for the spectacle itself was exciting enough. The two women came incessantly, with hysterical cries and without the slightest restraint.

I only regretted being in the group which was to service the chief, even though she was quite horny. As I approached her, I noticed that the other woman was also looking at me. But some other guy was taking care of her, so I thought no more of it.

One of my comrades had the job of taking off the bra of the chief, who was endowed with big, heavy, wobbling breasts.

Since I was near the end, I thought it would be only right to fuck her between her tits, where it seemed no one else apart from me had thought of putting his prick. So I made her half lie back on the sofa, squatted over her and began moving up and down in her bosom, which squashed itself obligingly around my cock and buried it more deeply inside.

This woman seemed so libidinous I felt like mistreating her. She urged me on with familiar 'Go on, darling's', which irritated me to the utmost. Finally, I couldn't prevent myself retorting: 'Shut up, slut.' And I abandoned her fat tits to stuff myself between her thighs which were sticky with come. I began hammering into her without any consideration. She grabbed onto the buttons of my jacket, grimacing with ecstasy. At the last moment, I suddenly pulled out of her insatiable hole and let her have the lot over her wanton face. She was exultant.

I got up, took one last look at the other woman, the one I would have preferred, who was taking her pleasure with one of the others. I went off without turning round.

I gathered up my clothes and went back into the corridor. At first, I wanted to walk for a bit to take my mind off things. But as I walked, I thought. And when I thought, I thought of this woman whom I hadn't had, I thought that she had satisfied herself with at least twenty firemen, and that didn't please me at all.

So I stopped walking and opened a new door.

 DOOR 12.

15

The Little Dancer

The little dancer took me by the arm and led me through the backstage area to her dressing room.

It was a narrow room, just big enough to contain a dressing table mounted with a mirror surrounded by lights and a swivel chair, a sink, a screen with tutus draped over it, and a small iron bed on which lay a large fluffy bear.

The little dancer placed my clothes over the back of the chair, picked up a sponge and turned on the hot tap.

'Come here,' she said in her clear, soft voice.

I joined her at the sink. She started washing me, rubbing the sponge into my forehead, hair and neck. She was obliged to stand on tiptoe and stretch out her hand to reach my face. It was as if she were performing some ballet steps around me and her body was so slender as she stretched, so graceful that I chose not to lower myself to make her job easier.

When she had cleaned up my head, she rubbed the water-soaked sponge over my shoulders, my chest, my back, my arms. Her movements were confident and serene, surprising for such young hands. She rubbed the sponge over my sex, my legs, my feet. I did nothing, easily forgetting all modesty, for this seemed totally natural to her. The water which she ran over my body also splashed her tutu, her pink top and her tights, but she seemed too absorbed in her work to notice. To finish things off,

she took her dressing gown which was hanging next to the sink and used it as a towel to dry me carefully, making sure she didn't irritate the scratches and bruises caused by the dozens of women who had had their way with me.

'Come here,' she said again.

And putting her bear on the floor, she pulled back the bedclothes and made me lie down.

I was so exhausted that I could have fallen straight asleep. But she hadn't finished her ministrations. From a drawer in her dressing table she took out a packet of cotton wool and a bottle of antiseptic, with which she delicately dabbed each of my wounds, the scratches and cuts distributed all over my body. Finally, she paid particular attention to my sex, anointing my testicles, my penis and my glans, with flower water, pulling back the foreskin then replacing it, before dusting all with a cloud of talc from a powder puff, which cooled the inflamation.

The women, in their fury, had worn me out so much that I felt not the slightest sexual excitement. As a result I could give myself over in total serenity to the expert hands of the little dancer, who maintained her angelic calm and acted with the professional conscientiousness, assurance and gentleness of a nurse.

'Now get some sleep,' she said, smiling.

And sitting down on the bed next to my face, she took my hand.

I closed my eyes and went to sleep, with her little fingers in mine.

I don't know how long I stayed like that, in that state of mingled dreams and periods of semi-consciousness. In my dreams, the little dancer was still caring for me, she was applying leeches to my body but these leeches were nothing but her lips, her mouth, which went all over me, and then she also massaged me, she undressed and massaged me with her naked body, her little naked body which moved over mine like a snake, she was wearing nothing but her shoes and the pink diadem in her hair

and she gave me a slow, gentle pleasure, a pleasure which half woke me and I felt myself growing erect again and I was excited but I didn't move, I thought about the little dancer and I felt full of love for her, I thought that it might be her, the woman of my life, I thought that I was going to take her with me and wait a few years before making her my wife, for she was still little more than a child but she was already mine, I was sure of that, I would teach her about love and pleasure and she would continue to give me everything she could give, she would be my wife till the end of our days, she who had sickened me of other women and rescued me from them, real women, brutal and voracious, who had found fault with me, while she had washed me, taken care of me and held my hand, with the same clear, admiring gaze, for I was her first man, the only man she had known and would ever know ...

And I sank back into sleep, happy and serene, and again I saw my little dancer in my dreams and felt her naked body against mine and the countless little games she played on my body and her breath on my skin and her fingers round my sex ... Then there came a point where the sensations became so strong that I opened my eyes.

I was turned over on my side, facing the dressing-table mirror. What I saw there made me close my eyes again. At first, I thought I was still in my dream, since the little girl was naked. Naked and kneeling before my sex. Then I had to yield to the evidence: what I felt around my penis was her fingers and the sensation was quite real.

I started sweating. I stiffened in order to stay immobile and I opened my eyes, gently lowering my head to look at her. She hadn't noticed a thing. Quite naked, she held my erect cock in her hands, without moving, like a saint in ecstasy before a divine apparition. Her cheeks were red, her lips brilliant. When I saw her bring her mouth forward – as if seized by a sudden inspiration – I couldn't prevent myself flinching. I was at the peak of excitement, but she had seemed so pure in my dreams

54

and she was still so fragile ... Then she raised her eyes towards me. And in her eyes was a petition, an incomprehensible, irresistible petition, which stimulated me almost painfully and which I interpreted by turning away sharply, just in time to come into the sheet, alone, out of her sight.

When I got up, she was already dressed and was doing her hair and humming in front of the mirror. So, her too! Do women always manage to take what they want from you while preventing you from taking everything you want from them? I put my clothes back on, promising myself that I would find a more satisfying adventure behind the next door.

'Goodbye,' said the little girl as she saw me out.

She seemed as reasonable as at the start, as if nothing had happened. From her demeanour I might have believed that I had dreamt everything but I remembered her expression at the moment when I was about to come. As if she were asking me to forget everything.

And I planted a kiss on her forehead.

She shone her torch into the corridor for me and I saw two doors:

DOOR 13,

DOOR 9.

16

The Hours

As I was about to open the door I heard my name called out, twice in succession. Two voices whispering into my neck. At the same moment the door opened in front of me and a splendid brunette invited me in.

I forgot the voices immediately. The brunette was dressed like a chambermaid in a tight black dress adorned with a little, starched white apron, with a matching cap in her hair, and had the most amazing curves. Tall, with the bearing of a queen, a more than generous bust, a well-defined waist, subtly rounded hips, legs which were both long and full ... And a finely-sculpted face in which her enormous, shining, almond-shape blue eyes fought for star-billing with her large, full mouth.

She asked me to follow her. We walked through a vast tea-room, decorated with mouldings from floor to ceiling and illuminated by crystal chandeliers. The room was crowded, men and women of all ages were seated on benches and chairs upholstered in red velvet, around tables laid with white cotton tablecloths on which hot drinks were presented, and cakes on porcelain dishes with gold borders.

The magnificent rump of the brunette, brushed down the middle by the bow of her apron, wiggled in front of me with each step she took, as the heels of her shoes, which were as dark as her dress, tapped out a rhythm on the polished floor. Other

waitresses, dressed in the same uniform, and all of them gorgeous, though no comparison with the exceptional beauty of my guide, came and went between the tables, carrying silver trays. None of the customers or staff raised their eyes to me. I felt like a transparent image, projected against a background, like you sometimes see at the cinema. Only the brunette in front of me, though she looked like a film star, seemed entirely real in her three voluptuous dimensions.

There was obviously not a table to be had but that seemed to be the last thing on my hostess's mind. She led me right across the room and into the kitchen. This was a hive of activity as the waitresses, some of whom I had already seen, took care of their customers' orders. They were all wearing the same tight black dresses, the same cute little aprons tied around their waists, the same white caps, they were all pretty and shapely, lively and gay.

As soon as I came in they all gathered round me, pulled me over to a large round table covered with teapots, jugs of milk, cups and assorted cakes, and invited me to help myself. I said I had greater need of a cool drink and they brought me a glass of something alcoholic with ice.

The funny thing was that there were no chairs around this table, nor anywhere else in the kitchen. So I stood there, sipping my drink and watching my hostesses come and go and occasionally come over for a sip of tea or a bite of cake. At first, I scrutinized the details of their faces and bodies, each more attractive than the last – except the fascinating dark-haired beauty who had led me here and had since disappeared. But when finally I was no longer totally blinded by desire I noticed something which should have been obvious from the start, namely the very strange thing all these girls were doing.

In the centre of the table there was a completely black hole, the bottom or sides of which – perhaps due to the lack of light – you couldn't see. And each time a girl came back in she took something out of the pocket of her apron, or her sleeve, or even the neck of her dress or her garter, and threw it into the hole.

The action was so swift and automatic that I hadn't paid it any attention, but I noticed it when I saw a pretty redhead lift her dress over one of her thighs and pull an identity card from her stocking, where she had tucked it away, and throw it without looking – she must have been so used to it – into the hole in the middle of the table. I had barely had time to notice her milk-white, freckled skin. Now she picked up a fruit tart between two fingers, stuffed it into her pretty red mouth, and danced away again, her little face with its pastel-coloured make-up lit by a childish joy.

Thereafter I saw that not one of them came in without some booty, at least one object clearly stolen from the customers, which might be a watch, a wedding ring, a wallet, a bottle of perfume or even a tooth or tuft of hair. All these objects invariably ended up down the same hole, where they threw them without looking, even the jewels. I could imagine them being able to pinch wallets, but how on earth did they manage to lift things so closely attached to a person's body as teeth, hair or even wedding rings?

I was on my way to the tea-room to watch them in action when the brunette reappeared, followed by all the others. 'That's it, it'll soon be time,' they said with a joyful exuberance. I had eyes only for the brunette, who was coming towards me. Good God! I had never had, or even seen, such a beautiful woman.

'My dear,' she said, taking hold of my arm, 'please excuse my neglect. I should have made the introductions sooner ... My name is Midday, or Midnight. And these are my sisters, the Hours.'

Then I saw that all the girls had arranged themselves in a circle around the table, at regular intervals, exactly like the hours on a clock face. There was only one space left, where the beautiful one went and stood, the one who called herself Midday, or Midnight, and was in effect the twelfth.

'You will no doubt have noticed,' the unsettling Midnight continued, 'that under the cover of serving we have been busy

divesting our customers of their belongings. So, by way of both punishment and reward for our efforts, each of us, at her appointed hour, must be treated in the following fashion: as soon as the clock strikes, our chosen host, in this case you, must stand behind the Hour in question (according to the number of strikes) and bugger her. I know it's a bit harsh, but I'm sure we can count on you?' she added, looking at me in such a way that it would be impossible to refuse her anything.

Since I had arrived here I had completely lost track of time. I only hoped, with a beating heart, that it was either midday or midnight.

I didn't have long to wait and dream. The clock began to strike and unfortunately I counted only three strikes. Faithful to the task, however, I placed myself immediately behind the third Hour, who was leaning on her arms on the table and had raised her dress to her waist and arched her back to reveal to me her tasty, round, naked arse. I looked at Midnight, undid my trousers and let them fall to my feet.

As soon as they saw my erect cock, the sisters went into a sort of erotic trance and started urging me on in the most crude terms. 'Go on, bugger her, the slut! Fuck her up her fat, shitty arse! Aren't we a pretty bunch of thieving sluts? Don't we deserve to have your big cock stuck up our bums?'

The girl was sticking her bottom out so much, and was so excited, that her hole had practically opened of its own accord, and I was in with two thrusts. Now she was hiccuping with pleasure, asking me to 'Say it, say it,' without making clear what it was she wanted me to say to her. Almost directly opposite, the little redhead, who was the eighth Hour, stuck out her tongue.

She and her sisters around the table had all tucked up their dresses and each had stuck two fingers up her neighbour's bum. I looked at Midnight, who was acting as uninhibitedly as the others and I said quietly, 'Slut.' The Hour I was buggering let out a cry of joy. I said it again, and again and again, more and more loudly, still shafting the girl, who was now dribbling with

pleasure and rage into a cup of tea, her hands full of squashed creamcakes.

'This is for you, you dirty bitch of an hour,' I said, giving her one last thrust of my cock.

And I laughed as I ejaculated in her tight arse.

I had rarely had such a good orgasm. 'Next time,' I thought as I got dressed, 'I will try to arrive around midday or midnight.' And as they got themselves ready to start serving again, I left via the back door.

Once I was back in the dark corridor I thought I heard two voices whispering my name. I turned round but saw nothing, and I was still too worked up after being with the Hours to attach any importance to it.

I walked on in the semi-dark, rejecting several doors along the way. I had the feeling I was being followed, but since my pursuers didn't deign to show themselves, I didn't care. Everything seemed possible here, the worst and the best. An unknown danger threatened at any moment to lay its icy hand on my shoulder, the wildest promises pulled me by the arm.

I had arrived at the end of the corridor. There was a door to my right and one to my left, and I would open one of them.

 DOOR 17,

DOOR 18.

17

The Ogress

'Ah, there you are, my dear,' said the fat woman lying in the bed.

The shutters were closed and it was almost as dark as in the corridor. Only a few rays of light fell on the covers which were lifted by an enormous mass of flesh.

'Come on, don't be shy,' she continued, 'come closer so I can see you a bit . . .'

She had a deep voice which could suddenly turn melodious and smooth, as when she said, 'my dear', for example, and generally at the end of her sentences.

I took a few steps towards the bed. It was covered with feathers. A hen started clucking, others followed suit. I peered into the darkness around me and saw that the woman's bed stood in the dead centre of a chicken coop.

'Don't be afraid, my pretty,' she said. 'It's just my pantry.'

And she threw the bone of a chicken leg she had just eaten onto the floor. A hen bolted in front of my feet, greedily grabbed the bone, raised its head, opened its beak and lowered it into its gullet until it had swallowed it completely.

'Come . . . come and see me . . .' the woman continued.

She reached out to me with her fat white arm. I moved closer. She had some blue on her eyelids and long tangled hair with small feathers and down sticking to it. She pouted suggestively,

with her fat lips puckered as if for a kiss. 'She must have a mouth like a suction pad,' I thought.

'Come here, my dear,' she said, pulling the covers back and patting the spot next to her that she had reserved for me.

I sat down on the bed. Her body was like a soft mountain moving slowly beneath the sheets. She pulled me towards her, simpering like a child and brusquely extracted one of her breasts, which she stuffed into my mouth. I hung on to it with both hands, to stop myself being suffocated, and started sucking it.

She took the opportunity to ferret around inside my trousers. I could feel her sausage-like fingers weighing up and appreciating my anatomy with a surprising dexterity. She managed to undress me completely with a minimum of movements. I started feeling her naked body. It was just fold after fold, layer after layer of fat. I felt like boring into it and losing myself inside.

She turned over on her back and this simple change of position was like a tidal wave in the bed. When everything settled down I climbed on top of her and cleared a path through the fat lips of her vulva and penetrated her. She squealed with pleasure, waking up the hens which started fluttering around and clucking. Anchored in this sea of flesh, I fucked her in an oblivious state, with my head between her breasts.

When I had finished, my only thought was to make a getaway. But she didn't see it that way.

'Oh, my dear,' she simpered, 'you gave me such a good orgasm . . . You're going to give me a bit more, aren't you?'

I mumbled some vague excuses as I tried to gather up my clothes.

'You're not leaving me already,' she began to whine. 'A poor woman like me who counts on these visits to have a little bit of pleasure . . .'

She had grabbed hold of my cock and started playing with it again.

'Oh, you can't put it away like that . . . It's still wet . . . Come here . . . Come here and I'll dry it for you . . . Come on, be nice

... Please ... Come and stick it in my mouth ... Please ... I won't hurt you, you know ... On the contrary ... You can leave straight afterwards, I promise ... I won't ask you for anything else ... Ah, I can tell you want to ... You know you'll be all right in my mouth ...'

'Luckily no one can see me,' I thought. I climbed her again, this time to go and sit on her face.

At least she kept her promises. She pumped and sucked away just as I had thought, like a suction pad. She sucked you in right to the back of her throat, right to the base of your shaft, and you felt as if she were about to swallow you whole. Within a few seconds my cock was as stiff as if I were about to fuck the most beautiful girl in the world.

I would have loved to come in her mouth, but the fat cow's fanny wanted its share of pleasure. Just as I was reaching my peak she dropped me and made me go back between her legs. She seemed to have an effective suction system down there as well. It didn't need much activity on my part, but this was enough to give her another orgasm, causing a series of jerks which almost unseated me. I hung on to her breasts and I came by surfing on these waves of vibration, which were most efficacious.

This time I got away as fast as I could. I gathered up my clothes, which were scattered over the bed and the floor, and stepped out of her reach to get dressed, while she tried to seduce me again with endless wheedling and promises. I took my leave of her, keeping a safe distance, and assured her in as kind a way as possible that she was bound to receive another visitor soon.

Once I was out in the corridor I spent a long time brushing at myself to remove all trace of feathers and down from my hair and clothes. Then I opened one of the following doors.

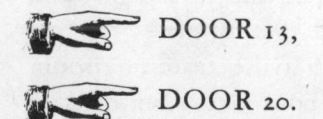 DOOR 13,

DOOR 20.

18

The Matron

I was beginning to get used to this place, this dark labyrinth where I found myself repeatedly thrown into the torments of desire and anxiety. For I still aspired to find behind one of these doors a new and ever more satisfying sensation, while having the feeling that I was being pursued by an invisible menace, which I was sure would eventually take form.

I no longer believed in the promise which had been made to me, that I would be able to realize all my fantasies here. For if I had entered the kingdom of fantasies, it was clear that I was ruled by them, not vice-versa. I was a plaything in their hands, they were amusing themselves with me and I simply had to be satisfied with the pleasure that their manipulations afforded me, sometimes succumbing to the illusion that I was their master. Basically, this place was like life.

I had barely opened the door when I was enveloped in the warm blast of a kitchen. Standing with her back to me in front of a broad coal stove, a thick-set, mature woman was stirring a large metal pot with a long wooden spoon. I closed the door behind me and gave a cough to announce my presence.

'You've come at the right moment,' she said, turning round and offering me the wooden spoon. 'Taste that for me.'

I stepped forward, presenting my mouth to the steaming spoon, which she pushed between my lips to pour out a wine sauce

which was both smooth and heady, and whose flavours continued to develop on my palate long after I had swallowed it.

'Hmmm!' I mouthed, making a gesture with my hands to tell her that it was perfect and there was nothing to add.

'Just as well,' she said.

Taking a teatowel in each hand she lifted the pot with her solid arms and placed it on the huge table, which was covered with a blue checked oilcloth.

'Because I have to do the cooking for everyone here,' she continued. 'And believe me, they're a hungry bunch. Yes, that's for sure. They don't just eat the food, they wolf it down. They're real pigs. If I didn't give them enough to eat, or feed them well enough, they'd happily eat me, and no mistake. Are you hungry?'

I didn't have time to reply before she had laid a place for me at the table, poured a glass of wine, cut a slice of bread from a large granary loaf and dished out a plateful of her thick, dark sauce. Then she offered me a high-backed, rush-seat chair and added in a familiar tone:

'Eat up, my little one, you don't know who will be eating you ...'

This all felt really good and I was quite ready for something to eat. I sat down, tasted the wine, which was old, dark, deep, fragrant, brought to room temperature, and then started on the ragoût, some sort of venison stew, or perhaps boar, a firm meat with a pronounced smell with slivers of wild mushrooms, which had been simmered so long that the wine in the sauce seemed to have reverted, through patient cooking, to its original essence of black grape, warm and sweet.

The matron slipped out for a few moments and returned carrying a bucket of coal. I started to get up to give her a hand but she dissuaded me with a single word in her strong, jovial voice. She opened the door of the stove with a poker and inside I could see glowing red embers. Then she tipped in the contents of her bucket, a rain of black bullets colliding as they fell. I served myself some more wine and stew.

Now she started preparing a milk drink in an aluminium pan. As I mopped up the sauce on my plate with the leavened bread I looked at the woman who had fed me. She was sturdy, and rather fat, but she was not unfeminine. The top of her apron was stretched over a bosom which still seemed firm, her slightly full stomach didn't entirely disguise the shape of her waist, her legs were shapely and her rump was as inviting as a pair of nice, plump cushions. As for her face, which wasn't made up, it bore the stamp of a natural beauty, the type that is not aware of itself and doesn't try to impose itself on you.

I poured myself another glass of wine and watched the dark red reflections shimmering in the glass. 'This woman must have been very good-looking,' I thought, 'when she was young and fresh. But her lines and her extra weight haven't made her ugly, quite the opposite. This woman is beautiful because she is what she is, she is at one with herself. There's probably nothing more satisfying, and more attractive.'

I had finished eating and drinking and I felt a gentle torpor descend on me, along with a confused desire to complete and enhance the pleasures of the board with those of the bed.

The matron sat in a large rocking chair next to the stove and looked at me with a smile.

'Have you had enough to eat?' she asked.

I nodded my head by way of response, for I suddenly felt extremely sluggish.

'But you seem worn out,' she continued. 'Come here, I'll give you my milky drink, it's an excellent pick-me-up.'

My limbs were so heavy, my head so foggy that I felt as if I were under the influence of a drug that was both a soporific and an aphrodisiac. I got up with difficulty and went slowly over to her, as if each step were a major feat of balance. As soon as I was within her reach she took me by the arm and sat me down on her knee.

'My poor boy,' she said. 'Those women have worn you out,

haven't they? Come here, my dear, and I'll give you something to make you better.'

I was so weary that I acquiesced, sitting in the warmth of her lap, and I closed my eyes and lay my cheek on her breast. She rocked the chair gently, I got an erection, but I would have gone straight to sleep if I hadn't suddenly realized that she was undoing my flies.

Straight afterwards she put her left hand behind my head and pushed a baby's bottle in my mouth while she took hold of my cock with her other hand and started to wank me gently.

'Suck, my dear, suck,' she said in a soft voice.

And I obeyed her, so that she wouldn't stop masturbating me.

In the bottle was a lukewarm, slightly sugary milk drink, no doubt the one she had just prepared. I began to pull on the rubber teat, in the same rhythm as I felt her chubby fingers moving up and down my cock. The milk squirted onto my tongue and palate, I swallowed it, with my eyes closed and my cheek still pushed into her bosom, her hand went up and down the full length of my member, squeezed it skilfully, I began breathing and sucking more quickly and more heavily, and she too speeded up her movement, following my rhythm so marvellously that I felt as if I had my own penis in my mouth and was sucking myself, my lips working on the teat as if they were trying to extract my own substance, sucking while wanked, wanked while sucking, and the rocking of the chair, wank and suck, I ejaculate, I extract the last mouthfuls and I ejaculate, with a shudder the length of my body.

She kept the bottle in my mouth and her hand on my cock for a few moments. Then she freed me of both when I opened my eyes. I saw her fingers hanging onto my still inflated member, dripping with sperm. She withdrew them, I got up, washed myself in the sink and rearranged myself. She was rubbing my come between her hands, as if smearing them with cream. 'To keep my skin soft,' she said with a wink. I ran my hand through

her hair, took her fingers in mine and, looking her in the eye, bent over to kiss her hand, then I left.

Once I was outside I realized that during all the time I had spent in that kitchen I had not said a word. I now felt just fine, totally relaxed and ready for anything. I opened the very first door that presented itself:

 DOOR 26.

19

The Street

When I went through the door I found myself in another corridor, but a much wider and lighter one. The light was natural and came in through a glass ceiling.

I raised my head and realized with a sudden excitement that I was underneath a pavement in a large city. My corridor exactly followed the course of this pavement where I could see dozens of people walking past. And of course some of these passers-by were women, and many of these women were wearing skirts, and from where I was standing I could see everything you can't see in the street, everything they concealed beneath their skirts.

I glanced around to check that I was alone in the corridor and couldn't prevent myself from swearing with pleasure. I couldn't believe my luck. Up above it seemed to be a fine afternoon in May and everyone was dressed lightly, though without displaying the excessive nudity of the summer months. As usual at this time of year, the women seemed happy to be able to go around in light dresses after the constraints of the trousers and thick tights of the winter months.

I didn't know where to look first. A young lady came by in flat pumps and a long dress, her legs bare. I walked beneath her for a while, admiring her firm calves, her long thighs and her white cotton knickers.

Then a woman in stilettoes passed her coming the other way

and I turned round to follow her. She had very muscular legs, the sort of lean, incisive muscles you often see on women who commonly wear high heels and which terminate at the top of the thighs in an accentuated roundness, because of the curvature such shoes inflict, and which isolate the whole buttock region, like a haven of undulating, greedy and idle femininity. By all appearances, this woman seemed to have been walking all her life in shoes like these, in navy blue leather, in which she clicked by above me at this very moment. I could see that from the movement of her chubby bottom, at once discreet and extremely lewd, inside her straight skirt, I could see it from the perfect scissor movement of stocking-clad legs, real silk stockings, grey, very fine, quite simple, held up by grey silk brocade suspenders which went up inside a pair of pale blue satin knickers. And these knickers had loose hems, as if the woman, in her stockings and knickers, wanted to grant immediate access to her sex, as if she wanted you at any moment, without having to take anything off, to be able to slip a hand, a mouth or a penis into her, as if her whole life were there, her whole truth, which she did not want to leave entirely naked, but magnified, exposed and protected like a treasure in its box, for there was her treasure and her secret, there, in that dark bush and bright pink flesh which sometimes, through the gaps under her knickers, I could just make out.

To see a woman in such erotic underwear is always a turn-on. But to see her from this exceptional point of view was almost unbearable. My cock was straining so hard against my trousers I had to free it. I continued walking beneath the woman in the grey stockings, my eyes riveted between her legs, with panting breath and my cock sticking up, but I didn't touch myself, for I promised myself I would find a way to have her rather than have to masturbate. My glans was already damp, I could have made myself come with one jerk, but I wanted to prolong this almost unbearable state of excitement for as long as possible,

which lent an extraordinary quality to the spectacle being offered to me.

Then the woman came to a halt at a kerb and waited. So I was able to observe at leisure the joints of her body, the top of her foot where the stocking creased slightly and, moving further up her leg, to lose myself between her thighs, in the shadows of her private parts, from the ribbon of her suspenders against the stockings to the narrow, loose hem of her flimsy knickers. Then she must have crossed the street and since my field of vision was limited to the pavement, I lost sight of her.

My first reaction was to try to follow her and I began frenziedly examining and probing the wall of the corridor in the hope of finding a gap, some sort of exit, a staircase, which would allow me to catch up with her. But the wall was despairingly solid. I gave it a punch and raised my head to the glass roof, where all the comings and goings made me forget my disappointment.

Dozens of girls and women walked along the pavement and it was impossible to follow all of them. I spent a few moments under the skirt of one of them, between the thighs of another, and so on, without really choosing, just as they came. I was like a little child, or a dog, mad and slobbering with joy, enraptured here by a thong in red lace stretched tight over tanned, muscular buttocks and a completely shaven pussy, there by some white stockings and flowery knickers beneath a pleated skirt, elsewhere by a bush of dark hair spilling out of some pink nylon panties which were too small and whose elastic dug into the fat, white flesh, or else by some fishnet stockings around hefty thighs and worn, without any knickers, with boots and a suede dress, or else by some white ankle socks and young girl's knickers under a cotton sailor's outfit ...

I probably covered a few dozen metres like this, my cock erect and my tongue hanging out, in pursuit of the black diamond of these young ladies. I reached the corner of the street and that's where I ended my hunt. A superb creature with long

blonde hair, in a tight white dress, her legs bare, was standing at the kerb, her arms crossed in front of her bust, one leg pushed out, her weight on the other. And I was the only one who knew that this statuesque blonde, whom all the men and indeed all the women eyed up as they went past, owed the golden colour of her hair to her hairdresser. For, although her dress was very short, and perhaps precisely because it fitted snugly on her little behind, she wasn't wearing any knickers. And her bush, which was very thin and neatly trimmed, was the most charming little thing it was possible to see in this underworld.

I lay on my back directly under her to admire her perfect long legs and the chubby freshness of her pale pink pussy, which was open wide enough to let me see her pretty, slightly shiny little button and the darker breach of her slit, towards which my cock rose of its own accord. This time I couldn't resist giving myself what my whole body was demanding of me, the deliverance of pleasure. People came and went around her, ignorant of this unfettered wonder beneath her dress, concealed merely by a few centimetres of white cloth, this exquisite cunt completely offered to my gaze, which I was wanking over, unknown to her, unknown to everyone; and, when she moved her hips to change leg and to consult her watch, she opened her buttocks and for a moment this slut unwittingly revealed her little arsehole and the entirely wooded valley of her mound and then I shot my load, my come flew into the air towards her, like a fountain, the spurts shining in the light from the glass ceiling, a light which fell right from between the legs of this girl.

Almost immediately, I saw her smile and wave. A tall, athletic-looking boy of Middle-Eastern origin, dressed in trainers, jeans and a T-shirt, arrived and embraced her. They kissed, holding tight to each other. She had closed her legs but she was kissing so fervently that I was sure that she was getting damp now. He passed his hand over her bottom, quickly because of the people around them, then took her inside the nearest building.

Directly beneath this, in my corridor, there was a door. I opened it without a second thought. Those two had a raging desire to make love and I didn't want to miss that. One way or another I would find a way to catch up with them.

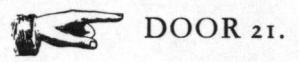   DOOR 21.

20

The Sheath

A young woman was trying on an evening dress in front of a mirror, a sheath dress which nicely showed off her curves. I held the door open with my hand on the handle, ready to leave and fearful of being indiscreet.

'You are very beautiful,' I said anyway.

She turned to face me, apparently not at all put out by my intrusion.

'You think so?' she said with a doubtful pout.

Apparently she wasn't of the same opinion. I entered the room and closed the door behind me.

'But of course. You are very, very beautiful,' I insisted with a smile.

'Well I don't think so. Look at that. It's too tight. It looks ridiculous, and indecent.'

'If you're lucky enough to have a body like yours, nothing is ridiculous. And the dress is very elegant.'

'It's fancy dress! I'd rather be dressed like you! You men don't have to wear things like this ... Yet you yourself seem to have a body worth showing off ...' she added maliciously.

'Do you want to see it?'

'Oh, it's wicked ... You won't believe it ... Can you imagine why my big sister made me buy this, for her bloody party ... And that's not all ... Look ...'

She lifted her dress and showed me her thigh, clad in a black stocking attached to suspenders.

'But that's pretty,' I said.

'Oh yes, very pretty. All the guys like that, don't they? Look, if I asked you a little favour, would you grant it?'

'With pleasure. What do you want?'

'Promise first.'

'I promise.'

'Right. Will you lend me your gear? Just for a short while ...'

'What for?'

'You promised ...'

'No problem ...'

I started to get undressed and was encouraged to see she was doing the same. Lovely girl, she really was. God knows why she had got it into her head to cover her gorgeous body with men's clothes several sizes too big for her ...

Once she had pulled on my shirt and trousers she looked at herself in the mirror with a big smile.

'What do you think?' she said, delighted.

'Not bad, but ...'

'No, but imagine I'm a boy. If I were a boy, how would you think I looked?'

'Well, you know, I'm more used to looking at girls than boys ...'

'All right. Imagine you're a girl and I'm a boy and you're looking at me. What would you think?'

'Very nice,' I said finally. 'I'd think you were very nice.'

'Oh, I would really have liked to be a boy. Just once, at least. But I obviously lack something,' she said, looking at my sex without coyness.

'Obviously,' I said. 'But I can lend it to you, if you like ...'

'Oh really? You'd do that?'

She seemed to be hatching a plan which brought a blush to her cheeks. She summoned up her courage and revealed it to me:

'And ... Would you mind dressing up a little ... I mean ... I put your clothes on, so maybe ... Maybe you could put mine on ... then we could really play ...'

'But I'd never squeeze into that!'

'Sure you would! It's elasticated! Here, let me! That's great! Brilliant!'

She managed to get me into her dress, then she lifted it up to put on the stockings and suspenders. Her joy was a pleasure to behold.

'See how nice you look!' she said, as she propelled me in front of the mirror.

The dress was even tighter on me than it was on her and, I had to admit, I didn't look bad at all.

'I'm concerned I might tear your stockings,' I said.

'Don't worry about it, I've got another pair. Now come, let's go lie down on the bed. I'm the boy, all right?'

She lay me down on my back with my dress up and my legs apart. She took off her trousers and sat on my balls, in such a way that my cock seemed to be part of her own sex.

'Have you seen my big dick?' she said, amusing herself by touching it and manipulating it. 'Do you want it, my big dick? I'll put it in you ...'

She penetrated herself with my cock and began to ride me, pushing up my dress to caress my breasts. She waited for me, and when she felt I was ready to come, she let go her own pleasure, thrusting her hips in a suggestive way and saying, 'There, take that ...!'

Then she offered me a cigarette and we had a quiet smoke in the bed.

'So, how was I?' she said. 'As a guy, how was I?'

'You were perfect, miss ... And how was I as a girl?'

'Hmm ... next time I'll try it with a real girl ...'

She looked at the time and realized that she was late. I took back my boy's clothes, as she put it, and as I left I wished her much pleasure next time round.

'That little girl will be very interesting when she grows up a bit,' I thought. And I went off into the corridor with a smile on my lips. The usual shadows followed me, until I opened another door.

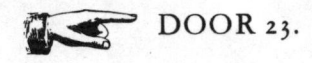 DOOR 23.

21

The Couple

'If there is a staircase,' I thought, 'I ought to be at the same level as them, in the same building.' And I opened the door, without even thinking about what I would do once I was in there with them.

At the same moment I suddenly seemed to go cool on the whole idea, my illusions and my enthusiasm dwindled away. From the beginning I hadn't managed to discover the slightest logic in the arrangement of this labyrinth. Why should one suddenly appear now? If any element of the logic of the outside world were at work here, how, for example, could people walk along a glass pavement without noticing? It was clear that in this place you could rely only the law of desire, a law which was obviously unfathomable, unpredictable, constantly changing.

Forget the couple . . . I wanted a woman.

Just as I was closing the door I felt a breath on my neck, then another, then both together. I turned round and peered into the corridor. As I was looking to my right, I heard a furtive footstep to my left. I swung round immediately, but everything was already silent again. I waited a while for these mysterious pursuers to show up again, but they had well and truly disappeared.

'You will find a woman, perhaps the Woman,' I repeated to myself, to get myself going. For I suddenly felt thoroughly

dejected. 'You shouldn't have masturbated,' I said to myself. It's reduced your desire and as soon as you've achieved the pleasure, it doesn't seem worth having.' I had masturbated so often during my adolescence. At that time it was a curiosity, a constantly new discovery, there was no risk of ever getting tired of it. But why still do it today, even at times when I could easily get my pleasure from a woman? Because it wasn't the same. Because I still needed this different sort of pleasure from time to time, this solitary pleasure that was like no other, not even the same as when someone else masturbates you. The whole secret, the whole attraction of this pleasure lay in that word: solitary. That's why it was an acute pleasure, which left me empty, with the sole desire to forget everything, or to start everything afresh, which is a way of forgetting.

I had entered an elegant lounge, which could have been in a large hotel. There was a packet of cigarettes and some matches lying on the low table. I took one, lit it, sat down in an armchair and started smoking quietly. It was then that I saw the tall, tanned guy from earlier, the one who had kissed the blonde on the pavement and taken her away with him.

He came towards me, introduced himself, shook my hand and asked if he could sit down beside me for a few moments. I acceded to his request without formality, in the same way as he had approached me.

Although masculine charms had no effect on me, I had to admit that he was a very handsome man, virile, sexy, refined in an understated way and with a manner that was attractive to men as well as women. He looked at me for a few seconds in a half-embarrassed, half-amused way and said:

'I have a favour to ask you.'

Whereupon, without waiting, he produced a photo from his pocket and handed it to me, adding:

'What do you think of this woman?'

It was a polaroid picture of the statuesque blonde from the street. She was standing, entirely naked, in a hotel bedroom.

'Congratulations,' I said. 'She is very beautiful.'

'Isn't she?' he said.

I must have communicated a tone of sincerity, even desire, for he seemed delighted.

'So this is the deal,' he continued. 'I'll just come out and say it: will you agree to come and fuck her with me? Before you reply I should make it clear that this would be as much for her pleasure as for ours. You see, we have been lovers for a long time. And every now and again we need these little threesomes, which satisfy us in a different way from what we can normally give each other. When we decide to make love with another woman, she's the one who brings her. And when we feel we need a man, then I'm the one who has to do the recruiting ...'

He paused for a moment, then added, as if to clinch the argument:

'I think you will please her ...'

I looked at the photo again and got up, saying simply:

'Well, that will be mutual.'

He got up in turn, smiling, and after giving me a fraternal hug, led me to the end of the room and showed me behind a curtain.

I recognized the room in the photo. The blonde was standing next to the window, naked. Her body was even more wonderful than I had imagined. She came towards us and as she looked at me, said: 'Thank you.' I couldn't tell whether this was directed at me or her lover, for having brought a second male. She took us both by the hand and led us towards the bed.

'This is what I propose,' my friend said. 'First we'll ask you to provide the services we require. Then, if you wish, our lady friend will be entirely at your disposal to realize your dearest wish. Is that OK?'

Before I made any promises, I asked what they required of me. It transpired that he wanted to treat his girlfriend to the joys of 69, without for once having to worry about giving her an orgasm, which always spoiled his concentration a bit as he tried

to achieve his own pleasure. While she, on the other hand, loved to come with her mouth full. My initial job, then, as she feasted on her lover's cock, was to graze on her gorgeous pussy. I had admired it enough, when it was out of reach, to find the prospect of paying it homage very enticing.

We got undressed and took up our positions, she lying on her back in the middle of the bed, her legs wide open, he crouched over her face. She opened her mouth to swallow her lover's imposing brown member, which was already slightly erect, while I went down between her legs and started licking to the very heart of her delicious, pink, glistening pussy. She smelt of briar honey, tasted of barley sugar and she knew exactly how to guide my tongue to where she wanted it: sometimes around her clitoris, sometimes at the edge of her lips, then all the way inside her vagina. Soon she began to arch back violently and she came with a muffled sound because of the cock filling her mouth, flooding my face.

When I raised my head, I saw that her lover had achieved orgasm at the same time as her, since he withdrew his member from between her lips and she ran her tongue over it to taste the last drops of sperm. Thus we had fulfilled our mission and we congratulated each other.

My comrade, who was now quite vigorously erect again, explained that his mistress only allowed herself to be sodomized by him, and only on one condition, that she could be taken from the front at the same time. For it was the only way she could get pleasure from being sodomized, and it was out of the question that she would do it without being able to come herself. My role this time, if I accepted, would be to fuck her in her cunt while he fucked her in her behind.

Once again we took up position, the two of us on our sides with her in the middle. She wanked me a little, as he was rubbing some lubrication into her arsehole. Then, on a given signal, we both penetrated her at the same time.

We began giving her her fill with thrusts of the hips, following

the same rhythm. I could feel his big dick knocking away at the same time as mine, on the other side of the lining. We changed rhythm together, again with a simple nod of the head, and made her moan and yell with pleasure. When we guessed that we had worn her out, we decided to come ourselves, together. We both grabbed on to the girl's hips and started pumping away without holding back, and without paying any attention to her reactions. I watched my accomplice's face for the first signs of orgasm, as he did mine. We felt our breath shorten at the same time and we shot our come together into the body of the girl who was now entirely at our mercy.

After which we slapped each other on the back like two old friends, together kissed the girl on the mouth and then had a bit of a rest. When, a few moments later, the blonde asked if she could do anything for me, I sat on the edge of the bed, made her kneel on the carpet and asked her to suck me off.

She went at it rigorously. Seeing that her lover had an erection again, I took pity on him and asked the girl to take care of him as well. She did her best to suck both dicks at the same time and, with the help of her hands, finally made us ejaculate, glans against glans, all over her face.

I reckoned I had fully made their acquaintance by now and I left them as cordially as I had met them. When I went out, through the back of the room, I found myself in a new corridor, deserted and dark like the previous ones. As I didn't relish the company of the sinister shadows who were still pursuing me in these corridors, I quickly decided to open one of the two doors which presented themselves.

☛ DOOR 24,

☛ DOOR 27.

22

The Black Woman

I was beginning to think that I was stupid to stay here, even if I did have such excellent company. After all, behind the doors of this corridor I had left there must be lots of other adventures and encounters to be had. That woman who was looking for me, for a start, whom I might never find if I stayed locked away in this room.

But it was as if I were ensnared in sexual desire, these two women and their friend smelt of sex, with them everything seemed permissible, I felt that they could give me much more, things that I wasn't even thinking about. For they seemed to be endowed with infinite experience, freedom and imagination, which they would use to push back my own limits and which could awaken the whole host of powerful, unfamiliar appetites I felt within me. I shared an obscene, unwholesome intimacy with them, and I wanted to revel in it to the very end.

I lay down on the bed along with Aurélie and Joseph, the black man. Anna had gone out. We grew sleepy in each other's arms. After a while, as we gently daydreamed, we started touching each other in every way that took our fancy, groping and feeling up our entangled bodies, in the way that animals sniff each other out of curiosity. Aurélie, who, in her sensual delirium, seemed to have reverted to being a suckling, attached herself indiscriminately to Joseph or me and sucked our breasts

or whatever part of our anatomies was in reach of her mouth.

'She's got a good mouth,' Joseph laughed. 'You'll see,' he continued, 'when you know her better you'll be very happy with her. She's a bit on the flabby side, and likes nothing better than being relieved by Anna, but you can do absolutely anything to her, or make her do anything. The only thing you can't ask her to do is to take any initiative. You're a total idiot, aren't you, fatso?'

Aurélie didn't react. Perhaps she hadn't even understood. I had taken advantage of her sucking craze to stick my dick into her mouth and she was sucking it with her eyes closed, as if lost in a world of her own.

'Don't worry, you're a good girl, carry on,' Joseph continued. Then he said to me: 'Have you had her between her tits yet?'

'Yes.'

'Ah, it's delicious, isn't it?'

And he put his dick to Aurélie's bosom, a large black rod squeezed between the two big white globes, and started moving it up and down.

'The trouble with a woman like this,' Joseph continued, 'is that once you have used her you want to discard her. Big mistake. You should hang on to her. You can't imagine how many times I've enjoyed having her to hand or lending her to friends. Don't be shocked, she loves to be used, she loves being a useful object . . . Doesn't she suck well?'

'Yes.'

'You see. And what's more, she's deliberately making the pleasure last . . . I mean her own pleasure. Look.'

Letting go of her breast, he quickly shoved two fingers into her pussy, then pushed them under my nose. They were damp.

Taken by surprise, Aurélie almost bit me. I felt a bit funny, partly because the vulgar way in which Joseph spoke about Aurélie made me ill at ease and partly because I could see that he was right, that it would be wrong not to make use of this girl as we wished. And what I wished now was to sodomize her.

Joseph was still rubbing himself off between her breasts, and I told myself it would be more polite to wait until they had finished. Besides, he was beginning to get excited, and so was she, which really pumped me up, with grunts of joy. I could see he was on the point of flooding her throat and I feared I wouldn't be able to hold back much longer from the other receptacle which I had my mind set on. 'Never mind,' I said to myself quickly. 'I'll bugger her later, that's what the fat slut is there for.' And I got ready to shoot off at the same time as Joseph.

But neither of us had the time to satisfy ourselves.

'What's going on?' someone said.

And Aurélie immediately let go of my cock, wriggled out of Joseph's grip and ran over to Anna, who had just come in. Joseph and I remained on the bed, spellbound.

Anna was extremely beautiful and quite stunning. Her ebony body was strapped into a skin harness, a pale, fine skin stretched over her dark skin like a drum, so tight it was like the inside of her own skin, as if, assuming the inside of her skin were white, she had been flayed, turned inside out and then sewn onto her own flesh in the places where her costume was.

For everything she wore had been cut from this skin: her elbow-length gloves, her corset tight around her waist, gripping her breasts below the nipples, her tiny pants which were so closely welded to her crack that it looked even more thoroughly obscene than if she were naked, and even her thigh-length boots whose elongated heels were tipped with thick steel screws. These boots, which she wore like stockings, went up as far as the top of her thighs where they were attached to her corset by suspenders which were also made of skin, but an unshaven skin, still covered with thick grey-brown hair, like that of a dog.

Yet the most gripping, chilling aspect of Anna's get-up was not any of this, but the objects which served as her headdress and belt. She had stuck over her head, after tying back the abundant mass of hair which fell down her back, a stuffed

hyena's head, with its jaws open and its lips curled back over its yellow fangs, which could only have looked more vividly real if it had started barking. Around her waist she had tied a cord of hemp whose two ends fell down between her legs where they were attached to a pair of scissors, pointing downwards, like a man's sex, with two small testicles and a penis of steel, hanging beneath her own female sex so tightly clad in the skin.

Anna stood there immobile, regal, her legs slightly apart as if on the bridge of a ship in a light swell, in an explicitly dominant pose.

'Didn't I forbid you to have pleasure without me?' she pronounced, in a voice in which softness contended with malice.

'Yes, mistress,' chorused Aurélie, who was prostrate at her feet, and Joseph, who was cowering at the end of the bed.

Anna looked straight into my eyes and I assumed she was waiting for my response. I looked at the others and thought that, if this was a game, they seemed to be taking it very seriously and I shouldn't be a spoilsport.

'Yes,' I said.

'Yes what?'

She didn't look as if she were joking either.

'Yes, mistress.'

I said 'mistress' simply to fit in with the others, but as soon as I had uttered the word, I suddenly felt infinitely weak. And when I felt myself becoming weak, I had an acute desire to be even weaker and to submit body and soul to this woman who, through the magic of a single word, had in actual fact become my mistress.

'Now, heel,' she said.

I threw myself to the ground and went to her, half crawling, half on all fours like a cringeing dog. Joseph did the same as me. Our cocks, still erect and damp at the tip, dragged along the floor and left a trail like two snails.

'That's fine, good boys,' said Anna.

And she opened her hands where she was holding three lumps of sugar, which she gave to us.

But as we were crunching our sugar lumps she treacherously scraped the steel tips of her heels along the glass floor. This was as painful as if she had stuck them into our teeth to the very nerve ends, and we started groaning with our hands over our mouths. After this, she walked away for a few seconds, leaving us to suffer, and came back with some cord, with which she tied our hands behind our backs.

'You were just about to come, weren't you?'

'Yes, mistress,' we replied in a chorus.

'And it's my job to make you come, that's what you're thinking, isn't it?'

'Yes, mistress,' we replied again, even more abjectly and feverishly.

'That's right, that's what everyone thinks: the black woman gives the black man pleasure, he gives the white woman pleasure and she gives the white man pleasure. At the top of the ladder, you have pleasure each time, and at the bottom never, which is how it should be ... And now you will show me if you really know how to have pleasure, each on your more or less privileged rungs of the ladder ...'

'You, Aurélie, because you think you have to play the role of slut or frigid victim in order to have pleasure, because you're afraid of the gaze of men, because you hate them to look at you and can't look at them, because the company of women is merely a refuge for you, I sentence you to come alone, without man or woman, with the back of this chair, completely deprived of your sight.

'You, Joseph, because you treat white women as whores, and feel you have to save black women from being whores by marrying them, because you're afraid of all women, I sentence you to come on this little teddy bear, which shouldn't frighten you too much.

'And you,' she continued, turning to me, 'because you think

that black women and black men are sexually superior to white women and white men, because you think sex is freer for them because it's more animalistic, because you think white women only enjoy sex if they're sluts, I sentence you to empty yourself in this shoe, where you will come as you normally do, like the heel you are.'

Whereupon she brought a chair to Aurélie, a bear to Joseph, and a shoe to me, which, in her stern but kind way, she obligingly fitted over my dick, and ordered us to comply.

I looked at the large scissors hanging between her legs and I was very afraid of what she might do if I didn't obey her. We all set to work, Aurélie on the back of the chair, Joseph on his teddy, I in her shoe. Before, the slightest touch would have brought us off, but now we had our hands tied behind our backs and even by trying to warm up our imaginations as we rubbed ourselves against our allotted objects we got no response, but only made ourselves more and more sore.

Anna went away, saying that she was going to return and that she was counting on us. And she did indeed return after a while. She looked as fresh and pretty as a peach and was draped in a long, brightly coloured sarong. She was carrying a baby in her arms, a little girl who was eating a banana and laughing.

'Oh, are you still there?' she said in an offhand sort of way. 'Well I've got things to do, so I'll leave you ...'

And she turned to leave. We protested loudly that we were still tied up and we wouldn't mind being released now.

'Tied up?' she said, bursting out laughing.

Her baby started laughing happily with her. And she left us.

We tried twisting our wrists, and our cords, which were quite loose, came open of their own accord. We hadn't come, but we no longer felt like it. I got dressed and left the room without saying goodbye.

I walked for a long time, alone in the dark corridor, where I felt I was being harassed by shadows, who even called out my name, but who always disappeared the moment I turned round

to try to see them. I stopped, alone in the dark, to curse them with angry cries and gestures. I'd had more than enough of these shadows. Finally, I opened a door at random.

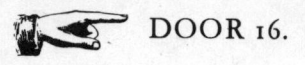   DOOR 16.

23

The Sorceress

It was an old, gloomy, dirty hut stuffed with bundles of firewood and earthenware pots. Under the chimney something was bubbling noisily in a cauldron on the fire.

At first, I didn't think there was anyone there, but as soon as I entered I heard the door being locked behind me. I turned round.

An old woman, bent double in old black clothes, was standing next to the door with a key in her hand and giving me an evil look. I started laughing.

'Would you be locking me in?' I said to her.

Her predatory little eyes stared at me without blinking and she stuffed the key into the pocket of her apron. Then she walked past me and stirred the simmering brew in her cauldron with a big iron ladle. I politely pointed out that it would only take one kick to open her rotten door or a slight squeeze of my hand to break her arm.

'I know what you're thinking,' the old woman said in a surprisingly clear voice. 'I'm not stupid. Whether you like it or not, you are locked up with me until I see fit to let you go.'

'Oh really?' I said.

I laughed again and went to sit down on the bench next to the fire.

'I'm joking, of course,' she continued. 'I lock the door

because otherwise it swings open all the time. With the draughts that blow all through the corridors ... Have you noticed the draughts?'

Now she was almost cordial. She trotted off to find two goblets, which she filled with a thick liquid.

'House liqueur,' she said, offering me a glass. 'I hope you like it ...'

And she drank hers down in one go. I followed suit. Her liqueur had a very spicy taste, which I couldn't identify. The old woman's eyes began to shine and she gave a toothless smile.

'Now you are trapped,' she said.

'Again? You're obsessed with it! Could you tell me why I have been granted the honour of being shut up by ...'

A sudden feeling of discomfort, accompanied by an unexpected and inexplicable erection, prevented me from finishing my sentence.

'Yes,' said the old woman. 'Of course I will tell you. I want your sperm.'

I hardly heard what she said. I feverishly lowered my trousers. My balls and my dick were hurting so much, I desperately needed to relieve myself.

'What the hell did you put in that fucking liquid?' I stammered.

'That's for me,' she said as she took hold of my cock.

She started wanking me with her emaciated hand. I ejaculated immediately.

She gathered the sperm in one of her earthenware pots and started again. My cock remained stiff and congested. When I tried to wank myself, it hurt, whereas she knew how to take best advantage of the state she had put me in. I don't know how many times she managed to get sperm out of me, but each time I had an excellent orgasm. Her hand was sordid, but she had virtuoso fingers.

When she had filled her bowl enough she took the key out of her pocket and opened the door. I got up and left.

In the corridor I wondered whether she had set this trap to get something to put in one of her potions, or whether she did it simply for pleasure. I decided to walk on a bit before going through another door, for I was completely exhausted.

During the whole time I wandered in the labyrinth I felt I was being followed by the shadows. When their presence became too oppressive, I opened a door.

 DOOR 24.

24

The Trout

It was one of those landscapes which reconcile you to life, even make you love it desperately. I found myself on a grassy slope scattered with rocks which fell away to the clear water of a mountain torrent. It was cool, in the early glimmers of a summer dawn, the air was extraordinarily pure and silent, despite the noise of the stream, as if suspended in expectation.

Behind me was a group of abandoned shepherd's huts arranged in tiers, built out of large grey mountain stone, some of which were in ruins. I was completely alone; alone yet in the company of warm spirits, of the men and animals who had lived here, of the night and the day, which were neither of this world; alone and wonderfully alive, in the company of the ghost of life, which seemed at this fleeting moment to have fallen into a catalepsy, but which was on the point of awakening; alone with regret at the passing of this moment and with a troubling hope for what would follow; alone as one always is with ghosts, particularly the ghosts of oneself, of what one has been and what one will become, that is, in reality, a multitude of ghosts, all the clear ghosts of dawn whose presence one can only sense in solitude.

I descended to the stream, which was quite broad and which, like all streams of its type, clicked its countless tongues against stones and rocks as it flowed, forming small niches where

the odd freshwater plants took root. And as I had hoped I saw flitting through the stones and the clear, bubbling water a small, silver trout, bright as a flash of lightning.

I followed it with my eyes until it disappeared downstream, past the bends of the torrent, then I climbed back up to the huts, following some instinct. There was some sort of wild spinach growing all around them, leaving virtually no place for any other vegetation, apart from a few nettles which I wove my way through.

There were five or six huts, most of them quite tiny, their roofs partially or fully collapsed. Their narrow openings, a door and the occasional window, were nothing more than holes where shadows took refuge. Only one of them, the best preserved, still had a full roof of slates as well as a door and a shutter closed in front of the little rectangular slit that served as a window. Inside, an iron bed, a stool, a table and a little corner fireplace virtually filled the place. I also found a fishing rod and a box of flies.

I returned to the stream, where I looked for the best place to cast my line. I walked along a stream bed of small, flat stones. A little further along there was a large white rock, with the water filtering gently around it, which overlooked a deep, dark pool. I turned my attention away from the stream to prepare my gear. When I looked round again I saw a naked young girl reclining on the white rock, a few metres away from me.

She was resting her head on her elbow and facing upstream and all I could see of her was the long wet strands of her green hair which ran like snakes down her back, the slender line of her back itself, accentuated down its middle by a deep, supple furrow, this line sinking into the hollow of her waist before curving around her hips as gracefully as a stringed instrument, an undulating line arriving at the delicate curves of her buttocks before giving way to the long line of the legs which disappeared from my view on the other side of the rock.

I was so affected by this I could at first neither move nor

utter a word. It was like coming across a doe in the depths of a wood. If I called out to her she might take fright and vanish. For the fact she was lying there like that probably meant she thought she was alone. But if I went up to her without alerting her to my presence, I might alarm her even more. I stood for a moment as if turned to stone, contemplating this slim, fragile beauty whose skin, almost diaphanous in the first glimmers of dawn, shone slightly with a cold, fascinating light.

Then she turned towards me, with a movement that seemed to me both excessively slow and quick at the same time, throwing me into a state of heightened awareness in which actions took place with a stupefying slowness, because they were broken down into an infinity of fragments, and simultaneously with lightning speed.

She turned towards me, her half-closed green eyes stared into mine, she opened her mouth, which widened slowly into a smile that was an obvious invitation, and then leapt down behind the rock.

At that moment the first drops of rain began to fall. I threw all my clothes onto the grass and dived in myself. She swam ahead of me, upstream; I saw her supple, lively body undulate through the icy water, setting my flesh on fire. To keep up with her I had to swim vigorously, with a butterfly stroke. I strained against the current with all my muscles and the effort aroused my passion. I could see just well enough to make out the fleeting form I was pursuing, but I wasn't worried. Her flight was nothing but a game, a way of galvanizing our energies to make her seem more desirable.

Suddenly she turned round and brushed past me. I tried to catch her but she slipped between my fingers and allowed herself to be carried off by the current. Her long green hair floated in front of me, as if inviting me to follow her. I too allowed myself to be carried along by the water.

We arrived at the white rock and floated around it to the other side. I was just in time to see her disappear into the pool.

The Trout

I was about to plunge into the little dark pool myself when I felt my sex gripped by a warm mouth under the water, the lips enclosed it like a glove and started sucking with such force that I felt that I was being sucked in whole, that my whole being was concentrated in that ever swelling, ever hardening piece of flesh below my belly which was being pulled downwards by burning sensations. I allowed myself to sink, to be dragged deliciously down into the bottomless depths of the pool where I could surrender myself for ever to the eager sucking of those lips, let myself go in the mouth of my cold, bewitching lover . . .

I was about to come. I searched for breath and that's what brought me to my senses. In a split second I realized that I was at the bottom of the stream, deep in the green water where I couldn't see a thing, and if I did not leave my irresistible fiancée at once I would remain her prisoner for ever. At the last moment I found the energy to pull myself free of her mouth and, at the peak of my orgasm, as if propelled, I returned to the surface with a spasm of my whole body.

From the bank I watched my sperm coming to the surface of the pool then flowing away downstream in silvery-white threads. It was raining. The dawn was over, the longest dawn I had ever been privileged to experience. The beautiful girl would not return to lie naked on the rock, would never return, with her bewitching smile, to ask me to follow her.

I cast my line and immediately felt a bite and a tug on the line; a trout started to leap and the energy vibrated through the length of my arm. It was a beautiful rainbow trout and it put up a long struggle, arching in the water with fierce, graceful leaps. Then it grew tired and I reeled it in, wrapping it in my shirt.

I gathered up my clothes, which were damp in the rain, and went back to the hut. The rain was bringing out the warm smells of the earth and grass and the cold, metallic fragrance of the stones. I lit a fire in the hearth with some wood I had found in another hut and stood in front of it for a good while, drying myself out. Then I went back to the trout. It had finally died.

I cut open its belly and filleted it. It really was a beautiful trout, fine and iridescent. I put a stick in its mouth, passed it right through its body and cooked it over the embers. I ate it with my fingers. It had the most delicate, exquisite flesh that I had ever tasted.

I returned to the stream to wash my shirt and then hung it to dry in front of the fire, with my other clothes. I dozed on the iron bed.

When my clothes were dry I extinguished the embers, tidied up the hut and went out. There was no more mountain nor stream, but one of those dark corridors full of doors I was already familiar with. The usual shadows dogged my steps but their whispering left me cold; I didn't even attempt to catch sight of them. I opened one of the first doors I went past.

 DOOR 25,

DOOR 26.

25

The Partition

I entered a small, quiet, comfortable hotel room. As there was no one about I thought I might as well stay there and get some rest, for I was sure I'd be receiving a visit. I got undressed, took a long shower and went to bed.

Then I heard the door of the neighbouring room open and close, as a man and a woman came in. From the conversation they were having and the various sighs, moans and shrieks which constantly interrupted it, I quickly realized how they intended to spend their time. At first I tried to make light of it. Then I tried to think of something else, in order not to hear anything.

But it was no use tossing and turning in my bed, their words got into my head, filled it entirely, inflamed my imagination. Finally they drove me so mad that I lost all control of myself. I leapt out of bed, went and sat next to the wall the voices were coming through and, with my cock in my hand and my ear against the partition wall, I listened to them to the end, not missing a word or a sigh, not even the tiniest sound of sucking or rubbing of skin against skin. I listened to them, breathing heavily.

MAN: Show me how lovely you are.
WOMAN: Do you want to see?

M: Yes. Yes I do.

W: Then sit down on the floor. Yes, against the wall. Now undo your flies. Take it out. My God, it's lovely! Take it right out. Please. I want to see everything . . .

M: We said we'd only look, at first.

W: Yes, I'm sorry. I won't do it any more. Look, I'll stay over here. Tell me what you want me to show you.

M: Turn round. Walk. Wiggle your bottom, that's right. Now come back to me. Again. Again. Don't worry, I won't touch you. Lift your skirt.

W: You have to fondle yourself at the same time, slowly.

M: Lift it a bit higher . . . Show me your knickers.

W: Oh, I like that. It's lovely when you fondle it.

M: Show me your bottom. Your stockings are creased around your ankles. Hitch them up. Bend over and hitch them up. Are you wearing see-through knickers and will you now show me your arse, slut? Rearrange your skirt . . . Yes, tight over your thighs . . .

W: Don't get too excited, you pig, or you'll come too soon. Look how hard you are! I'm completely wet.

M: Be a good girl and pull that chair over. Yes, here. Sit down. Cross your legs. Yes, you can stroke me with your shoe. Uncross them. Again. More slowly. Lift your leg high when you do it.

W: Like that? Can you see all right like that?

M: Yes, like that. It's just at the right height, I can see everything. What are you doing?

W: I'm lifting my skirt and spreading my legs.

M: God, your knickers are all damp.

W: I'm so excited . . . I want to do it now . . . please, come . . .

M: No. Not straight away. Take your knickers off. Good. No, don't change position. Put your legs over the armrests. Now fondle yourself.

W: Oh yes, I want that. But you too. I want to do it as I watch you. Yes, do it again. See how well I do it . . . Look . . . With my

two hands ... Oh, give me the candle ... There, on the table next to you ... Thank you ... Look, I'm doing it for you ... for your cock ...

M: That's good. You're beautiful. Carry on. Right to the end.

W: And you too?

M: Me too what?

W: You'll ...

M: Say it. I want you to say the word and come at the same time. Yes, I'm wanking, I'm wanking. Yes, you're so nice, you've got it, go on, go on, go on ... And say it ...

W: You're ... wanking ... aaaah ...

M: Now you'll feel it ... Get down on all fours ...

W: That's it, that's what I wanted. I did it to have that.

M: Was it a good orgasm?

W: Yes, yes. But your dick is bigger ... It's better, I prefer it ... I adore it, I adore it ... It goes all the way in, I adore it ... That's it, that's it, it's coming back ... iaaaah ...

M: Come over to the bed.

W: Yes. Wait. I want to take off my skirt and blouse. You get undressed too.

M: It's nice, that basque. Keep it on but take your breasts out of the top.

W: Come and suck them ... Hmmm ... Now the other one ... Gently ... Yes ... Now lie down. Leave it to me. I want to take advantage of you.

M: Hmmm! I love it when you pinch my breasts like that.

W: I know. And when I suck them?

M: Hmmm ... And your nails ...

W: My nails, they like to walk all over ... There ... and there ... and ... wider ... and ... there ... No, don't be afraid ... there, gently ... Isn't that good? Come on, turn over. Onto your stomach. Wait, I'll stick it underneath. There ... Hmmm ... No, wait. Turn over again. I want my body to touch it. I want it all over. There ... On the soles of my feet ... You see, I can roll it like a lump of modelling clay ... Behind my knees ...

That's great, behind the knees! On my navel ... In my arms ...
On my breasts ... On the other ... Between the two ... In my
throat ... In my eyes ... And there ... Tap it against my cheeks
... Under my nose ... Yum-yum ... Come into my mouth, you
lovely thing ... Oh, let me have it. Let me have it a little
longer ...

M: OK, but afterwards I want to put it in ... behind ...

W: ...

M: Do you want to?

W: Wait ... I don't know.

M: Please ...

W: I don't know ... I'm afraid ...

M: No, you're not afraid ... You're afraid to start with, then
you never stop coming ...

W: Yes, but not today ... Please, not today ...

M: OK. Come here then. Put your legs over my shoulders. And
your hand ... Yes ...

W: Yes, like that ... Go on ... All the way in ... More, more,
more ...

M: You're beautiful when you come.

W: That was so good. Come on now. Here ...

M: You've changed your mind?

W: Yes, I want to now. Look, I want to so much, it'll go in on
its own ... Go on ... You see ... You see how much I like it?
Oh, I can feel it ... It's so big ... Oh, my love, you're
buggering me ... And touching me at the same time, from the
other side, and ... I'm coming ... I come so much when you
bugger me ... I can't stop coming ... Oh, please, put it right in,
say you're buggering me and put it right in ...

M: Here, take that ... in ... your ... arse ...

They both groaned together for a while, then there was silence.
Then I could hear kissing and giggling, and water running in
the bathroom.

I went to the bathroom as well. I had come over the carpet

and wall. The sperm had formed into little drops which were running down the wallpaper. I did it for that woman I hadn't even seen. Now I knew she was the one I wanted. At least I would recognize her voice when I met her ...

I went out into the corridor, feeling confident. I passed a few doors before opening one, for I didn't want to risk meeting her straight away. For the time being I was happy to hold on to her voice, for it was with it that I had made love.

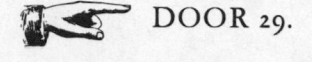 DOOR 29.

26

The Net

It was a sort of large railway station concourse, absolutely deserted and silent. As soon as I entered I heard a piercing voice call out:

'Please! Help!'

The voice resounded and echoed all the way around the walls of the hall. I raised my eyes towards the glass roof, through which the daylight fell. Right up there, just under the apex, a woman was hanging in a net hammock.

'They've tied me up!' she shouted out.

I saw that all along the walls there was a whole network of rope ladders, which went right up to the top of the ceiling, forming a gigantic spider's web, which was also reminiscent of the rigging of a sailing boat or the paraphernalia of a tightrope-walker in a big top.

Hanging above the void from this complex, unstable system of ropes, I began to climb towards the light. The exercise required the total concentration of every muscle and I didn't dare look up or down, so as not to be seized by vertigo. But the more I climbed, the more a gentle euphoria came over me, which finally took possession of me entirely and made me forget everything, except my exciting aim to get to that woman in the air who was waiting for me and to deliver her.

I reached the top of the ceiling and the sun-drenched net. The

woman was lying on her back and was skilfully bound, in a manner that seemed to be designed less to torture her than to accentuate her womanly assets. The knotted cord was wrapped around her flesh in such a way as to make it bulge and stand out.

Her breasts were fastened around their base and were separated into two distinct entities. Her hands were tied behind her back. Her thighs and her legs had been separately wound round with string, then tied together by cords around the ankles and knees. It was no longer merely her body that was desirable, but each parcelled-out piece of her body which was placed at the disposal of whoever wanted to make use of it.

'You came,' she said, full of gratitude.

I carefully climbed into the links of the hammock, which began to swing, and crouched down over her. I passed my hands under her waist to free her wrists. She thanked me, her voice full of tears of happiness. As soon as her hands were free she pulled me towards her and gave me a long kiss.

'You set me free, you are my master,' she said. 'Now tie me up. Separate my legs and tie them up in the air, wide apart. Tie my hands apart too. I wanted to be spreadeagled and tied up to receive you inside me.'

From under her behind she pulled out a black latex hood which she slipped on; it had no opening, not even round the eyes, other than a round hole where her mouth was.

The hammock swung gently, my head was spinning. I was lying on her bound-up body and I got an erection.

I sat up above her again, took off all my clothes and let them fall to the ground right down below. Then I tied her in a spreadeagled position, as she wished. During this whole operation my cock and my balls were rubbing against her, on the flesh of her thighs, her stomach or her breasts, and on the cord which girded them. The net swung wildly, but that only served to increase my excitement.

When she was well tied I lay on top of her, between her wide-

open thighs, and penetrated her. I heard her come. Only her tongue, which she sometimes stuck out, protruded from her hood. The rope irritated my skin, the net swung, the woman cried out, I arched back to push myself as deep as I could inside her bound-up body, this headless body which was nothing more than a bundle of wanton flesh to be perforated ... I ejaculated in heavy spasms.

Then I sat down next to the hood and introduced my cock into the hole, where it was immediately swallowed. My arms in the air, I hung onto the cables and, kneeling above the void, my head sucked up towards the light, I fucked the black hole.

When it was all over, she took off her hood, I undid all her ropes and we lay a while wrapped up together in the net, looking at the sky. Then we climbed down and I left her, tenderly.

At the corner of the corridor, I opened a door.

 DOOR 27.

The Questionnaire

I entered a large, warm, wainscoted library. I slowly wandered round the room, whose walls were entirely covered with books. Along the shelves, alphabetical by author, were all the great texts of world literature, ancient and modern works all mixed together, in their original language or in translation, as well as books I had never heard of, no doubt rare editions of little-known or anonymous authors, works of poetry and philosophy, erotic and esoteric writings … One section was reserved for art books, another for travel books, yet another for scientific works.

I poked around the shelves, flicked through the volumes which most excited my curiosity. I felt as if I were in the company of old friends, beings whom I mainly didn't know, but who were nonetheless close to me, because they offered an intimate relationship from the very start, because they needed me as much as I needed them, because they loved my hands and my eyes as I loved their pages and their signs, because we made a great team and shared a mad dream, because they were there to help me in my quest, to help me make my life into a quest, even if I did not know its true object. And a kind of great silent music emanated from this library and I stood in the middle of the room listening to it for a long while.

Then I sat down at the desk, on which lay a ream of paper, a

pen and this questionnaire, to which I wrote down my answers, attempting both to allow my fantasies to emerge and to gather within me everything that was profound and authentic.

Questionnaire

– Have you made love with two twin sisters?
– Have you ever spied on the woman next door with binoculars?
– Have you sodomized your fiancée at night in the middle of a wood?
– Have you paid a woman to have sex with you?
– Have you been sucked off under the table, at your office or during dinner?
– Do you remember losing your virginity?
– Have you made love on a ladder?
– Have you masturbated in an unusual way, in an unusual place or in unusual circumstances?
– Have you made love wearing yellow oilskins and a sailor's cap?
– Have you ever been madly in love?
– Have you ever written love letters? Have you received any?
– Have you ever waited for a call from your lover with your heart in your mouth?
– Have you been jealous?
– Have you ever received a telegram cancelling a date?
– Have you ever cried first thing in the morning because you were alone?
– Have you been deceived?
– Have you been unfaithful?
– Have you ever desired someone you shouldn't have?
– Have you ever experienced a great platonic love?
– Have you been abandoned?
– Have you caused suffering?
– Have you ever been drunk with happiness?

- Can you remember times when you have met your lover, after a separation, in a railway station or at an airport?
- Do you like solitude?
- Have you ever had the feeling that a love could lead you to your death?
- Have you ever really loved?
- Do you want to rediscover an old love?
- Are you fickle?
- Are you in love right now?
- Have you ever made love passionately, to the point of exhaustion?
- Would you recognize your lover's smell?
- Do you do everything you dream about with your lover?
- Do you think that anything goes?
- Do you feel responsible for someone's death?
- Do you feel you have destroyed many things?
- Have you felt your love sometimes turn into hate?
- Do you think you can stay with your lover after your death, whether she is dead or alive?
- What would you be like without love?
- Are you prepared to give everything or abandon everything for love?
- Do you like one-night stands?
- Do you believe in eternal love?
- Do you sometimes feel that you will always be in search of an absolute and impossible satisfaction?
- Do you sometimes have the feeling that you couldn't possibly be any happier or more satisfied?
- Under what conditions do you obtain your best orgasms?
- Do you use objects when you make love?
- Which?
- How?
- What is your type of woman?
- Which part of the female body do you like best?
- Do you often think about sex?

– Do you like specialist films and magazines? Do you read exciting books?

– What is your favourite fantasy?

– Do you like others to fantasize about you?

– Do you like your body?

– Do you like your sex?

– Do you like to see your sperm spurt out? Why?

– Do you want to live, love, come?

I probably stayed in this library for many days. Sometimes immersed in a book, sometimes filling in my answers on the questionnaire, sometimes searching in sleep for the rest and the dreams that would contribute to my pleasure and my quest.

When hunger caught up with me, the wolf I had become in this adventure left the wood and went out once more into the dark corridor.

It was a very long corridor, well enough lit for me to see several crossroads, a number of landings between two flights of stairs, and countless doors. As I was driven by hunger, I didn't hang around or bother to choose. In any case, whatever door I opened, it would be myself that I found behind it.

 DOOR 32.

28

The Angels

As I reached the door, I felt the hands of the shadows, my pursuers, touching me on the shoulders. This time, however, it didn't worry me. I didn't turn round, as I was certain they would eventually show themselves to me of their own accord and that the moment of our meeting was not far off. That's what they were trying to tell me when they touched me; it was also an encouragement to take the next step that presented itself.

As soon as I opened the door I was assaulted by some sugary music, rather like supermarket muzak, and by a smell of the same kind, a whiff of baking, popcorn and cut flowers with the obligatory presence of certain artificial essences.

I entered a long corridor, lined with deserted toilets. Overlaying the synthetic music was a babble of laughter, whispers and sighs. I went a bit further and reached one of the wings of a huge auditorium, entirely decorated in sky-blue velvet drapes, with a vast pit separated into tiers, a whole host of boxes, dress circles, balconies and three overhanging galleries. From the orchestra pit to the gods, massed clouds of angels fluttered round and intertwined in great confusion.

Naked and beautiful, and for the most part bisexual, these creatures' sole activity seemed to be an uninterrupted pursuit of pleasure, in chairs which were often half broken and submerged in the clouds of feathers and down which fell from their wings and filled the whole room.

Yet the enormous stage, whose curtains had obviously been ripped down a long time ago, since there were still a few dirty, discoloured red shreds hanging, and whose boards were invisible beneath a thick layer of dust, was empty.

I walked slowly up the stalls, clearing a way through the first section. From all sides, angels brushed past me as they flew hither and thither, taking no heed of my presence, carried away with their incessant babbling, perpetually smiling, eternally youthful. They all had well-proportioned bodies, slim, slightly muscular, with supple, appetizing flesh and fine, entirely smooth skin. Many of them had the attributes of both sexes, magnificent, firm, round breasts together with a penis and testicles. Some of them were exclusively female or male, others were totally sexless, with a strangely smooth strip of flesh between their legs, others were hermaphrodite.

Some of the latter had female genitals above their male genitals, while others had them the other way round: their male cluster hanging over their female slit. They coupled in what struck me as the most perfect possible way: the upper cock of the first in the upper slit of the second and the lower cock of the second in the lower slit of the first. Each was simultaneously penetrator and penetrated, each was at the same time the man and woman of the other. And I imagined that they must experience the greatest ecstasy.

The other angels also embraced incessantly and without any distinction of sex, stuck together, fluttering one to the other, from the stalls to the balcony and from the dress circle to the boxes, in total disorder, adopting every position imaginable for creatures free of the laws of gravity.

The pricks were constantly erect, the vulvas constantly swollen. The display of all these hairless genitals might easily have been obscene. But what struck me as particularly strange – for since I had entered the little circus I had noticed the place was detached from this particular obligation, unlike the outside world – was that all these sexes, including the female ones, were

covered as far as the anus with a sophisticated form of condom, a very fine film of latex wrapped so tight over the skin it was almost as one with it. All these condoms were delicately tinted, in all the colours of the rainbow, as I soon noticed. 'If these creatures need protection,' I thought, 'perhaps the world I have found behind this door is, in spite of all appearances, closer to that which we normally call the real world ...'

I noticed that, between the thick piles of feather and down, the floor was bestrewn with popcorn. I snacked on enough of this to placate my hunger, then I went to the back of the room where I found the stairs up to the upper galleries. I left all my clothes on a landing as I wanted to blend in with this mass of naked bodies, and I climbed up to the gods.

It was the same atmosphere up there as in the pit, perhaps even more confused, because of the relatively cramped spaces between the seats, and more fantastical, because of the pleasure the angels took in using the balcony rail for their unusual acrobatics.

I also had a high-up view of the stage, which stood deserted and abandoned in the middle of all this tumult and seemed even more desolate than ever. I noticed that none of the angels ever looked at it, as if they knew the sight of it would be too sad, almost unbearably so, and that it would spoil their pleasure.

I decided to imitate them and, turning my back on the stage, I mixed in among the throng and tried little by little to get involved in their games. I began by lavishing caresses on those around me, trying at first, in line with my tastes on the outside, to choose angels of the female type. But the sexes were so mixed up and there were too many of them. When I found myself kissing the buxom bosom of some creature who turned out to have a cock as big and erect as mine, I gave up trying to make these distinctions, which were entirely meaningless here.

I started touching everything that came my way and so I ended up, for the first time in my life, with a cock in my mouth, one belonging to a hermaphrodite angel who had stuck it in

without asking as it flew level with my face. Because of its condom it had a slight aniseed taste and I was happy to keep it in my mouth as I admired and caressed the nice pussy opening up beneath its balls and which was also covered by a thin film of green latex. Almost immediately, a male angel came up behind it and penetrated its female sex as I was taking care of its other sex.

'We're spoiling you, aren't we, my pretty,' I thought. 'It won't be long before you come ...' And I began to wonder how, when they had come, they managed to remove and replace their condoms, which seemed stuck to their skin. But a moment later they both withdrew to fly away elsewhere, in different directions, without having achieved orgasm.

As for me, I was very excited. I got hold of a female angel who was standing next to me and penetrated her without waiting. It had big doe eyes and was the first really to look at me, with a truly angelic, charming smile. I caressed its long, silky blond hair and told myself that, despite my desire, I would be patient and give it enough time to take its pleasure from me.

That's when I noticed what I had missed in my haste. Once again I had ended up with a hermaphrodite. The feeling of its cock pushing its way between my buttocks left no doubt on that score. I was shocked and pulled away sharply. I immediately regretted being so brusque and wanted to apologize; but it was no use, for it had already flown away to new skies, still smiling and not the slightest bit bothered.

All these adventures had left me with a keen sense of frustration. 'You're not relaxed enough,' I told myself. 'Be like the others, let yourself go, and you will experience the same bliss.'

Around me it was turning into a party. The male and hermaphrodite angels were now taking each other in a line, one behind the other. The chain was already several dozen strong and was growing by the second. Without thinking, and with a burst of energy, I penetrated the open, pink arsehole stuck out in front of me. And then another angel came up behind me, since that

was the law of the chain, and this time I went along with it. I felt the tip of its cock gently open my anus and then slide inside, finally penetrating me all the way. It started to give me a sweep, to the same rhythm as I dug into the one in front of me, the rhythm of the entire chain. The pain had given way to a strange joy, and I groaned, from both rage and pleasure, violence and submission, the desire to hurt and the desire to come.

Around us the female angels were making love with each other, or were having it done to them by the sexless angels, who were perhaps the keenest to fuck all the sexes, even if they only had their mouths and hands to do it with. Other angels, ones with cocks, left the chain to join in their games, and I promised myself I would do likewise, once I had finished with the males.

I noticed that, curiously, none of them had bothered to come before seeking new pleasures. Whereas I, since this was my first homosexual experience, intended to see it through to the end, to experience the sensation of ejaculating in the firm behind of another male while feeling my own arse being invaded and pummelled by another dick. And I didn't take long. I let out a cry, my come shot out like an arrow.

Immediately, the angel I was buggering cried out too, separated from me and collapsed to the ground in tears. At the same time, the one who was in me pulled out sharply and in an instant the chain fell completely apart. There was an air of dejection throughout the whole gallery, which gradually turned into anger and delirium. Some angels pulled out their feathers, others clawed their breasts or spun round and round. Their faces slumped before my eyes, their bodies collapsed, their splendid flesh sagged, fattened and went horribly out of shape, lines appeared at the corners of their mouths and across their cheeks and foreheads ... Then they turned towards me, tried to intimidate me by spreading their wings, which creaked and crumbled pitifully and, all together, pointed their fingers at me.

'What's going on? What have I done?' I asked, flabbergasted.

'He came!' they cried in a tearful chorus.

'I don't understand . . . Why shouldn't I have come?'

'He has blasphemed! Destroyed everything! We never come, you wretch, we have learned to forget about it! We forgot! That's why we are so beautiful! So pure! So perfect! Look what you've done to us!'

They grabbed hold of me, shook me violently, their eyes full of hate. I suddenly felt a strong sense of injustice and rebellion, and started to shout out myself:

'It's you who are wretched creatures! The sad audience of a void which you refuse to see! What are you doing in this theatre with no plays, imprisoned together, desiring each other but never able to come?'

But these words only made them more furious. Several of them even seemed to have gone mad. They covered their ears with both hands, screamed hysterically and shook their heads from left to right, as if to deny what I had done and said. Others became violent and came at me like a lynch mob. Fortunately my pleasure had caused them to lose a lot of their strength and I managed to get away.

I left the gods, collected my clothes from the landing and got dressed, and then left by the first exit I found at the foot of the stairs. I felt bruised and weak. Sad too, as if these deplorable creatures had managed to contaminate me with their taste for non-existence. I spat on the ground, to show what I thought of them.

I was in the middle of a crossroads of corridors and there was only one door available.

☛ DOOR 33.

29

The Dog

It was completely dark. I hesitated for a moment with my hand on the door, then my curiosity got the better of me and I entered.

I felt my way forward along the wall. There was a corner, leading in, then another, leading out, as if marking a change of room. Then I heard a metal grille descend and I found myself locked in a cell, behind bars.

I started calling out, without success. I made several tours of my meagre space, hoping to find a possible exit, and I shook the grille several times with all my strength, before I finally curled up on the ground and tried to sleep in order to banish my anxiety, caused by a feeling that time had been halted by my incarceration, by the silence and the dark.

In the end I got to sleep, but I was brutally woken up by kick to my thigh. A harsh light was shining on me. I screwed up my eyes and saw, under the raised grille, a woman dressed in thigh-length boots and PVC underwear, who was holding a lead that was attached to a dog collar round my neck.

'Come out of your hole, you filthy beast,' she said.

And she gave a violent tug on the chain. I was about to get up when I received another kick from the pointed toe of her boot.

'On all fours!' she ordered, in a tone which brooked no discussion.

116

I obeyed her. As I walked behind her I raised my eyes from her stiletto heels to her little bottom, which was barely covered by her very narrow pants and which minced nicely. She was slim and well built and very sexy in her tight, shiny synthetic-leather undies. Her corset, laced at the back, accentuated the curve of her hips.

I followed my mistress into the sitting-room. In one corner of the room a fat man in a silk dressing gown was lounging on the sofa and smoking a cigar.

'This filthy beast has been naughty again,' said the fat man, looking at me in an evil way. 'If this carries on we will have to tan his hide.'

'Don't worry, I'll put him in his place,' said the woman.

She led me to the kitchen. My knees were beginning to hurt. She put a big pile of mince in a bowl, went back to the lounge and placed it at the foot of the sofa.

'Eat,' she said.

And without letting go of my lead, she sat down next to the fat man, opened his dressing gown and started to wank him. I tentatively placed a hand on her thigh, hoping to be given permission to join in their games, but I received a kick in the ribs.

'You fat pig!' the woman shouted. 'Are you going to eat your meat?'

I bent over the bowl, took three small mouthfuls and swallowed them with some difficulty.

'That's better, good dog,' said my mistress, stroking the back of my neck. 'In return, you can lick me,' she added, offering me her foot.

I began to run my tongue from the pointed toe to the high heel. The fat man watched me, his eyes alight with lechery. The woman had just gone down on his little dick, which began to stiffen, and she started to suck it.

I continued to lick her boots assiduously. When I saw that they were both too wrapped up in their fornication to notice

me, I undid my trousers and, while she was busy with her sucking, I rubbed myself off against her leg, like a real dog would do.

I came more quickly than the fat man. They hadn't noticed a thing. I slipped out of my collar and went discretely to the door, glancing back at my semen running down the vinyl boots. I felt like laughing.

I did up my flies in the corridor and opened the following door.

 DOOR 30.

30

Jane and the Marsupilami

Everything was green. Everything except the turquoise stream and the red wood of the palm-roofed huts in the clearing. It was virgin forest, impenetrable, filled with the calls of humming birds and cockatoos.

I left the edge of the forest and headed towards the huts, which stood at the side of a path.

There were no more than a dozen of them, and there was no one to be seen, but there must be civilization here because two of them had signs over the door: the sign on the longer one said BAR, and on the shorter one, whose roof was equipped with a load of sophisticated antennae, the sign said BANK. They seemed to be in good nick, not abandoned.

I carried on as far as the stream, which I could see sparkling through the leaves, and I discovered that it was bordered on both banks by walls of stones, carefully placed on top of each other, about fifty centimetres high. I sat on top of the little wall and watched the shimmering stream. Then I saw a monstrous head rise up out of the water, which snorted noisily then began to emit guttural cries.

I leapt to my feet. But it was just a man, a local, his face half covered by an old diving mask, and he was celebrating. He came out of the water, his arms raised in victory, laughing and dancing comically on his frail legs which emerged from his

soaking, over-large shorts. The tanned skin of his chest was marked diagonally, from the left collar bone to the sternum, by the scar of what seemed to be a knife wound.

He came towards me, still hopping and delirious with joy, and opened his hands in front of my face. I recoiled a little, for the nearness of what he was holding made my eyes light up. In each palm he held a large, shiny nugget of gold.

'Gold, mate!' he said. 'Gold.'

And taking off his mask he pointed to the stone walls.

'See all that? I pulled all that out of the stream to see more clearly. Nice work, eh?'

He looked proudly at his work, thousands of stones patiently collected and piled up.

'Now there's nothing left but nuggets. I need only dive down and help myself. Here, mate!'

And he shoved a nugget into my hand.

'Take it! Take it! I'm giving it to you!'

He was delighted to see the surprise and incredulity on my face, delighted by his own generosity. His small hazel eyes shone.

'Hee-hee! Come on, the drinks are on me.'

He dragged me off to the bar. On the way I looked at the nugget. It was shaped like two buttocks, or a heart, depending on which way you looked at it. I wondered whether to keep it or sell it. It depended on how much it was worth. These days it's probably better to find a bank card than a gold nugget. I put it in my pocket.

The bar was dark and made entirely of wood; it looked like a saloon. As we came in the four drunkards leaning on the bar slowly turned their heads, as one man, towards us, without blinking; their bodies stayed totally still and relaxed. There was a sly-looking old man, a tall beanpole with a stupid smile and two ruddy-faced types, of average height but solidly built, who must have been in their early thirties and looked like brothers.

'The drinks are on me,' my goldminer repeated for the benefit

of the barman, a tall chap with a handlebar moustache, who lined up six glasses of beer on the bar.

After this, everyone bought a round. In the ceiling a large fan stirred up the oppressive air as they recounted their latest goldmining adventures, or trotted out their old stories, which they all knew, and which were all about discovering ever more extraordinary seams and making and losing fortunes in a matter of days.

My 'friend' led them to believe that I had found a nugget right under his nose, just like that, by bending down, and he invited me to show it off to them, making out that he had never met anyone as lucky as me, and he seemed to derive some mysterious kudos from all this. The others looked at my treasure and shook their heads, clearly impressed. Since I had become some sort of hero, I offered to buy another round.

I must have knocked back a few pints, but it was just as hot. The conversation became more and more meandering and my shirt was sticking to my skin. I asked where the toilets were. I was shown a corridor at the end of the room.

There was no light other than the vague glimmer of the sign marking the toilets at the end of the corridor. I went towards it, staggering a little because of the beer. When I tried to lean against the wall to guide myself, I found that, on both sides, my hands touched against bars.

At the same time I realized there was something alive behind these bars, for I could hear sounds of rubbing and breathing. My first thought was that I was in a narrow alleyway in a circus menagerie, between cages of monkeys and other wild animals. But my head was too befuddled to ponder this any further and my most urgent preoccupation was with finding the toilets, where I could throw up and piss out all the excess liquid that was swilling round my body like a choppy sea.

As I returned to the bar, I heard myself being called to on all sides, from the cages. The voices were whispering, but were unlike those of the shadows in the corridors, who always called

me by my name, whereas these used the language of prostitutes:
'Looking for business, darling?' and other such things. Although
I was still drunk, I got the message: in this village consisting
solely of a few huts belonging to goldminers with primitive
methods, there was nonetheless a bank, a small one, but still
connected by modern systems of communications to the banking
establishments and stock markets of the world, a bar with
a plentiful supply of beer and other alcoholic drinks, and a
brothel.

I leant against the bars of one cage to see if I could make
anything out inside and the door opened of its own accord. At
the back of the room, to the right, I saw a bed, on which lay the
voluptuous form of a naked young woman with her back
towards me.

'Come, oh, please, come quickly,' she whispered over and
over again, her voice burning with desire.

I took off my clothes, dropped them on the ground and went
to lie down next to her on the bed. She still lay obstinately with
her back to me, but she had such ample hips and such a splendid
bum that far from complaining about her position I grabbed her
by the hips and stuck my cock between her buttocks. She slid it
out and pushed it into her cunt, for she was so excited it seemed
she was smeared with lubricant between her legs. She said not a
word throughout.

She had soft skin, a supple body, she was amazingly docile
and her vagina was so elastic it sucked and squeezed your dick
with the combined talents of an expert mouth and hands. It took
me a long time, because of the alcohol, and I felt the pleasure
slowly rising within me and came in the girl's belly. I went
straight to sleep, holding her in my arms and still inside her.

I didn't realize until I woke up: I had fucked an inflatable
doll, her lascivious invitations had come from a tape recorder on
the bedside table. Now that my eyes were used to the dark I
turned it over and looked at it from all angles. She was bloody
shapely, she had a nice pair of pointed breasts and a pretty face,

with large eyes that seemed to be imploring you for something, and juicy lips opened just wide enough to take you in.

'So you lied to me, you dirty little whore,' I said.

And to punish her I stood above her, my legs apart, and pissed on her face. Then I grabbed her by the hair and stuck my dick in her mouth.

'So, bitch, what do you say to that?'

She didn't say a thing, but it felt as if she had a vacuum-cleaner nozzle between her lips. I held her by the hair and pulled her head backwards and forwards, her large eyes looked more and more surprised, and she sucked my gland like some highly efficient orgasm machine, while I took advantage of the situation to shower her with insults and obscenities. All this filth, which was my revenge for the treachery I had suffered, went to my head. I started to grip her throat between my hands, pressing with all my strength with my thumbs and, at the moment the latex exploded under the pressure, I ejaculated.

I crawled around the cage on all fours, looking for my clothes. But they had vanished. I found nothing except a sort of loincloth in imitation leopardskin, a ridiculous-looking thing which I put on anyway, for want of something better.

Apparently the bar was closed. There was no one about and the door was locked from the inside. I was almost relieved, for I wasn't keen to be seen in this garb. I looked outside through the window. No one there either. Apart from the little old man squatting on the ground in the shade. Perfect. I opened the door and went towards him.

As soon as he saw me he guffawed and slapped his thigh, then, pointing at me, started laughing like an idiot, punctuating it with high-pitched hiccups. I would have liked to punch his face to shut him up but he looked too frail.

'Where are my clothes?' I asked him in a sufficiently threatening tone of voice to make him reply.

Between hiccups he pointed to the top of a tree. As I approached the enormous trunk I saw that my clothes had been

placed on a large branch, neatly folded with my shoes on top. Luckily there was a solid-looking creeper hanging from this branch.

I started climbing, as if on a climbing rope. The branch was several metres above the ground. Each time I stretched to pull myself up, my sex, which was dangling free below the end of the cloth that was supposed to protect my modesty, rubbed gently against the vine. When I reached the top I had a hard-on and I was almost sorry the climb was over.

There was something strange about this tree. It was in fact a false tree, a prop tree. The wood, the bark, the leaves, the creepers were all imitation. I raised my eyes to the other trees in the jungle to see whether they were as false as mine. That's when I saw, sitting comfortably in the branches of a neighbouring tree, a superb creature of flesh and blood, a quite beautiful woman dressed only in a loincloth like mine. And indeed it was my loincloth she was staring at, licking her lips.

I too lowered my eyes to the object of her curiosity and greed and I saw that my cock, still erect because of the creeper and now even more so because of the sight of this naked pin-up, had lifted the edge of the cloth and its tip was sticking out.

I looked back at the girl, who was still interested in my manhood, so interested in fact that she started to fondle her breasts, then moved her hands over her stomach, her thighs, and then finally opened her legs wide, lifted her loincloth and caressed herself ardently, still staring at my cock, which was stiffer than ever.

I grabbed hold of a creeper and this time used it to swing across to her, without taking my eyes off her. The sight of her there, panting, her head back in the leaves, together with the contact of the creeper, almost made me come in mid-air. But I managed to contain myself and reached her at the very moment she achieved orgasm. As she was coming, I stuck my cock against her stomach, which made it stand up even more. Then I

penetrated her immediately, placing her magnificent legs around my neck.

My child of the wild had platinum-blonde hair, immaculately plaited and lacquered, eyes made up to seem slightly bigger, painted lips, entirely hairless legs, armpits and sex, twenty polished nails and skin imbued with some luxurious perfume. The white bikini marks showed the very narrow portions of her body which modesty prevented her from revealing on the beach. She started arching back again and crying out, and I forced myself to make the whole thing last as long as possible, for the show she put on as she took her pleasure was so intense that you wanted to see it start again straight away.

After a while I thought I'd seen enough of the front view and I turned her round and took her doggy fashion, from the flip side. She hung onto the branches and jerked her hips furiously, mewling and moaning, shaking her mane of hair every which way. It was all too much for me.

I was about to come with her when a hairy monster, yellow with black spots, seemed to fall from the sky and ripped her away from me. Before I knew what was going on she had grabbed hold of him with a cry of joy and, with a few leaps, he had carried her away to the top of the neighbouring tree.

I found myself alone in less time than it takes to say it, my sex erect in mid-air and sorely abandoned. Over yonder, my Jane was trembling with joy and playing with the tail of the Marsupilami, for indeed it was he (I had recognized his victory cry, that distinctive 'houba, houba' with which he taunted me). It seemed I was out of the running. With his tail he could satisfy her in all sorts of unbeatable ways, like, for example, tying her up and penetrating her at the same time. And she had an even better orgasm.

So I made do with playing the voyeur. I ended up sitting astride a branch watching them. My sperm spurted out like a fountain and fell from branch to branch, from leaf to leaf, to the ground, where it would fertilize the earth. I went back to my

branch, lost the loincloth, put my clothes on and climbed back down the creeper. When I reached the bottom I remembered to look for the nugget in my pocket. It was still there. And how beautiful it was! I turned it over lovingly between my fingers. I looked across to the huts and, through the foliage, tried to make out the banks of the stream. I should go and bid farewell to the man who had shown me such generosity, even if I hadn't the slightest desire to see the others.

I was walking towards the river with my hands in my pockets and the nugget in the hollow of my hand, when I felt the nugget soften and go out of shape in the warmth of my palm. I could barely bring myself to look at it. When I opened my hand it was smeared with brown stains, by a dark-brown paste seeping out through the tears in the gold paper.

I threw the chocolate nugget to the ground, in the synthetic grass, licked my palm clean and returned to the place where I had come in, the door at the back of the scenery which returned me to the dark corridors, where two doors offered themselves to me.

☞ DOOR 28,

☞ DOOR 31.

31

The Player

'Hurry, hurry, Miss Mariella is waiting for you!'

The man dragged me through the changing rooms to the treatment room. Lying on the massage table, a tennis player in a white skirt welcomed me with a smile.

'You're Paul's replacement?' she said as she held out her hand. 'I presume he's explained it to you. He always massages my calves and thighs before I go out on court.'

'Of course,' I said, returning her smile.

She had magnificent legs, long, lean and muscular, and if she took me for the replacement for her physio, then I had to play the role and not disappoint her. If I tried hard enough I'd soon find a suitable way to warm up her precious muscles.

Miss Mariella closed her eyes and waited for me to set to work. I approached the table. In that position she looked like some delicacy laid out for my delectation. I grabbed her left leg, pulled it away from her right. Her skin was elastic, smooth and tanned. I bent her knee and started to massage her calf, running my fingers the whole length of her firm, supple flesh.

A half-smile of relaxation spread across her face. She was so feminine and ravishing, with her fine, chestnut hair pulled back and gathered in a coloured tie, a few short curls hanging loose, with her oval face, her high cheekbones, her little nose, her discreet make-up, her air of determination mixed with an impression of freshness and gaiety.

I moved up to her fine, round knee. Under her white top her plump little breasts rose gently with each breath. At the hem of her pleated skirt I could see where her knickers fastened between her legs with three press studs. I spent a long time massaging her thighs, moving as far up as my role permitted. I had an erection.

Then she got up and told me to keep an eye on her during the match, in case she needed my services. I crossed my fingers to wish her good luck and went out into the stand as she emerged on court.

The crowd raised the roof as she stepped out. Her opponent was there too, a tall blonde, severe-looking, slim and well-built. Throughout the whole match she played a stream of hard strokes to the back of the court, while Mariella, lively and mobile, continually came up to the net and covered the whole clay court as if she were performing figures in a ballet, as if she were fulfilling the rites of some cosmic ceremony which consisted of glorifying every inch of a demarcated space.

I was sitting in the front row. When she was playing at the far end, I could see the killer look in Mariella's eyes when she served, a look designed to weaken the unwavering psychological strength and the solid physical and technical qualities of her opponent. And when she was at this end I could better admire the play of her legs and her knickers.

Her knickers, which she revealed completely when she was waiting for her opponent to serve, bouncing on the spot and swinging her racquet from left to right, or every time that her skirt flew up when she raised her arms and threw her body forward to make a serve or a smash.

Twice, during breaks, she called me over to give her right thigh a quick massage, where she had felt a slight tightening of the muscle. But the match was very close and I felt that she didn't even see me, didn't see anything of the outside world, so focussed was she in herself. Finally she won the match in three sets, 7–6, 6–7, 8–6.

She greeted her victory with a raised fist. All the time she was out on court she was radiant, as if filled by the applause raining down on her. But as soon as she returned to the dressing room I could see that she was extremely serious and, far from being relieved after the tension of the match, she seemed even more wrapped up in herself and her anxiety.

She dragged me into the treatment room. She opened a metal locker and, standing on tiptoe to reach the top shelf, took out a riding crop, which she handed to me. Then she crouched down on the massage table, undid the studs on her knickers, pulled the two halves up over her waist, and, offering me her gorgeous, naked bottom, which was whiter than her tanned thighs, she said: 'Let's go.'

I mumbled something, incredulous, unable to believe what she wanted me to do. She turned towards me with a blank expression and repeated: 'Let's go.'

Her plump little bottom was sticking out in front of me. It was as if it were looking at me. I raised the crop and whipped it gently.

When the lash touched her flesh she gave a jerk. The blow left a light mark on her skin, which started to turn pink. I hesitated a moment. But she arched her back even more to incite me to continue. I struck her again, several times in a row.

I continued cautiously, so as not to hurt her too much. Her buttocks were now covered in bright red stripes, but she still wanted more. Her backside jerked under each blow, but otherwise she didn't flinch.

However, she finally let out a moan of pain. Then, I don't know why, I had a taste of blood in my mouth, and I started wielding the crop with all my strength. The lash descended, she gave a cry, a trace of red appeared on her buttocks.

I was breathing hard, it was hypnotic. I raised my arm again and hit her again and again and again, getting more and more excited as she moaned and cried at the violence of the blows, as the shiny red tears seeped through each break in her skin.

Finally I got onto the table with her and, kneeling behind her, with my trousers down, I roughly penetrated her bruised arse and fucked her. She screamed, twisted, choked hysterically and I had to hold her by the hair as I thrust my hips into her. Then she started sobbing. I came as I had beaten her, with a sort of savagery.

'Thank you,' she said as she got up.

She wiped away her tears, much calmer now, and passed a white towel over her bottom, which became stained with red. I was beginning to regret what had happened, all the more as I hadn't seen her achieve her pleasure.

'But you didn't come,' I said.

'That's not what I look for in pain,' she replied. 'Pain doesn't give me any pleasure.'

'Then why . . . ?'

'Because I need this pain to distract me from another sort of pain, much more terrifying – I don't know what to call it or where it comes from, but when it appears, it threatens to become unbearable. In a way, I choose to suffer so as not to die of a greater suffering.'

'This unbearable pain, why not try to forget it through pleasure instead?'

'I love pleasure too much to spoil it in this way. I take my pleasure when I feel good. That's when it's best . . .'

As I left the room she gave me a little farewell wave and said:

'Do you think we might understand something about life one day?'

And she headed off into the showers.

So as not to follow her I washed myself in the sink and wondered whether I had really lost control or whether this feeling of being out of control wasn't just a trick invented by my mind to free me of the weight of what I had done.

I went back out into the dark corridors, where I wandered for a long time before I opened a door.

☞ DOOR 33.

32

The Collection

I found myself in a lift. I would probably have stepped straight out if it hadn't been occupied by a young girl who greeted me with a smile. She pressed a button and we started to go up.

We were standing in opposite corners, facing each other. She was simply dressed in jeans, boots and a jacket. She had a large photographer's portfolio at her feet and was carrying a square 6 × 6 camera round her neck. She was checking me over from head to foot with a frank, direct gaze.

'Do you want me to turn round?' I joked.

'I want to show you something,' she said.

She bent down, took a file out of her portfolio and came over to me. The file contained a collection of pornographic photos, bodies and sexes of men and women, couples in action.

'Did you take these?' I asked.

'I have several clients ... Collectors ... They pay well.'

'Good for you.'

'Would you like to pose for me?'

'For a rich female collector?'

'Yes. Here in the lift will be fine. Open your shirt, drop your trousers, that's all ... Thanks, that's great. Oh! I'm sure they will adore ...'

She measured the light down between my legs and took a first series of snaps in close-up. She made me strike different poses and encouraged me:

'Very good ... Yes, like that ... Very nice ...'

Then she knelt at my feet and started to suck me. I thought the shoot had turned her on, but I realized she only wanted me to get an erection for the rest of her reportage. As soon as I was stiff, she started shooting off film.

She photographed me from every angle, with my dick erect, then she asked me to pretend to be wanking. Finally she had the good grace to finish sucking me off. But my contribution was not yet at an end. When she felt that I was on the point of coming, she placed my cock back in my hand and picked up her camera. I ejaculated right onto her lens.

When I left her she blew me a little kiss. The doors closed and the lift whisked her away.

I walked in the corridor for a while, trying to imagine what effect my photos would have on the rich collectors who would buy them. What would they do with them exactly? I hoped there was at least one pretty woman among these sluts ... A pretty woman who would dream about me as I was dreaming about her ...

Then I stopped thinking about it and opened a door.

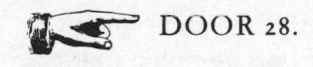 DOOR 28.

33

The Exchange

I entered a rustic house, a barn made of roughly hewn stones cemented with earth. In a corner of the large single room a log was burning slowly in the fireplace. Opposite, there was a pile of wood stacked against the rough white wall, the only wall where the stone had been covered and along which there were several shelves of books.

The room was a mixture of roughness and comfort, with a concrete floor tinted pink, a colourful carpet whose white background showed the dust, a sofa in black fabric with a small white motif, two rattan chairs painted white, two armchairs in blue fabric and, in the kitchen, all the latest electrical goods, a large trestle table and two rough wood benches.

Three Chinese lampshades in red paper, which hung down between the beams of the low roof, made the place look a bit like a gambling den, while the bathroom door, which still hadn't been painted and had no latch, contributed to the unfinished feel of the whole thing. In the centre of the room a large square opening in the ceiling revealed the loft, which was reached by a ladder. There was a wooden rail running around this hole and I was expecting to see a brace of girls in petticoats leaning over it, smiling at me. I placed myself in the centre, right beneath them, perfectly placed to make my choice. But no one came.

I stood in front of a large mirror with a dark red frame and

checked how I looked, as if I were waiting for an important meeting, and then I climbed up.

The loft was divided into three levels, which marked out three small bedrooms or sleeping quarters. One of these was separated from the others by various bits of cloth hanging from the beams. I pulled them apart and went inside the end room.

It was almost entirely taken up by a large bed with metal posts facing a French window which framed a magnificent, luminous mountain landscape, entirely white with snow. In the bed a woman reclined on a couple of large pillows. She had a cardboard folder resting on her lap, on which lay a white sheet of paper which she was covering with blue ink.

'Hello,' she said. Indicating the bed, she continued, 'Please sit down. If you just give me a couple of minutes ... I just have to finish a little description then I'm all yours ...'

And she continued writing.

Behind the bed two sets of shelves full of books formed a sort of partition on each side of the two red curtains which marked the entrance to the room. It was the same theatrical dark red as the frame of the large mirror on the ground floor, and it appeared here also on another large oval mirror and on the bed spread. Leaning against the lowest part of the roof there was also a board on which were pinned a number of postcards and photos, among which I recognized pictures of Kafka, Poe, Céline in his garden, Rimbaud, Verlaine sitting in a bistro in front of a glass of absinthe, Baudelaire, Tolstoy with his beggar's stick ... And a reproduction of *Philosophy Meditating* by Rembrandt, another of an engraving representing a ruined Roman church in a landscape of sand and pines ... And photos ... A small boy reading on a beach, his chin resting on his knee, a plump, naked baby sitting in a chair sucking its thumb, a young woman in shorts sleeping on a park bench – the same woman who was lying on the bed writing – a young man in a hat and dark glasses lying full-length on a road, the same man reading

on a hotel bed with a full moon shining in the night sky through the window ...

I turned to look at the mountain.

'Do you see that summit over there with the tall aerial? It's the Pic du Midi,' she said, without stopping writing. 'That's where they take the best photos of the sun's corona. And at night they observe the sky ... It's beautiful, isn't it?'

She seemed to be lost in wonder. I agreed politely, wondering what she was driving at. She didn't say any more. I reached out my hand to touch her leg through the covers. But she pulled it away, apparently amused by this. She was still absorbed in her writing.

'Haven't you finished your description yet?' I said, slightly annoyed.

'Yes, just done. Now we'll be able to talk.'

But she carried on writing. I leaned over her piece of paper and I saw that she had just noted down the exact question I had just asked her and the reply she had given. And at this precise moment she was recounting that I was reading her piece of paper.

'What do you think you're doing?' I asked.

This time she looked me in the eye, still scribbling away. Her eyes were dark, shiny and wide open, making her look almost stupid or as if she were hallucinating.

'I'll explain,' she said. 'Let's not be formal. It is I who am writing your adventures.'

'You're a reporter?'

'Not exactly. To be a reporter I'd have to follow you ...'

'Ah, I get it. You're the one who's been following me in the corridors?'

'No, not me. I stay here, in my bed. To tell you the truth, I invented all this, the kingdom of Eros, the doors, the shadows who follow you in the corridors, the adventures, the characters, the Woman ... and you, of course.'

'I see. If I understand you correctly, I only exist in your imagination.'

'Of course not, not solely. Here, touch yourself. You see you are made of flesh and blood. Particularly flesh – I hope you have had plenty of opportunity to verify that since you have been in here ...'

'How can I be in your head and in my body at the same time?'

'I don't know. I am in your head, too, and still in my own body. You see, at this precise moment you are inventing me as much as I am inventing you ...'

I was silent for a moment, then I continued:

'If everything is written ... that means I am not the master of my own actions nor of my own destiny ...'

'Nothing is written in advance. Everything is written as we experience it. It is simply a matter of how we perceive time. Do we ever know where the present is? In the past, in the future, it is everywhere and nowhere ...'

'Perhaps ... All that's very well, but there's one thing I don't agree with. You see everything I do, you even see me in the most private situations, but I can't see anything of you. So why don't we talk about you for a bit? For example, to turn things round a bit, what turns you on?'

'You're being really unfair. Or you're blind. I'm constantly exposing myself. You see as much of me as I see of you: all these corridors you walk down are in my mind, all these doors you open are inside me. You see, we have millions of doors in there,' she continued, tapping her head. 'There are people who, their whole life long, open only a few of these doors, while you and I transform this labyrinth into the most thrilling area of adventure and exploration. Each time you open a door, you open it both in my head and in yours. So you know as much about me as I know about you ...'

'Ye-c-cs ... But all the same, you make me do what you want, yet it doesn't work the other way round.'

'Do you believe that? You should have heard me when I had enough of your erotic frenzy. I admit that on those occasions I

slagged you off in the most inelegant terms. Sometimes I had it up to here with your insatiable sexual appetites. But I carried out my task ... For you ...'

'I can see now why you made me do some bizarre things ... And now, may I know what is going to happen to me? Will I find the Woman?'

'That all depends on you. On the way you deal with the final tests. But first the time has come to meet the shadows.'

'And ... what about you and me?' I added knowingly, leaning towards her.

'You and I are everything. That's enough, isn't it?'

She got up, climbed down the ladder, opened the door of the barn and went out into the corridor with me.

This time they were there. Two motionless silhouettes in the dark, one wrapped in a dark red cloth, the other in a black cloth. My heart started pounding against my chest.

'Meet the Shadow of Lost Love,' my companion said.

The red shadow came towards me, took me by the hand and said in a warm, affecting voice: 'Come.'

'And here is the Shadow of Yourself.'

The black shadow advanced, took my other hand and said in a serious, penetrating voice: 'Come.'

At the end of the corridor an illuminated sign indicated the exit. I realized I had reached the end of my journey. There were only two doors left, but I could just as easily give them a miss.

I turned to my companion, who was leaving me already.

'And the Woman?' I asked.

'Outside,' she said. 'You will find her outside.'

Terror and desire were battling it out in my veins. Now, no doubt, I was not far away from the great moment. Everything would depend on the choice I would make between:

– following the Shadow of Lost Love:

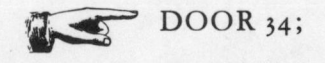 DOOR 34;

– following the Shadow of Myself:

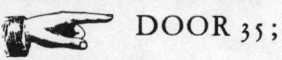 DOOR 35;

– not following either of them:

 DOOR 36.

34

The Shadow of Lost Love

'Who are you?' I asked the Shadow of Lost Love.

In the dark I could only make out the dark red shape and the white glimmer of her long hair. She lowered her head and her face was hidden in the darkness.

'Come, please . . .' she moaned.

Suddenly I recalled a memory from my childhood. Our dog had disappeared. Despite searching all over we didn't find her until a week later. She had been discovered by a hunter at the bottom of a dry well in the forest. When we returned to the spot with him, bringing ropes to get her out, we heard a soft whining. That timid lament expressed all her exhaustion, but also her love and faithfulness. Lying at the edge of the hole, the child that I was hid his face in his hands and started crying with the dog, out of compassion and fear of emptiness.

And now it was as if the Shadow of Lost Love had fallen down a well and was waiting for me to save her.

She ushered me through a padded door into a small, circular pink room. The bed, which was also round, stood in the centre of the room. It was the only piece of furniture, but it still almost filled this confined space. The vaulted ceiling cast a weak, opalescent light over everything.

The Shadow had turned her back and moved ahead of me. Her strange, magnificent white hair fell down to her waist,

making a striking contrast with the scarlet cloth wrapped around her like an ancient tunic.

'You see how my hair has turned white since I've been waiting for you, my love?' she said. 'But you are here at last and once again, and more than ever, we will be united in the most burning passion ... See, I am yours.'

She moved her right hand over her left shoulder, the cloth fell, she was naked.

She was so beautiful she made me breathless. She was like a statue. Venus rising from the waves, seen from behind. I approached her and placed my hands on her hips, which seemed to have been sculpted by a god.

'You are beautiful,' I said.

Was it her beauty that so moved me? Or did she seem so beautiful because of the emotion which emanated from her? When I asked her to turn to face me, she refused.

'You mustn't see me,' she said.

'But why?'

'I don't want you to see me. I beg you ...'

I was taken aback.

'Get undressed,' she whispered.

'Look, this is stupid.'

'Please ...'

I took off my clothes. Then I picked up my shirt, ripped a strip off it and tied it round my eyes.

'I can't see you any more,' I said, placing my hand gently on her shoulder.

She turned round and gave me a long kiss on my mouth, pressing her body against mine.

I pulled her onto the bed, which was just behind us. We continued to exchange kisses and caresses. I felt feverish and clumsy, no doubt because of the emotion which had taken hold of me since I had followed this woman and because she had forbidden me to look at her. Even though her body was superb to touch, I couldn't get an erection.

She moved down my body and took my sex in her mouth. But, despite all her efforts, nothing happened. I felt more and more uncomfortable. To take her mind off my discomfiture and to gain a little time I moved down between her legs and kept my face pressed in there for as long as possible. She held me by the neck, raised her hips, doing her best to achieve her pleasure. But it soon became obvious it wasn't working for her either.

Suddenly I could no longer tolerate this blindfold over my eyes. I ripped it off angrily. And I saw her.

Naked, lying on her back in the middle of the round bed, her alabaster body was as I had touched it, perfectly proportioned. Her long hair lay loose around her face and shoulders like a soft halo of light. She had the features of a madonna, overwhelming in their grace and humility. Her lips were tender and pink, like the nipples of her small, round breasts. Her waist curved harmoniously, her stomach was firm, her navel fresh and pretty as a heart, her silky mound as white and fascinating as her hair, her thighs plump, her calves smooth, her feet slender, her ankles fine, her hands delicate, her arms soft and gentle, her shoulders voluptuous, her neck elegant, her earlobes subtly outlined and joined directly onto her delicious face ... everything about this woman was ravishing, everything was perfect. Except her eyes. Her glassy, turned-up eyes had no life in them.

I probably observed her for quite a while, motionless, kneeling before her body. Suddenly she realized what was going on. She sat up straight and felt for my face. I didn't hide away. When she verified that I had taken off my blindfold, she lay down on her stomach and started crying, her head on her arms.

'Don't cry ... Please don't cry ...' I said, caressing her slowly.

She was more beautiful than ever. I felt a surge of desire. My cock was so erect it almost hurt me. But I wanted to be nice to her. I gently coaxed her to turn over. Tears flowed copiously from her white globes and soaked her cheeks, her hair, her

throat, right down to her bosom. I finally got her onto her back and penetrated her.

She let out a deep sigh and then continued crying her eyes out, with moans both of pleasure and pain. I leant over her to kiss her wet lips, her wet neck, her wet breasts, then I looked at my cock, which she couldn't see, moving all the way in and out between her thighs, which I held wide open; and again tasted the salty liquid coming out of her turned-up eyes like a slow, plaintive, delicious orgasm and I asked her not to cry, even though her tears were bringing me to the pitch of excitement.

At the last moment I pulled out of her to ejaculate over her blind, already damp face. The sperm came out in large spurts and formed into heavy blobs at the sides of her mouth, on her cheeks and at the corners of her white eyes.

I tenderly wiped her face with the strip I had torn from my shirt.

'Oh, my love,' she said, 'I don't ever want to be separated from you again.'

'Me neither,' I said, taking her in my arms.

She was the woman I had always loved.

'Will you leave me?' she whispered.

'Why do you say that? I love you, I want to stay with you.'

'But I can't leave here. They won't let me leave, I know they won't.'

'Don't worry. I'm here. I'll take you with me. Trust me.'

'Oh, if only we had never left each other ... Do you see what the sorrow has done to me? My hair has turned white, I've lost my sight ...'

'But you are even more beautiful ... And I too have been unhappy ... So unhappy ...'

I held her more tightly in my arms and started crying softly, like her.

I couldn't say how, but these tears flowing out liberated me. I penetrated her again and we made love, embracing tightly. At

the moment when I came I felt as if my sex was joining our tears, crowning and exalting their sweet sharpness.

She rested her head on my shoulder and went to sleep. I lay there pensive, staring at the walls and the vaulted ceiling. It seemed as if the room had closed in on the bed. The room was becoming smaller and smaller, more and more oppressive; my mind became confused; sometimes I recalled a specific memory of my former lovemaking with this woman lying at my side; other times I had a strong feeling of deceit and unreality.

'My love,' I whispered, 'I will never leave you again, never . . .'

Yes, that's probably what I wanted. Wasn't this an extraordinary opportunity to kiss and to love forever my Lost Love, the love most people regret their whole life long?

I got up, taking care not to wake her, and went out into the corridor.

Then I saw coming towards me, still dressed in black, the Shadow of Myself. The door of her room was still open behind her and I could see her bed, in the shape of a boat.

'Here,' she said, offering me a pebble. 'Keep this with you.'

I bent over to see it. It was a beautiful polished stone. I put it in my pocket.

Now it was time for me to leave. But a nagging anxiety prevented me from leaving alone. The feeling that there was no going back pierced me in the chest, and I tried to banish it by giving myself a choice. Confronted by the final exit, whose green light I could see not far ahead, at the end of the corridor, I convinced myself that I was still free, since I could still:

– go back and find the Shadow of Lost Love and bring her with me as I had promised her:

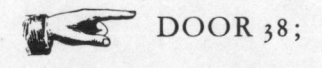 DOOR 38;

– or take the hand of the Shadow of Myself, to whom I felt irresistibly attracted, and take her with me to the exit:

 DOOR 39.

35

The Shadow of Myself

'I am so happy to meet you,' said the Shadow of Myself.

'Delighted,' I replied, somewhat gauchely.

And I gripped her hand, which was already holding mine. I thought a smile spread across her face, which I could only just make out in the dark. I thought she was probably amused by my awkwardness. This woman intimidated me, but I felt a pressing need to get to know her. I felt sure that we could do great things together and that's what made me so nervous.

'Would you like a drink?' she asked. 'We'll be more comfortable in my place than out here in this dark corridor ...'

I followed her and she led me into a large, square-shaped room, covered from floor to ceiling in an ancient mosaic with extraordinarily rich and exquisite colours.

There were a few black cupboards standing against the walls. Near one corner of the room a round table, surrounded by chairs, was laden with bottles of alcohol and food. There was also a large bed in the shape of a boat, covered on the inside with a kaleidoscope of thousands of tiny mirrors.

I turned to the shadow, anxious to see her face. She was just taking off her cape to reveal herself fully; she was naked. She was a very attractive woman, mature but still slender, not skinny, with small but firm breasts, a well-defined waist, nicely

chiselled legs, full buttocks and thighs which accentuated her femininity.

She was wearing nothing but black boots of shiny leather with high, rounded heels, tightly laced to halfway up her shins. And, in her Egyptian-style black hair, a large crown of diamonds. Her big, dark, shining eyes were elongated over her temples by very pronounced make-up, her mouth was painted blood-red, as were the very long nails on her slim fingers. She carried herself like a queen, she was magnificent. And despite her striking, theatrical appearance, her face displayed a childish gaiety and an extremely sharp intelligence.

'Let me see you,' she said.

And she started to undress me.

'You are handsome,' she continued, when I was naked.

I returned the compliment, took her face in my hands and kissed her. Her body throbbed against mine, warm and sensual. She was very excited. She rubbed her sex against mine and this contact alone seemed to bring her close to orgasm.

'Do you know I watch you every night?' she whispered in my ear. 'When you are lying naked in bed I lean over you, I give you erotic dreams and then I slip under the sheets to caress you and suck you ...'

I lifted her up, she put her hands around my neck, her legs around my hips and I impaled her standing up. She let out a deep sigh of satisfaction and started babbling incessantly: 'Make me come, make me come ...'

Without stopping I carried her over to the bed. I held her by the legs, with her boots resting on my shoulders, and she accompanied each of my thrusts with a languorous undulation of her pelvis.

'I deserve it, you know,' she said. 'For every time you make love, every time you wank or you fuck another woman I am there with you, it is I who caress your balls to excite you and to help you spurt out of yourself ... Like this ...'

Moving her hand under my buttocks, she started scratching

my balls with her long nails, commanded: 'Make me come now,' and then immediately came, throwing her head back and jerking violently in spasms which started at her waist and reverberated through her body, which was as tight as a bow. I myself could not resist the scratching of her nails and I came at the same time, with such a feeling of joy and liberation that I was laughing when I finished ejaculating.

I let myself fall by her side and softly caressed her face and breasts with my hand. She was like me, exhausted and happy.

'Is it true what you said?' I asked. 'You come into my bed at night? You are always by my side when I make love?'

'Of course. And not only when you make love. At every moment I am with you and I love you.'

'So you are my guardian angel?'

'If you like ... Except that I am not there simply to protect you, but also to make you dream, love, come, conquer ... And to suffer too ... Hope, despair ... To excite you, to satisfy you ... I am at your command and you obey me ... I am your servant and your mistress, your whore and your ally ...'

Her speech became more and more broken up, for, as she talked, she was wanking us both.

'Oh, let's wank ourselves off, shall we?' she said, already panting for breath. 'I love it when you do it ... I am there every time, watching you ... And you excite me so much that I do it too ... I love wanking myself so much ... Let's do it together, shall we?'

She got up, opened one of the black cupboards and took out an empty bottle, a gold ingot in the shape of a phallus, a tube of lubricant, a pair of scissors, a shaving stick and a razor.

'First we must prepare,' she said.

She sat in the prow of the bed with her legs wide open and handed me the scissors and asked me to trim her pubic hair, which was very bushy. I started to cut it. She grabbed onto the sides of the bed with both hands, out of fear and excitement. The steel blades skimmed her white skin and her glistening red

lips, which were swollen with desire, and rasped and chopped shut over her black pubes. I cut it all off, all the way down between her buttocks.

Then I daubed on the shaving cream and finished off with the razor until her pussy was completely smooth and bare. Finally I smeared her generously with lubricant over her lips and clitoris and also, as she wanted, over and inside her anus. During the whole operation she moaned and panted, but held back from coming.

Then it was my turn. I lay back against the stern with my legs apart. She rubbed lubricant on my balls, my cock and right down into my bum with such dexterity and application that I had to hold myself back from coming. She turned round to sit in front of me and we started to wank together, promising each other to make it last as long as possible.

I closed my hand around my cock, which was already stiff, and started to move it up and down the shaft as I watched her touch herself at the same time as me. At first she put the neck of the bottle in her mouth as if it were a dick. She pushed it into her cheeks and to the back of her palate, licked it and sucked it, without taking her eyes off me. Then she rubbed it over her whole body, lingering around her earlobes, the tips of her breasts, her stomach, before placing it on her clitoris, where she received it with a more pronounced jerk and moan. Finally she pushed it into her cunt and moved it in and out to the same rhythm that I wanked myself and, rubbing her fingers in a circular movement around her clitoris, she excited herself by talking to me in a voice raucous with pleasure:

'Wank yourself, wank yourself well, my love ... Go right up to the tip ... It's sliding nicely, I've lubricated it well, haven't I? Go down to the base ... Oh, your dick must be so warm and hard ... You must be feeling the blood pounding under the skin ... It must be so good to have it in your hand ... Rub it well, my darling, it is so lovely ... Rub it gently ... And caress your balls with your left hand ... Your big, swollen balls ... Yes ... More ... Go right down to your arsehole ... Wank it as well,

your nice little hole ... Stick your finger in it ... Oh, you're going to make me come ... Wait ...'

Then she took the gold ingot and put it in her cunt instead of the bottle, which she gave to me, begging me to put it in my behind. For we had to enlarge our anuses for later, she insisted.

'Please, trust me,' she said. 'We will enjoy great pleasures together, but they won't be normal pleasures. It is necessary, do you understand? Do as I do, my love ... See, first I loosen up, then I make it vibrate against the edge, it's good, isn't it, and then, gently ... It slides in easily ... Now let's wank ourselves hard ... If only you knew how handsome you are ... Move it around in your behind, wank your big dick which is making me come, and now, now ...'

I ejaculated at the same moment that she convulsed in orgasm. Because of the bottleneck in my body I felt a strange pleasure, slightly disagreeable but heightened, which caused my sperm to fly far ahead of me and land on her boots.

We sat there a good while, dazed and motionless. Then she crawled towards me on all fours with a malicious look and whispered in my ear:

'Are you hungry?'

On the table there were several plates of seafood, dishes of cold meats, salads, cheeses, pastries, baskets of fruit, red and white wines ... I was famished. She had a ferocious appetite too. We ate and drank heartily, chatting and joking, ever more gaily as the food and wine warmed us up.

We finished off our feast with a large joint, which we smoked as we reclined comfortably in our chairs, face to face, our legs apart and resting on the arms. In the centre of their brown aureoles on her little breasts her nipples were stiff and erect. Her vulva, denuded by the razor, opened like a shell. She slid a bit further down in her chair and I saw her anus open as well.

She got up, grabbed my balls and said:

'Now it's time to shit.'

She took two little plastic pots out of a black cupboard and

placed them on the ground. We sat down on them side be side
and started pushing as we held hands. When we had finished,
she reached out and grabbed my shirt, which was lying on the
ground, and tore off a strip, which she divided in two, to wipe
ourselves with. Then she tipped the contents of one pot into the
other and said:

'It's our shit that unites us.'

We returned to the boat and started making love with our
mouths, lying head to toe. This lasted for hours, perhaps, and
we didn't change position, except occasionally to roll over, so
we each had a turn at lying on the bed. When we had come,
I got up and I saw that she was still convulsing, with her
legs apart, until a large black spider emerged from her vagina
and ran around the room before seeking refuge in the empty
bottle lying next to the bed. Then the shadow fell back,
appeased.

Later, I took her by the arm, dragged her to the table where I
made her bend over and rest on her hands. I sodomized her,
repeating over and over:

'It's our shit that unites us. And our fucking come,' I added at
the moment when I came.

For her come was running down her legs as much as mine
was inside her body.

When the moment came to part, she picked up the bottle,
which was lying next to the bed. Inside, instead of the spider,
there was a pebble. She threw the vessel to the ground where it
smashed noisily.

'Keep it,' said the shadow as she handed me the pebble.

It was a beautiful polished stone. I put it in my pocket.

Once I was in the corridor, I wondered whether I would now
elect to:

– leave and look for the Woman:

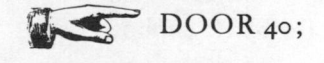 DOOR 40;

– leave and set off alone:

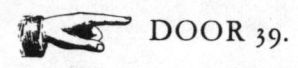 DOOR 37;

– or take this shadow that I loved out with me, for she was perhaps the one, my Woman:

DOOR 39.

36

The Monster

The two shadows waited, squeezing my hands.

'I'm sorry,' I said. 'You are certainly very charming and I admit I am attracted and touched by your invitation. But it is time for me to bring an end to my wanderings in this labyrinth. Outside there is a real woman waiting for me and I don't want to compromise my chances of finding her.'

And, letting go of their hands, I headed for the exit.

At the end of the corridor, the illuminated sign called to me like a hope, a deliverance, an adventure. Would this last one be a happy one? There was a stab of apprehension in my desire to breathe the air of the outside world. Inside this dark kingdom, even if the journey had not always been easy, I had been exposed to some strange encounters and singular pleasures. Would I find so much emotion in the light of day? Would I be able to develop with the same mixture of anxiety and desire, with the same playful spirit? Wouldn't I simply succumb to the repetitive banality of everyday life, the tyranny of necessity? Would I be able to avoid the traps this world holds in store for that unfortunate creature we call human, the feeling of absurdity, the temptation of blindness, the submission to fate, boredom, renunciation, fear? Would I be able to love this woman who was waiting for me?

Before I reached the end of the corridor, I turned round. I

saw the shadows, half submerged in the dark. They were embracing each other. It seemed as if they were exchanging a lovers' kiss. Then they disappeared behind one of the doors.

They had followed me in secret during my whole journey and I was throwing up the one opportunity I would ever have to see their faces uncovered. I turned round and went quickly back to the spot where I had seen them disappear. The door was still open.

I slipped quietly through the gap and found myself in a huge, square-shaped room, entirely covered by a mosaic, as in an ancient palace. The two shadows were there, naked. I recognized the Shadow of Lost Love by her long white hair. She was a gorgeous girl, like a living sculpture, an aesthetic masterpiece full of grace and softness, the very incarnation of a profoundly human ideal.

The Shadow of Myself was a more mature woman, but still beautiful and just as fascinating, with her dark, intelligent, extraordinarily lively gaze and her dominatrix appearance. She was perching on laced-up, high-heel boots, which were tightly moulded around her fine calves, and was wearing a glittering diamond crown in her black hair, which was cut short and square like an ancient Egyptian's. Otherwise, she was as naked as her companion. The cloths they had been wearing in the corridor, one purple and the other black, lay on the floor.

They hadn't heard me come in and I stood there in the doorway, not daring to disturb them. They both possessed a strange charm, which almost held me entranced. The pubic hair of the Shadow of Lost Love was the same silky white as the hair on her head. I never tired of looking at her body, her curves, her voluptuous hips, her round, pearly breasts ... And I was not the only one who had succumbed to her beauty: the Shadow of Myself had fallen at her feet, which she was kissing fervently.

The white shadow began to moan and for the first time I realized that her eyes were turned up, unless they had no pupils, for there was nothing between her lids but two white globes.

How had I not noticed this before? It was as if this sightless beauty had the power to divest you too of your own sight.

This discovery almost made me sick, and yet I realized that it served only to increase the fascination of this woman. For although I had been greatly admiring her naked body, although I had also been deriving much pleasure from observing her companion's body, although I had seen them indulging in lovers' foreplay, it was only at the moment when I saw this empty gaze that I got an erection.

At the same moment, the Shadow of Myself turned towards me and gave me a knowing smile, signalling to me not to make a sound. Then she took the white shadow in her arms and, with an ease and strength that astonished me, carried her to the bed, which was shaped like a boat. She then carried over a chair from the corner of the room where she signalled me to sit, still without making a sound.

The Shadow of Lost Love lay motionless in the boat in the position in which she had been laid, on her back with her legs open. When I reached them, the black shadow came to me, undid my belt and my flies and let my trousers fall around my feet. I wanted to embrace her, but she prevented me.

'It's too late,' she said. 'You didn't want to follow us when the time was right ... Now you can do nothing but regret us ...'

'Is he there?' the white shadow cried out, sitting upright with a haggard look. And she started crying and mumbling: 'Oh, why did you leave, why did you leave?'

This time I reached out my hand to her, but again the black shadow stopped me.

'Don't do that,' she said. 'Believe me, you must not do that. I have another task for you, the destiny of all three of us depends on it. Please, listen to me and stay there, for we will have need of you soon. For now, enjoy the only pleasure we can give you.'

She sat me down gently in the chair, took my right hand and closed it round my cock. She had been so persuasive, had

seemed so superior in her knowledge of the mysteries of life that I started to desire her even more ardently than her young companion. However, I trusted her completely and was ready to submit to her orders, even if I was prevented from touching either of them.

She joined her companion on the bed and set about consoling her. Large tears flowed incessantly from her white eyes, drenching her face and neck, trickled down to her nipples, making them stand up. She took her in her arms, opened her mouth with her tongue and gave her a long kiss as she caressed her breasts, her stomach, between her thighs, until the tearful beauty opened her legs to offer her pussy to the expert fingers that were massaging it.

Then the Shadow of Myself got up and took a little plastic pot out of one of the black cupboards that stood against the walls of mosaic. Then she made the white shadow crouch on top of the bed, held the pot between her open thighs and said with authority:

'Stop crying and piss.'

The girl complied immediately. I watched the stream splash down from between her intimate lips and I had to lessen the pressure of my hand on my cock so as not to come.

The black shadow placed the pot at the foot of the bed and pushed her face into her warm pussy and started licking and titillating her clitoris, then the whole vulva. Her young friend moaned, panted and arched her magnificent back with the pleasure of it. Finally she penetrated her with her tongue while rubbing her pink button with her thumb. Then she seemed to be possessed and arched back violently when she came, with guttural groans.

When they swapped roles, when the white shadow slid her face into her friend's intimate parts, I forgot the order I had been given. I was starting to get tired of being a spectator of their women's games. The white shadow was lapping away assiduously, on all fours between her mistress's thighs, sticking

out her tongue regularly and artlessly, like a cat before a bowl of milk, while her delicious behind bounced up and down in the air, as if it were held by some invisible phantom. She was obviously missing something, something that only I in this room could give her.

Who could have resisted the sight of this sublime rump, this adorable bum so in need of love? I climbed onto the bed, placed myself behind her and penetrated her. They both cried out, no doubt through a mixture of surprise, anger and pleasure, and I came deep inside the belly of my beautiful Lost Love.

They chased me off the bed, still screaming and gesticulating more than ever, in a state of terror, as if they were expecting some terrible consequence of my disobedience. The white shadow in particular seemed to be completely demented. She began clawing at her face and body until it bled. I helped the black shadow prevent her hurting herself further. I took off my shirt and ripped off a strip with which I tied her wrists to the prow of the boat.

She was lying on her back and she gradually calmed down. That's when I noticed how pale she was. Her skin had become transparent and there were large blue veins standing out all over her face and body. At the same time her stomach began to swell alarmingly. I looked at the Shadow of Myself, seeking help, some explanation. But she was merely crying and trembling silently, stroking her friend's brow.

As she was now, if anything, too calm, I wanted to untie her hands. But she started writhing again, supporting herself on her feet, with her legs apart. Her face, however, showed no pain, or anything at all. It was as if what was happening to her were totally foreign to her. In truth, it was as if she were dead and something were seeking to get out of her.

'It's now that we need you,' said the Shadow of Myself.

And the tone of her voice surprised me. She opened one of her black cupboards and handed me a large kitchen knife.

Sometimes I can't seem to remember very well what really

happened then. Other times, even when I think I've forgotten everything, the images return with a hallucinatory clarity. At those moments I feel that my whole life consists solely in walking a wire, or a network of wires, in a sort of trance which allows me to forget the constant risk of falling and the efforts I have to make at each instant to preserve such a fragile balance.

A huge black cockroach was extracting itself from the belly of the Shadow of Lost Love. At the same time she was losing all her blood, which was flowing out of her sex in long, shining streams. I held the knife in my hand and was unable to move.

Now the monster had managed to get out from between the thighs of the white shadow and it raised its eyes to me, surprising, large, sad eyes which seemed to be asking for mercy.

'It's a female,' said the Shadow of Myself, 'her belly is full of vermin. Kill her, before she has time to lay. Kill her, or they will spread everywhere!'

The creature was still looking at me with its strangely human eyes. I went up to the bed, sank my blade into its shell, just behind the head, pulled it out, sank it in again, over and over, with all my strength. It writhed clumsily on its thin legs, while a thick white liquid oozed out of each of its wounds. The thought came to me that it was my sperm, and I felt despoiled and betrayed. I continued to strike it to make it give back everything it had taken from me which I hadn't wanted to give. The creature fell on its back on the ground, wiggled its foul legs a little, then ceased to move.

'It's over,' said the Shadow of Myself as she stayed my arm.

She took the knife and slit the monster's belly. Inside, thousands of tiny cockroaches swarmed feebly, in their death throes.

The black shadow looked at me, then turned away to vomit. Bent double, she retched violently and ejected a stone, which she caught in her hand. On the bed, the white shadow was dead. I slumped to the ground, put my head in my hands and started to cry.

'It was necessary,' said the black shadow, placing her hand on my hair.

I lay prostrate for a long time, as if hoping that the passage of empty time would wipe away everything that had happened.

'Get up now,' the shadow finally said. 'Come and help me.'

The mosaic floor was made up of trapdoors, which opened onto tombs.

'So you live over a cemetery,' I said to the shadow, somewhat disgusted.

She looked at me as if I were stupid and said simply:

'Obviously.'

We buried the two bodies and cried together over Lost Love, over that white shadow we had both loved, who was so beautiful and for whom we now had to grieve. Then I helped her to clean the room.

When the time came to part, the Shadow of Myself gave me the pebble she had thrown up. It was a beautiful polished stone.

'Keep it,' she said. Then she added: 'From now on you and I will be allied forever.'

I gave her a long kiss. We made love, we cried again and we went to sleep in each other's arms.

Then I put the pebble in my pocket and left her. I knew we would remain close whatever happened and that I could count on her, as she could count on me.

As I headed for the exit I told myself that once I was outside I could still choose between:

– leaving with the Woman I was about to meet:

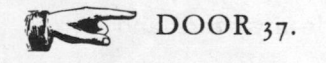 DOOR 40;

– or leaving alone:

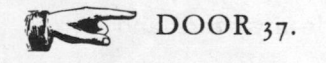 DOOR 37.

37

The Hermit

This afternoon Emilie came to see me. She had bought a mountain bike. She was flushed and out of breath when she arrived, but was very happy with her new toy, which she had proudly described to me in full detail. She said she could come and see me more often now. It was a long way on foot.

As it was a nice day I had put the table outside the cave to draw on. She took some cherries and some tobacco (for me) out of her rucksack. I made some tea and we sat out in the sun to have a chat.

She wanted to speak about Alaska again, but this time she had brought a little notebook to take some notes. She said that she would go there one day, to the same place I had been. She said that one day she would go everywhere I had been and write my life story. I know what she meant by 'one day': she meant when I was dead. I didn't say that to her because it would have upset her. But we both know that I am an old man and my days are numbered.

Emilie is the only one who doesn't try to convince me to come down to the village. They all think that, if I continue to live far away from people and doctors, I will die up here, alone, on the mountain. I'll die where I want to die.

Emilie went quite red when she told me about this book she wanted to write about me. I could see it was her way of

declaring her love for me. Then she asked if I would authorize her to do it and if I would help her by recounting everything. This time it was her way of asking if I recognized this love.

Well, I didn't answer straight away. Wouldn't she be better off having fun with people of her own age, rather than wearing herself out climbing up here to see me?

'Just for the book,' she added, as if she could read my thoughts. 'Please, it's very important to me ...

I said yes.

*

My name is Emilie, I'm seventeen years old. The hermit is dead. I loved him.

It wasn't me who found the body. It was the baker's son when he went up with his weekly delivery of bread and provisions. He had been dead for several days. I would have so wanted him to know why I'd stopped coming recently.

It's more than a month since he agreed to tell me his life story. I wrote everything down, the journeys, the jobs, the loves ... On this subject, I tried not to give anything away, but I was quite jealous. Oh, he had loved women! And, to listen to him, they had all left him the fondest memories. One day I couldn't stop myself saying, about one of them:

'If she was really that good, why didn't you stay with her?'

That's when he told me about the little circus. How, in his youth, he had made a journey through a strange labyrinth, looking for the woman of his life and how, at the end of this journey, he had finally given up on this woman. Naturally I asked him why.

'I don't know,' he replied. 'My life would certainly have been just as fine if I had lived with this woman ... But you only have one life and you have to make a choice. I chose to live and die alone ...'

'But you have never been alone!'

'Many women have loved me, that's true ... They've kept me company ... Like you, today, my dear Emilie ... But deep inside I have always remained alone. I have often suffered, but I have also found precious joys in it. For it was what I wanted: to be in dialogue with my shadow ...'

And he took out of his pocket a beautiful polished stone, which he rolled in his hand before putting it back in his jacket.

I didn't know that would be the last time I saw him. I wasn't sure I understood what he was trying to say. I should have gone back, so he could tell me more about it. But immediately after he had told me this story about the little circus, one arrived, the next day, in the village. Normally I'm not interested in this sort of thing, but now all of a sudden I was quite fascinated. As soon as I saw it, in the early afternoon, I stopped to have a look.

Everything was quiet, the people were no doubt having a siesta in their caravans, for it was very hot. I went up to some of the animal cages and stopped in front of the tiger. That's how I met Pablo. He came up behind me, asked jokingly if I wanted him to teach me his trade, for they needed a woman trainer. Oh, Pablo, Pablo with the dark eyes, the white teeth and swarthy skin, I told you I did. That's the first time I'd done that, agree to something just like that. You took me into your caravan and we loved each other straight away.

That evening there was a show and the following day I left with him, with the little circus. I only got back yesterday, at the end of the summer. And I discovered the hermit was dead. I would have so liked to tell him what was happening and to ask his advice. And, above all, to tell him I hadn't abandoned him.

I wonder what he was thinking about at the moment he died. I looked for the stone in his cave, I asked whether it had been discovered on him, but it was nowhere to be found.

38

The Madman

As soon as I went through the curtain, as soon as I left the little circus, she disappeared. The Shadow of Lost Love. Outside the sunlight was so bright I squinted, then I felt nothing any more, I no longer felt the shadow's hand in mine, I turned round and couldn't see her any more. What was left to me now? The stone, I had given it to her, but they took everything back, my beautiful shadow, the stone, everything. At first, I admit, I thought it wasn't so serious, I barely remembered a thing, I took a couple of steps in the light and already everything was forgotten, I got into my car and drove, I drove very quickly along the road, it was good. It was later that I realized, realized I had nothing left. I loved all those women but not one of them loved me any more, not one of them loved me as I wanted, and I felt so depressed that I stopped everything, anyway I couldn't make love any more, I went to see a woman you pay and it didn't work I felt like lying down in the gutter lying down and flowing away with the water in the gutter. I took drugs and stopped eating meat I rediscovered religion and then stopped I went back to women but they liked me less and less and I didn't even remember the Shadow of Lost Love any more I walked on beaches and gathered stones but I couldn't even remember that she had taken my stone away, oh, why did I want to abduct her? Sometimes I remembered, I looked all over for the little circus, I

was like a tramp a vagabond I wandered everywhere looking for it and I finally forgot like always forgot what I was doing but I carried on anyway you have to do something then I stopped and started again women didn't like me any more and I liked them too much. I became a poet and burned everything I became an artist and smashed everything I went mad and I understood everything I grew old and I left, I went to die in the mountains. In the village they told me there was an old hermit in the mountains, a wise old man, so I set off it was a foggy day and the path was arduous, the hermit was waiting for me in front of his door and I saw that he was my double. I want to die I told him die in the mountains and he opened his door to me I went into his cave, he went off somewhere else, went off to live, and I died.

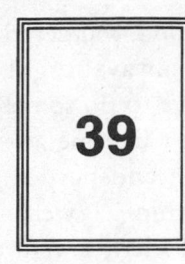

39

The Dead Man

They are all there: my widow and my family with their crocodile tears, my so-called friends, my supposed closest associates and even a representative from the government. A fine cortège behind an empty coffin. Oh, the reckoning up and the backbiting isn't over yet. My inheritance, literal and metaphorical.

They never found my body. The sea swallowed it up.

I soon realized what the mistake, my mistake, was. I should never have taken the Shadow of Myself out of the little circus. That's how I lost her. As soon as I passed through the curtain, she disappeared. Vanished. Later I realized that I had also lost the beautiful polished stone that she had given me.

After this nothing was ever the same as before. Gradually I realized that I had become incapable of loving, that I could no longer feel joyful and carefree. The world disgusted me. I turned to money and power. I amassed as much of both these things that I was able to take from others. The more cynical and contemptuous I became the more women and men tried to win my favour, while still detesting me.

I married a woman who soon had nothing on her mind but divorce and alimony, the best deal she could get from me. But rather than granting her this favour, I had her bear my children, whom neither of us loved. Since I couldn't have pleasure myself, I didn't allow anyone around me to have any.

I treated myself to loads of girls and orgies of every sort. I stocked up on products enabling me to fuck repetitively for hours on end, more and more. I bought a boat. I brought the world's most beautiful women, and the most depraved, to fuck them on this boat. I invented a love story, I invited the woman I had designs on, to love her on this boat. I got erections, I ejaculated a thousand different ways with a thousand different people on this boat. But all to no avail. I never had an orgasm.

One night I left the six bimbos who were slaving away to give me pleasure and went to the bridge. I leaned over the prow of the boat and saw her in the dark water. The Shadow of Myself. I jumped in.

At the bottom of the sea I saw a brightly lit corridor. She was there at the other end. She was waiting for me. My heart was thumping in my chest and I started walking towards her.

I'll soon be there. The corridor is getting darker and darker, but I am sure she is still waiting for me at the end. I hope she is, so much.

40

The Jugglers

I waited for her at the exit of the little circus, that's how we missed each other the first time. For she was waiting for me too, a short distance away. How we didn't see each other I'll never know. Anyway, we waited for each other, then we both had the same idea: to go to the show that evening.

We didn't see each other there either. It was only after the show that we recognized each other. In the little bar on the other side of the square.

Most of the people from the circus were there too and we hung out with them, because it was a good way for us to get closer to each other, in the general conviviality. At the end of the evening she and I were standing side by side at the bar, laughing together with some of the other. It was a laughter which hid a whole host of things ...

It was very late and everyone was starting to leave. We asked the landlord whether there was a hotel in the village. He said there was one, but it was full. Then the jugglers said, 'Don't worry, little lovebirds, we'll find you a bed.' And they lent us their caravan. That was our first night of love.

And the last, for a long time. She had her bike, I had my car. Before leaving we exchanged telephone numbers written on books of matches. And we lost them. Both of us. I realized I didn't even know her name. I couldn't even look her up in the

phone book. As she didn't phone me, I thought she didn't want to see me any more.

A year passed. I had a few flings, but my heart wasn't in it. From time to time I looked at the stone which the Shadow of Myself had given me. And it gave me hope, in love, in myself, in everything.

I thought I had put her out of my mind, but the following summer, when I saw, by chance, that the little circus was performing in a village I was driving through, I stopped. That's where I found her again. She had been passing through too, and had stopped.

From that moment we never left each other. We were both tired of our former lives. We travelled with the circus for a while, where we learned to juggle. We worked out a new act between us, with a touch of something very personal and poetic, which went down very well.

Later we left the circus to try some other things. We had children, grandchildren. Arguments, reconciliations. Happiness, pain. Everything that makes up a life.

This very afternoon we shared a little celebration of love and sex. Play, passion, pleasure ... Once again, with virtuosity we threw back to each other everything we had learned behind the closed doors of the little circus. We are still jugglers ...